Praise for

Under the Lights

"With humor, emotion and captivating characters, *Under the Lights* will make you believe in love, second chances and happily ever after."
—Jaci Burton, *New York Times* bestselling author

"Small-town romance with a dash of heat . . . This charming tale is a feel-good read that will have readers eagerly awaiting the next installment in the series."　—*Publishers Weekly*

"It is a real pleasure to read about a place and people that are thoroughly likable."　—*RT Book Reviews*

Praise for the novels of Shannon Stacey

"A sexy, comical, feel-good read that left me impatient for the next installment."　—*USA Today*

"Books like this are why I read romance."
—Smart Bitches, Trashy Books

"Stacey is an author who knows how to write fun, relevant dialogue within the world of romance."　—Harlequin Junkie

"Stacey writes such fun, warm characters with the backdrop of a great small town that I was totally engrossed."
—Smexy Books

"One of the best contemporary romance series . . . Very realistic."　—Fiction Vixen

"If you're a fan of big families, cute romances and friends-to-lovers stories, then this book is definitely for you."
—Under the Covers Book Blog

Homecoming

SHANNON STACEY

JOVE
New York

A JOVE BOOK
Published by Berkley
An imprint of Penguin Random House LLC
375 Hudson Street, New York, New York 10014

Copyright © 2016 by Shannon Stacey
Excerpt from *Under the Lights* copyright © 2015 by Shannon Stacey
Penguin Random House supports copyright. Copyright fuels creativity, encourages
diverse voices, promotes free speech, and creates a vibrant culture. Thank you for buying
an authorized edition of this book and for complying with copyright laws by not
reproducing, scanning, or distributing any part of it in any form without permission.
You are supporting writers and allowing Penguin Random House to continue to
publish books for every reader.

A JOVE BOOK and BERKLEY are registered trademarks and the B colophon
is a trademark of Penguin Random House LLC.

ISBN: 9780515155860

First Edition: September 2016

Printed in the United States of America
1   3   5   7   9   10   8   6   4   2

Cover illustration by Danny O'Leary
Cover design by Judith Lagerman
Cover photos: *Football and field* © David Lee / Shutterstock
Book design by Laura K. Corless

The Boys of Fall series is about community and family, whether by blood or by bond, and this book is dedicated to my community. Whether you're family or friend or somebody the Internet brought into my life, I wouldn't be able to write what I do without all of you. Thank you.

Acknowledgments

Thank you to Kate Seaver and everybody at Berkley for all of your hard work bringing the Boys of Fall series to life. And thank you to my agent, Kim Whalen, and to Jaci and Stuart for always being on my team.

01

Sitting in a hospital waiting room with a pack of scared and sweaty teenage boys while wearing a little black dress and high heels wasn't Jen's idea of a fun Friday night.

Nothing could have dragged her out of there, though. Not even the promise of flip-flops and her favorite yoga pants. The police officer leaning against the wall and staring at the ceiling was Kelly McDonnell, one of her best friends. Kelly had been the first to arrive when the 911 call came in from football practice. Kelly's dad—Coach McDonnell—had collapsed on the high school's field and they were afraid he was having a heart attack.

When Kelly called her from the emergency room, Jen had been in her car on her way to a second date with the first guy in a long time who actually had potential to make her forget the man she spent too much time thinking about, but she hadn't even hesitated before canceling. Kelly needed her.

"Miss Cooper, do you think it'll be much longer?"

Jen looked at the young man who'd asked the question in such a low voice, it was almost a whisper. PJ, the team's cornerback, bore the same solemn expression as the rest of the football players in the room. Coach was more than the guy who taught them to play football. He was a mentor and a role model and, when need be, a father figure.

"I don't know, PJ. If it's too much longer, we'll start working on how to get you all home."

"We're not leaving," Hunter Cass said. The running back gave her a look that practically dared her to try asserting authority over them.

As the school's guidance counselor, her authority didn't technically extend to hospital waiting rooms. This was her hometown, though, and as far as Jen was concerned, her sense of responsibility for these kids didn't end when the dismissal bell rang, and it never had.

"Nobody's making you leave right now," she said. "But if we don't hear something soon, you guys will need food and rest. And your parents will want you home before it's too late."

She could tell he wanted to argue with her but, after a glance at Kelly, Hunter shut his mouth and leaned his back against the wall again. Jen almost wished he had pushed back because she wouldn't feel so damn helpless. Keeping teenagers in line and on track was her job, and she was good at it. But she had no idea what to do for Kelly or her mom.

Coach McDonnell's wife, Helen, sat quietly on the couch opposite Jen's. She was leaning forward, with her elbows resting on her knees, and was staring at her clasped hands. She hadn't really said anything after thanking the boys for being there, and Jen's heart was breaking for her.

It was at least another fifteen minutes before a nurse walked into the waiting room. "Officer McDonnell? Helen? You can come with me."

Jen tried to read the nurse's facial expression before the three women stepped out. She couldn't remember the woman's name off the top of her head, but they'd met a few times. The hospital wasn't very big, but it served a large area—including Jen's hometown of Stewart Mills, New Hampshire—so it was inevitable they'd crossed paths. And based on those few interactions, Jen could see the nurse had been relaxed and didn't appear to be dreading talking to Coach's wife and daughter.

The boys, though, managed to ratchet the tension up to an almost palpable level. Jen hoped she was right in her assessment of the situation because if the news wasn't good, she had no idea what she was going to do with an entire football team of emotionally devastated boys. Especially after the roller coaster this year had been. The low of the budget cuts that canceled the football program, which had kept many of the boys on track in the economically depressed town. The success of Eagles Fest, the community-wide effort to raise the money to keep the boys on the field. Losing Coach now would be a low they wouldn't recover from for a long time.

When the door opened and Kelly walked in, Jen knew she wasn't the only one holding her breath. Her friend had been crying, but whether they were tears of sorrow or relief, she couldn't tell.

"He's going to be okay." Kelly paused for a moment to let

the boys react to the good news. "He had a heart attack, but he's awake now and hooked up to a bunch of monitors."

"Can we see him?" one of the boys asked.

"Not for a while. They've moved him to ICU, which is family only. We don't know yet how long he'll be in there or if they'll put him in a regular room. Cody, you're a captain, so you're going to be my liaison. You and I can keep in touch, and you can keep the rest of the team up to date. I don't need all of you calling my mother or my dad's cell, okay? Or me."

Cody Dodge, tight end for the Eagles, nodded, as did the rest of the boys. Jen smiled and stood up, stretching her back. "I'll make sure everybody has a way home."

Kelly nodded. "You mind sticking around after? I'm going to go see Dad, but then I'll need to get the cruiser back and change, and I don't want my mom here alone."

"Tell her I'll be right here if she needs anything."

It took almost half an hour to empty the waiting room of football players, and then Jen pulled out her phone and relaxed against the couch. She checked her email and caught up on Facebook, managing to kill the time until Kelly walked in and plopped down next to her.

Jen dropped her phone in her lap and reached over to squeeze her best friend's hand. "How is he?"

"Pale. Weak." Kelly exhaled a long, shuddering sigh. "Frail. He looks frail."

"His body might be having a frail moment, but he's strong. He'll be okay."

"Yeah." Kelly turned sideways on the cushion to face her. "He wants Sam to come back to Stewart Mills and coach the boys."

"What? No. No, he can't. Nope." Jen shook her head, just

in case Kelly wasn't clear that this ridiculous idea was getting a big old *oh, hell no* from her. Sam Leavitt was supposed to go home to Texas and never come back.

"It's his only request and it's pretty important to him."

Kelly couldn't possibly be considering this, Jen thought as her mind spun. "You don't call a guy who lives in Texas and ask him to run up to New Hampshire to temporarily coach high school football for a few weeks. There are assistant coaches."

"Did you see any assistant coaches here tonight?" Kelly waved a hand around the waiting room. "Dad was running practice alone. Charlie quit because he got offered a better job down south. Dan's wife is having a baby any minute and, since it's their first, he's running home every ten minutes."

"Joel?"

"Joel's the gym teacher, so he works them out and puts them through their paces, but he's not a football coach."

Jen couldn't believe this was happening. "Decker played for the Eagles. He could coach. I know Chase has to work in New Jersey, but what about Alex? Now that he's moved in with Gretchen, he's in Stewart Mills enough."

There had to be another option. Kelly's fiancé, Chase Sanders, and Alex Murphy, who'd fallen for their friend Gretchen, had both come back to town after fourteen years away to support Eagles Fest. Their team had been the first in Stewart Mills to win the championship, and the highlight of the fund-raiser had been the exhibition game between the current team and the alumni team. There were other options. Almost *any* option was better.

"He wants Sam," Kelly said quietly. "You know how he

is. There's more to it than what he's saying, but I think he believes Sam still has unfinished business here and it's important to him that Sam come home and coach."

Unfinished business. That was seriously bad news. The three men—Chase, Alex and Sam—had returned to town, along with a couple of the other guys. Chase had fallen in love with Kelly. Alex had fallen in love with Gretchen.

And Sam had set the bar for sweaty, toe-curling sex with Jen on the hood of her car.

As far as she was concerned, that business was finished and needed to stay in the past. He wasn't the kind of guy for falling in love.

Sam looked at the cell phone vibrating its way across the glass-topped patio table and sighed. He was pretty comfortable, with his ass in his favorite camp chair and his feet up on a cooler of cola on ice.

The name on the caller ID screen caught his attention, though, and he reached for it. He'd exchanged a few text messages with Kelly McDonnell since Eagles Fest had ended and he returned to Texas, but she hadn't called.

He hit the button to answer the call. "Hey, Kelly."

"Hi, Sam. Are you busy right now?"

He looked over the exceptionally flat horizon, watching the hot breeze play with the sand. It was cooler in the shade of his trailer, under the awning, but the only thing he'd done for the last hour was stay out of the sun after a long day of working in it. "Nope. What's up?"

"Let me open with the fact he's going to be fine."

Coach. Despite the reassurance meant by her words, fear sucker-punched him in the gut. "What happened?"

"My dad had a heart attack last night. But he's okay. I promise."

Sam dropped his feet off the cooler so he could lean forward and rest his elbows on his knees. "Was it bad?"

"They've seen worse, but he's going to be benched for a while."

At least he'd be okay. Coach was strong and nothing could keep him down for long. "I'm glad you called to let me know. Even if, the last time you called, it was to sucker me into going back there to play football against a bunch of high school kids."

"Yeah . . . about that." Kelly hesitated and Sam braced himself for more bad news. "Dad wants you to come back to Stewart Mills again—to step in for him and coach the team."

He wasn't sure what he'd been expecting, but that wasn't it. "I don't get it. There are other coaches. Other guys."

"He wants you."

Sam rubbed the bridge of his nose. "Why?"

There was a long moment of silence, and then she sighed. "To be perfectly honest, Sam, I don't know. What I do know is that it's important to him. And you know how he is. He probably thinks you needed a little more time in Stewart Mills. But whatever his reasons, they're personal and he's not sharing them with me."

There was a time—essentially the last decade and a half—when thinking of his hometown had brought up painful memories of a shitty childhood, an alcoholic mother who couldn't protect him from it, and what was an adolescence headed toward self-destruction until Coach McDonnell got hold of him. Coach had taught him to be a part of a team—a brotherhood, even—and how to be a man.

Since the trip back for Eagles Fest, though, thinking of his hometown evoked the sweet memory of Jen Cooper's legs wrapped around his waist, her back arching off the hood of her car as her fingernails dug into his forearms. His mind had been evoking that particular memory a lot lately.

"Sam?"

Kelly's voice dragged him back to the present, which hadn't included a woman's company since he left New Hampshire. "I'm still here."

"What are the chances of you coming back here?"

He thought about what he had here in Texas. A decent job as an oil-field electrician. A good truck. A mobile home that suited his needs well enough and didn't demand much upkeep. And he had some friends he'd hit the local bar with once in a while, even though he stuck to soda.

Then he weighed that against what Stewart Mills held for him. There was the only man who'd ever given a shit about him and who needed his help. And a mother struggling to stay sober, who wanted to make amends Sam wasn't ready for yet. And there were the good friends he'd gone too long without, but he hadn't known just how long until he saw them again.

And there was the woman who'd shifted the earth under his feet with just a touch.

"I know it's a lot," Kelly said. "The season can go into November if they make the play-offs, and the doctor hasn't given us a time frame for Coach's recovery yet."

"They'll make the play-offs," he said. He'd seen them play and they were damn good.

She laughed softly on the other end of the line. "Maybe that kind of conviction's why he wants you."

Maybe. But Sam suspected the old man simply wasn't done with him yet and had seen an opportunity to bring him home. "I'll be there. I have to wrap up a couple of things, since my boss won't be happy about an extended leave of absence. And I'm going to drive this time, instead of flying out so I'll have my truck. It'll probably be a week."

"Thank you, Sam. It'll mean everything to my dad."

"He means everything to me," Sam responded, and he was surprised to find himself a little choked up. "He's really okay?"

"He really is. Weak, like I said, but the damage wasn't too bad. He won't be sneaking any more hash omelets at O'Rourke's, though, if my mom has anything to say about it."

"I think Mrs. McDonnell will have a *lot* to say about it."

When the call was over, Sam propped his feet up on the cooler and leaned his head back against the chair.

He'd been in Texas a long time—longer than any of the many other places he'd lived over the years—but he had to admit it had never really felt like home. He'd stuck it out in New Hampshire until he got the high school diploma that meant so much to Coach and Mrs. McDonnell, and then he'd hit the road with no destination in mind but anywhere else. He'd worked a lot of odd jobs, landing in Texas, before going back to school so he could make more money.

But in fourteen years, he'd never really settled down. He'd never bought a house, instead making do with short-term rentals. He hadn't found a woman he wanted to spend the rest of his life with or started a family. He didn't even have a dog. Maybe, deep down inside, he'd always known he'd go back to New Hampshire someday.

The first time had been a whirlwind of activities and emotion. But this time he'd be there long enough to work through some things. Maybe he could even work on forgiving his mom and making peace with his past.

Luckily, his employers thought highly of him and were willing to give him an extended leave since the alternative was him quitting. Then he packed a couple of duffel bags of clothes, along with a couple of boxes of things he'd need for the next couple of months. After dropping off a check for three months' rent in advance with his landlord, who'd keep an eye on the place, he was ready to hit the road.

Nine days later, Sam drove into Stewart Mills and paused at the main intersection. He let his truck idle at the stop sign a little longer than was necessary to avoid getting a ticket, since there was a crop of new signs and it was easy to forget them. Then he started toward Coach's house because, dammit, he needed a hug from the man.

When he left after high school, he never thought he'd ever return to this town. But now he was back in his hometown for the second time this year, and this time he'd be staying awhile.

02

"I am *not* okay with this." Jen grabbed the corner of the fitted sheet and snapped it over the end of the mattress. She was helping her best friend make up a bed for Sam Leavitt to sleep in and she couldn't make sense of it.

"You've said that every five minutes since you got here," Kelly said. "I'm about to slap you in the back of the head because your brain seems to be stuck on that song like an old jukebox."

"He wasn't supposed to come back." That's what Jen's brain was *really* stuck on. He wasn't supposed to come back to Stewart Mills anytime soon, and especially not *so* soon. At the very least, he could have waited until Jen found a man who could finally kill the memory of Sam's hands on her body. Then she wouldn't have to worry so much about temptation.

Of course, it would probably be easier to find that guy if she went out once in a while, but there weren't exactly any social hot spots in Stewart Mills. And the guy she'd been meeting the night Coach had his heart attack turned out to be a jerk.

"I know you're not happy about it, but he's supposed to be here today, so you should work on not saying that out loud quite so much. And he's going to be pretty busy. You'll probably barely see him."

"He'll be hanging out at the high school. You know, that big brick building where my office is?"

Jen took the bottom end of the top sheet and spread it over the foot of the bed. They were making Kelly's old bed at Coach and Mrs. McDonnell's house so it would be ready for Sam to sleep in. She tried not to imagine that tall, lean body stretched out on the new tan sheets, but her mind seemed determined to torture her. Would he snuggle under the blue-and-tan-plaid comforter, or throw the covers back?

What did he wear to bed? Being a guest in Mrs. McDonnell's home, he'd probably wear sleep pants or sweats. At the very least, he'd wear boxer briefs, like the navy pair he'd slid low on his hips that night they had sex under the summer night sky.

"Okay, you're definitely going to have to work on *that*," Kelly said, breaking into her thoughts.

Jen looked at the perfectly tucked sheet end. "Work on what?"

"You were just thinking about having sex with Sam on the hood of your car. I can tell because you'd look like you're having the world's worst hot flash except for the fact you're biting your bottom lip to keep from smiling."

"Damn." She was *definitely* going to have to work on that.

If just wondering what he'd look like lying on a bed was enough to flush her skin, what was going to happen when she actually ran into him? Just the memory of his mouth made her want to fan herself. When she could stare at it—watch his lips moving—she was going to be in trouble.

"Will it really be so bad?" Kelly asked. "I mean, he's a good guy and you said the sex was freaking amazing. If it's that good on a car when neither of you saw it coming, just imagine how good it could be when you have the space and privacy to take your time and explore a little bit."

Oh, she had. Jen had spent more time than she wanted to admit picturing in very graphic detail just how many delicious ways she and Sam could curl each other's toes. "Sexual chemistry's great, but it's not a good foundation for a long-term relationship."

"Of course it is."

"It's important, but don't you think having personalities that complement each other and similar life values and goals are more important? Too many people use having a healthy sex life as proof they have a healthy relationship, and it's not always true."

"You can't overthink love so much, Jen."

She tossed a pillow at her friend, frowning. "We're talking about sex, not love."

"You're the one who brought long-term relationships into the conversation."

"Not only am I thirty years old, but my two best friends will be getting married soon and I'll be the fifth wheel. So I'd like a relationship, yes, but I'm not holding out much hope for the kind of love you and Chase have. Or Gretchen and Alex."

"Tell me why you can see yourself having great sex with Sam, but not a relationship." Jen shrugged. "No, I'm serious. Because I'm your best friend and I'm going to nag you into getting all the hot sex you can unless you've got a reason you shouldn't that I can wrap my head around. And based on the look in your eyes when you think about him, it's going to have to be a damn good reason."

"I'm scared of him." She hadn't meant to say it out loud. She wasn't even sure it had been a cohesive thought until she opened her mouth and the words came out.

She watched as what she'd said sank in and Kelly's expression changed to her "cop face," as Jen and Gretchen liked to call it. She even drew herself up into her "cop stance," even though she didn't have the heavy utility belt to rest her hands on. "Scared of him?"

"Not like that. Not physically scared." She watched Kelly relax a little, though her face was still guarded. "He's rough and . . ."

Kelly lifted an eyebrow. "And . . . rough how? Or should I say how rough?"

"Again, not like that." Jen blew out a breath and sat on the edge of the bed they'd just made. "He's got a lot of baggage, with his parents and his background and stuff. And he's a runner. He took off for fourteen years. I'm not just looking for great sex. When push comes to shove, I'm looking for somebody to spend the rest of my life with, and the father of my children."

"I've known you my whole life. You're one of my two best friends. And, professionally, I've seen you counsel so many kids through crises. So I know you're not dismissing a man's ability to be a good father because his father was abusive and his mother is a recovering alcoholic."

Jen felt the hot flush across her cheeks. "Of course not. Let's just say I didn't get the impression he's a guy who believes in white picket fences, minivans and happily ever after."

"I don't know about picket fences, but he believes in family. Maybe it's *my* dad and not his own, but twice now he's uprooted his life because I asked him to on Coach's behalf."

"If I ever need help with football, I'm sure he'll be on my list of people to call."

Kelly laughed. "Considering how often the guys on the team are in your office, you might want to put him on speed dial."

"Not funny."

"A little bit funny."

Jen shook her head and then looked around the room that had been Kelly's growing up and then again after her divorce brought her back to Stewart Mills. There weren't many of her personal belongings in it, so it looked like a typical guest room, but Jen felt a pang of nostalgia thinking about the many hours they'd spent in the room as teenagers, talking about movies and music and boys.

There were three of them. Jen. Kelly. And Gretchen Walker, who'd completed their circle of best friendship when she moved to town to live with her grandparents in fifth grade. There had been no secrets between them, and they never broke each other's confidences. They knew how rough Gretchen's life had been before her no-good parents had essentially traded her for her grandfather's new truck. They all knew Kelly had secretly crushed on Chase Sanders, the star running back for her father's football team, and had pretended not to like him in order to hide it.

And they all knew Jen's head had been filled with fantasies of bad boys that her very strict, white-collar parents would disapprove of. Boys who grew up to be men like Sam Leavitt, she thought, fussing with the knit throw blanket draped over the easy chair in the corner so Kelly couldn't see her face.

But she'd grown up and her view of her parents' marriage had grown with her. What had seemed boring then was now stability. What had seemed, when she was a teenager, like a lack of passion for each other, she could see now was the kind of quiet, constant love that got two people through decades of marriage together.

Teenage Jen may have daydreamed about guys like Sam, but adult Jen wanted what her parents had. Quiet, constant and stable.

A door slammed outside and Jen whirled to the window. "That's not him, is it?"

Kelly pulled back the curtain to peek. "Yup. Sam's here."

"I wanted to be gone before he got here, dammit." She knew it was childish, but she wanted to avoid him for as long as possible. "I can go out the back."

"Really?" Kelly rolled her eyes at her. "You're being ridiculous. Besides, he parked behind you. You're blocked in."

"Shit." Jen closed her eyes for a moment and drew in a deep breath, centering herself. She dealt with awkward situations a lot being a guidance counselor, whether she was working with the kids or meeting with parents, so she could certainly handle saying hello to a man she'd known her entire life. "You're right. I'm being ridiculous. We had sex.

It happens. Maybe not as memorably as that particular sex happened, but it does happen and there's no reason for me to avoid him."

"I'm glad you're going to be adult about it even if it does mean I don't get the joy of watching my mom catch you trying to sneak out the back door."

Jen snorted, all too able to imagine Mrs. McDonnell calling her out. "Yeah, I think I'll just give him a polite 'welcome back' and ask him to move his truck."

Sam wasn't surprised when Mrs. McDonnell opened the front door before he could ring the bell. She pushed open the screen door and hauled him in for a hug.

"Thank you so much for coming, Sam. I can't tell you what it means to us."

"I seem to have a hard time saying no to McDonnells." He pulled back to look at her. Based on Kelly's age, he guessed her mom was somewhere in her early fifties—not that he'd ever ask—and she was a beautiful woman. But he could see the toll that worry had taken on her lately. First the stress of Eagles Fest and fighting to fund the football team, and now her husband having a heart attack. She was having a rough year. "How's Coach?"

"He's . . . as well as can be expected, I guess. He's weak and he needs to avoid stress and not cheat on his diet while he recovers—or ever again, if I have my way—but God knows it could have been worse. Come on in and see him."

Sam tried to brace himself as he followed Mrs. McDonnell to the living room. Coach was not only the closest thing he had to a father, but he'd always seemed larger than life somehow. His brush with mortality had Sam off-kilter and he had to concentrate on keeping his face relaxed.

Coach was kicking the foot of the recliner into place as Sam walked into the room, throwing aside a fleece throw. He looked tired and pale, with shadows around his eyes. He'd also lost a few pounds since Sam last saw him, but when they made eye contact, he saw that Coach might be down, but he wasn't out.

"Don't get up," he said, walking over to the recliner.

"You drove halfway across the country just to do me a favor. I think I can get up out of my chair to say hello." He pulled Sam into a hug and slapped his back. "Thanks for coming, Sam."

He heard footsteps on the wooden staircase and turned, expecting to see Kelly. She had her own place, but Sam imagined she'd be around a lot to help her mom out while her dad recovered.

Kelly was coming down the stairs. But right behind her was Jen Cooper, and once his gaze locked onto her, he couldn't seem to look away. She was so damn pretty, with long blond hair and blue eyes. Her skin was soft—and damn, he knew just how soft it was—and she had a smile that warmed him like a crackling fire on a winter night.

When her eyes met his, her cheeks turned pink and her lips parted as her chest hitched in a quick breath. *Oh yeah, she remembers*, he thought. When she looked at him, she remembered how explosive they'd been together and, like him, she was doing her damnedest not to show it.

"You made good time," Kelly said, giving him a quick hug. "We didn't think you'd be here for a few more hours."

"The flow of traffic was good. Hi, Jen. It's good to see you again."

She gave him a tight smile from the bottom of the staircase. "Hi, Sam. Welcome back."

"Welcome *home*," Mrs. McDonnell said. "He may live in Texas, but Stewart Mills will always be home."

Because Jen was in his peripheral vision, Sam saw her lips tighten and the look she gave Kelly. The coach's daughter was obviously amused by it because she grinned at her best friend. Sam tried to ignore them both and keep his attention on Mrs. McDonnell, but it wasn't easy to ignore Jen being in the room.

"I'm glad I'll be here for fall," Sam said. "I miss having seasons. I'd forgotten how much I love fall foliage and the chill in the air."

Coach laughed. "Guess you've also forgotten starting your truck when it's ten degrees and there's a mound of snow plowed up between you and the street."

"I should probably buy a coat before long," he said, but he was actually hoping to be back in Texas before there was snow on the ground.

"I hate to say hi and run," Jen said, "but I have some errands I need to do. I think you parked behind my car, but Kelly can move it for you."

"I don't mind moving it," he said.

She shook her head, probably more vehemently than she meant to. "You just got here and you're talking to Coach and stuff. We can do it."

And she wouldn't be outside with him, out of earshot of two people he was certain had no idea anything had ever happened between him and Jen. Kelly probably knew, but he seriously doubted anybody had told Coach and Mrs. McDonnell. He wondered if she just wanted to avoid talking to him or if she was afraid they might find themselves wrapped around each other again.

Sam wasn't sure how he felt about *that* possibility yet, so he tossed his keys to Kelly. "Thanks. I'll see you around, Jen."

"Probably."

"Oh, I'm sure you will," Mrs. McDonnell said. "Sam will be spending a lot of time at the high school."

Jen gave Coach's wife a huge, fake smile. "Great!"

He heard Kelly chuckle as she followed her friend down the hallway toward the front door, confirming his suspicion she knew what was up.

"Do you want something to eat, Sam?" Mrs. McDonnell asked. "You should at least have something to drink before you start unloading your truck."

"I'm good, thanks. I ate on the road, and I won't be carrying too much in. I made a few calls from the road and I'm looking at an apartment as soon as I can arrange it. I guess the owner of the building is going to have Chase remodel it when he's done working in New Jersey and, in the meantime, doesn't mind me staying there on a week-to-week basis. Gives him some money without worrying about a tenant getting in the way of renovations."

"Well, you know if it's not right for you that you're welcome to stay here as long as you need to. I'll just let you and Coach talk, and give a yell if you need anything."

Once she was gone, Sam took a seat on the couch opposite Coach's recliner. "Are you really doing okay?"

"I am. I've felt better and it's frustrating as hell having my wife and daughter and a bunch of doctors fussing over me, but I'm trying to look at the bright side, which is that I'm not dead."

Sam laughed, even though the thought of it made his heart stutter. "I'm glad you're not. What about your business? Is that under control?"

"Yup." Coach was a plumber with his own business and, though he'd slowed down in recent years, most of the town looked to him when they needed somebody. "My buddy's kid is coming up from the city two or three days a week to cover for me. He's been in the market for a camp a little north of here so he's looking around after work. Killing two birds with one stone, so to speak."

"Good. You know I'll help out if you need me, but I'm not licensed."

"We're good. I just need you to focus on the football team."

It seemed like a good opening. "What did you really drag me out here for? You've got assistant coaches and there are plenty of guys in town who know the basics. Decker played ball for you. He could have stepped in."

"Deck's got a business to run. And the coaching staff was already down to bare bones. A couple of the guys I had made other commitments when the funding for the team was cut at the town meeting in the spring. Charlie was damn good, but he got offered a job down south he couldn't pass up. Dan's wife just had a baby and there were some complications, so he's needed at home a lot. And Joel, who's the gym teacher, helps out with the workouts, but he doesn't have a head for football."

"Come on, Coach. You and Kelly didn't ask me to drive up here from Texas because there wasn't a guy in the entire county capable of wrangling some high school boys on a football field."

"They've had a rough go, son." Coach's eyes turned somber. "This town's economy went to shit, dragging their families down and tearing some apart. Then they thought they lost the one thing that kept them out of trouble and gave them dreams of college and maybe something more to budget cuts. No sooner did they have hope again before I go and end up in the hospital. They're shaken up."

"I spent a lot of time with them when I was here for Eagles Fest and they're good kids."

"I don't just need somebody to blow a whistle and call plays from the sidelines," Coach said. "I need somebody who knows what they're feeling—who knows what playing ball together as a team can mean when it's the only thing in your world you can control."

Sam took a moment before he spoke again, hoping the words wouldn't jam up behind the lump in his throat. "It wasn't the game, Coach. It was you."

"Hell, I'm not magic. I was just a guy who believed in you and taught you boys to believe in yourselves and each other."

"You saved me." It was that simple in Sam's mind. He'd been hell-bent on destroying himself because it was the only way to escape the hell that was his home, and he wasn't long for a cell or a coffin when Coach had seen him throw a brick through the liquor store window because they wouldn't sell him a bottle. Some sort of deal had been struck between Coach and the chief of police, and Sam ended up choosing showing up at football practice over doing time in jail.

"You saved yourself. I may have thrown you a rope, but

you hauled yourself up. You worked your ass off and learned to define yourself by your own actions and nobody else's. I need you to get my boys through this, son."

Mixed emotions churned in Sam's stomach. The weight of responsibility and expectations, along with the pride that Coach's faith in him brought to the surface. "I'll do my best."

"That's all I've ever asked of you." Coach yawned and Sam noticed his eyelids were looking a little heavy. "Besides, I think you've got some unfinished business in Stewart Mills."

He was pretty sure Coach meant giving his mother a chance at repairing their relationship, but it was Jen Cooper's face that flashed through his mind. He wasn't sure he'd consider the pretty guidance counselor unfinished business, but he had a feeling that whatever chemistry had brought them together during the Eagles Fest street fair was still just as potent as it had been on that summer night.

03

Jen was surprised when a knock on her doorjamb interrupted the endless reading of paperwork. Usually somebody in the main office called back when she had a visitor, and the students seldom knocked except on the rare occasion when her door was closed.

Looking up, she saw Gretchen Walker and smiled. Then she saw the chocolate Lab beside her and laughed. "Cocoa! You must have been pretty stealthy to sneak in here."

The dog walked around the desk to sit next to her and lifted her paw for a high five. It was the only trick she knew, so she never missed an opportunity to show it off. Jen slapped hand to paw and then scratched the dog's neck.

Gretchen sank into one of the visitors' chairs, pulling her long, dark braid over her shoulder so it wouldn't get caught

Shannon Stacey

behind her back. "I delivered your ugly pumpkin babies and nobody said anything about Cocoa, so here we are."

Jen laughed. "Mrs. Fournier must have been thrilled to have them."

"It's hard to tell with her."

Jen had asked Gretchen if she'd be willing to donate some small pumpkins to the health class, and that she'd happily take the rejects that wouldn't sell. After her grandfather's passing and in a tough economy, Gretchen had planted some pumpkins to supplement the farm's income, and it had grown into a surprisingly good business venture.

The Stewart Mills High health class had, for decades, taken part in the longstanding tradition of making students pair off and care for eggs to teach them how difficult their lives would be as parents. Gretchen had her own thoughts on how ineffective the exercise was as birth control but, until Mrs. Fournier retired, the babies would stay.

After an unfortunate incident the previous school year, they had reconsidered eggs, however. One of the students lost hers and it wasn't found until *much* later, when it broke between the seats of her mother's minivan. It had taken two hundred dollars to clean it well enough so the family could ride in it without gagging, and Jen had floated the idea of using tiny pumpkins instead. It was one of the few times she and the health teacher had seen eye to eye on an issue.

"I guess they're going to draw faces on them and everything," Gretchen continued.

"Some of the big school systems actually have robotic babies, from what I've read. And the teacher can access data from the baby and see how well the kids are actually taking care of it." Jen shrugged. "Considering we had to nickel-and-dime the school budget right down to explaining to the committee the only way we could save any more on toilet paper would be a *bring your own leaves* policy, we won't be having robotic infants anytime soon."

"Pumpkins are cuter, anyway." Gretchen smiled. "And speaking of cute, I heard you ran into Sam yesterday."

"Did Kelly at least let me get out of the driveway before she texted you?"

"I doubt it. So?"

"So what?" When Gretchen just stared at her, one eyebrow arched, Jen sighed. "I have to see him in about an hour because he's having his first meeting with the team after school, and Kelly and Coach both think I should be there. I need to mentally put him in a box with a big old *professional colleague* sticker on it."

"But he's only a temporary substitute professional colleague. That's barely a colleague at all."

"It's Sam Leavitt, Gretchen. We didn't hang around with him when we were kids, but we knew him. He was bad news, and not in the sexy-bad-boy kind of way." Okay, maybe a little bit of the sexy-bad-boy kind of way, but if he'd ever actually noticed her, she probably would have run.

"Kelly told me you were focusing on who he was then instead of who he is now. That doesn't seem like you."

"I don't really want to focus on him at all." But she didn't expect her friends to get that message any more than her subconscious had, judging by the steamy dream she'd had last night.

Cocoa started to fidget, making a soft whimpering sound while looking at Gretchen with her big eyes. "You need to find some grass, girl?"

"Thanks for bringing the pumpkins by. I would have found somebody to pick them up."

"I had a few things to do in town and Cocoa wanted to ride in the truck. Alex is in Providence to empty out his apartment, so she's been pacing the house and driving Gram and me crazy."

Jen walked them through the maze of narrow hallways to the main office so Gretchen could sign out of the visitors' log. Then she gave Cocoa a high five and watched them leave before heading to the staff break room. She wanted a coffee, and the powers that be wouldn't allow individual Keurig coffee brewers. First the coffee brewers and then mini-fridges for the half-and-half, they had said. It was a slippery slope to having to go without pens in order to pay the electric bills.

Kelsey Jordan, the new social sciences teacher, was sitting at the break table, reading what looked like a badly handwritten paper. She looked up when the door opened, and smiled. "Coffee time?"

"You know it. Free period?"

"Yeah. I decided to hide in here rather than in my room because there are cookies here."

Jen grabbed one of the aforementioned cookies from the plastic-wrapped tray. "I need to fortify before the football meeting. Trying to gauge the emotional status of a roomful of teenage male athletes is like trying to win a staring contest with an owl."

"Speaking of the football team, I saw the new coach in the hallway a few minutes ago."

Why hearing Sam was on the premises should send an

excited sizzle down her spine when she'd known he'd be there was beyond Jen, but she barely managed not to choke on the snickerdoodle she was chewing.

"He's wicked cute," Kelsey said, and Jen was reminded that Miss Jordan was young and single. And pretty.

"I guess," Jen said, hoping the heat on her cheeks didn't show on the back of her neck. She shouldn't have worn her hair up today.

"So do you have dibs on him or what?"

"Dibs? He's not the last buffalo hot wing." Jen grabbed another cookie before carrying her coffee to the table. "Or cookie."

"I know the three guys—Sam and Alex Murphy and Chase Sanders—were tight in high school and are still friends. And you and Kelly and Gretchen are best friends. Kelly's marrying Chase and Gretchen's marrying Alex, so . . . you know."

"I don't have dibs," she said, and then she sipped her coffee to keep from saying more. Maybe the new fill-in coach would hook up with the pretty social sciences teacher and Jen could be done with him once and for all.

She set the snickerdoodle on the table, her appetite for sweets suddenly gone. If that happened, Kelsey would be a lucky woman. Jen knew just how amazing Sam's hands felt on naked skin and how, even though he was having a rough night, he'd made sure she was breathless and weak-kneed from pleasure before he went looking for his own.

If Sam actually set out to romance a woman . . . Jen shivered just thinking about it.

"You okay?" Kelsey asked.

"Huh? Oh, yeah. I just got a chill." She ate the cookie

and washed it down with the rest of her coffee so she could get out of there. "Everything okay with your classes?"

"So far, so good. I don't know the kids as well as some of you, since I haven't been here long, but I haven't noticed anything that concerns me."

"That's a good thing, though it's still early in the year." Jen got up and washed her mug out in the sink before setting it in the drying rack. "You know where to find me if you need me."

"Yeah, you'll be hanging out with the hot coach."

"I meant in my office on a daily basis, not for the next hour." Jen forced a laugh to take any accidental sting out of her words. "But, yeah, I'll be with the football team this afternoon."

And the hot coach, she thought, yanking open the break room door. *So do you have dibs on him or what?* In her mind, she ran her tongue from his sternum over his Adam's apple and under his jaw to his chin, licking him so nobody else could have him.

Jen almost walked right into a couple of seniors and mumbled an apology as they split apart to avoid a collision. She turned the corner and then ducked into the girls' restroom to splash some cold water on her face. She really needed to get it together before she walked into the meeting.

And no dibs.

When the door to the room they were using for the football meeting opened, Sam turned, expecting to see one or more of the players. Or maybe one of the guys who were supposed to be assistant coaching.

It was Jen, and she looked just as surprised to see him as he was to see her. She glanced around, as if hoping there were other people in the room, before putting on a polite smile. "I guess I'm early."

"Not as early as I was. I guess I was anxious."

"You'll do great," she said, and he wasn't sure if she believed that or if it was some kind of reflex response that came from her job.

"Thanks."

"How's Coach? He must be glad you're here."

"He seems good. Mrs. McDonnell's making damn sure he follows his doctor's orders, so he's cranky as hell, though. And this morning he asked me to smuggle him a cheeseburger."

Jen laughed, a happy sound that relaxed him. "I know you're conditioned to do what Coach tells you, but I think that's the wrong play in this situation."

"You got that right."

"Have you seen your mom yet?" His shoulders stiffened and he gave a sharp shake of his head. "Are you going to?"

For a few seconds, he thought about not answering. He didn't care for personal questions and had a tendency to ignore them, especially if they came from women who might be trying to take his emotional temperature. But there was a possibility Jen's only motivation in trying to get into his head was her concern for the boys on the team. His mental state could affect them, so it was slightly her business. *Very* slightly.

"I wouldn't have come back if I wasn't willing to see her, even for Coach," he finally said. "That would be cruel."

He could tell by her expression that Jen agreed, which he liked. But it was awkward having her ask about his mom, because she was the reason he'd ended up alone with Jen the first time he'd come back to town. He'd run into his mom and it threw him, so he'd started walking. He wasn't sure how long he'd been walking when Jen drove by before stopping and picking him up.

They'd started talking and ended up by the old dam, where a whole lot of making out in cars had happened in his teenage years. Talking became touching and, before long, touching became sex on the hood of her car.

"You have to stop looking at me like that."

"Like what?"

"Like you're thinking about that night out by the dam."

Busted. He shrugged, letting the corner of his mouth turn up in a half smile. "Usually when I look at you, I end up thinking about that night at the dam."

Her cheeks turned a shade of pink that complemented the creamy sweater she was wearing. "It was a stress release. That's what we decided."

"I don't think we ever talked about it, so when did we decide this?"

"No." She waved her hand at him. "By we, I mean Kelly and I. We decided it was because you were so stressed out by seeing your mom and I was so stressed out by the whole football funding thing and . . . we just released some of that stress together."

"Is that what it was?"

"Of course it was. We have absolutely nothing in common. I mean, we're not each other's type *at all*, so what else could it be?"

Since Sam was confident Jen had no idea what his type

was, he had to assume what she meant was that *he* wasn't *her* type. At all. And for some reason, even though he hadn't come back to town with the intention to pick up where they'd left off, that hurt.

He was saved from having to answer, though, when the door pushed open and a stream of teenage boys entered. They were talking to each other and, on the surface, the mood looked good. But he could see the tension in them and a thread of anxiety buzzed through the chatter.

Sam remembered some of them from Eagles Fest. He and the other alumni guys had worked with the team on the fund-raiser to-do list before the kids kicked their asses in the Eagles versus Eagles alumni exhibition game.

He saw Hunter Cass, who was not only the running back but tended to be the mouth for the team. He'd had a rough summer, but appeared to be back on track. PJ the cornerback was with him, talking as usual. The kid never shut up and had made it clear he was playing football just to pad his qualifications for being a head coach someday. He considered himself the secret weapon because he was observant as hell and quite the strategist. Ronnie was one of the defensive line, and the thing Sam remembered most about him was his notoriously bad sense of direction. The kid could get lost in the school cafeteria.

While he waited for them all to find seats and settle in, Sam looked over the clipboard he'd brought from the tiny closet off the gym that served as Coach's office. Running down the names and positions calmed his nerves.

It became obvious to him after a few minutes, however, that the teenagers wouldn't quiet down until he told them to. He looked out over the group and then slapped the clipboard down on the desk. They all shut up and turned to him, expectation written all over their faces.

Sam had no idea what to say. All day he'd been running words through his mind, trying to come up with some kind of inspirational speech worthy of Coach McDonnell. "Hey, guys."

"Hey," they all said together.

Screw it. He'd come up with a pep talk another day. "So you've played some scrimmages. You won your first game."

"Dude, we're pretty good," Cody Dodge said from the back row.

Sam smiled, remembering that the tight end called everybody *dude* to the point Chase had wanted to strangle him. "I was on the losing end of our exhibition game, so I know you're pretty good."

"Yeah, but you guys are like old, dude. We're pretty good in our division."

He heard Jen try to disguise a snicker as a cough and chose to ignore it, even though it was tempting to remind the woman they were pretty much the same age. "You boys don't really know me, but I hope the fact Coach McDonnell asked me to step in for him temporarily is enough for you as far as accepting me as part of the team."

"You came all the way from Texas to help us raise money to keep playing," Hunter Cass said. "And now you came back again 'cause Coach got sick. You're already one of us."

Emotion welled up in Sam's chest, catching him off guard. He picked up the clipboard again and sat on the edge of the desk to give himself a few seconds. When he left Stewart Mills after high school, he never thought he'd see it again. When he'd returned for Eagles Fest, he was surprised to realize he'd missed it—missed the people and the community bond. Now, on his second trip back for an extended stay, the feelings seemed magnified.

When he saw Jen fidget in her seat through the corner of his eye, he guessed she was about to fill the silence and forced himself to get it together. "Where's Shawn Riley?"

A hand went up in the back, and Sam looked at the tall, lean kid with closely cropped dark hair and some scruff on his jaw. According to the sheet, he was a junior, but Sam didn't know much else about him.

"You're the quarterback?" The kid gave one sharp nod, but said nothing. "So you lead the offense, then?"

"I mostly do that," Hunter said. "I like to talk and Riley likes to be quiet."

Maybe Sam was biased since he'd played quarterback in high school, but he didn't think the running back should be the touchstone for the offense. "A team's gotta have confidence in the quarterback."

"Whoa, dude," Cody said. "We have confidence in Riley. Cass just does the cheerleading and shit. He gets us fired up and does all the talking."

Sam wasn't sure if the kid was allowed to say *shit* in the school building, but Jen didn't call foul, so he just went with it. And he noticed the rest of the guys were nodding as Cody spoke, so it was obvious to him they all had Shawn Riley's back.

His cell phone buzzed on the desk and he glanced at the screen. Because he had it set to preview texts on the lock screen, he could see the message from Jen. Don't push at Shawn. Talk after.

If there was an issue with the quarterback, it seemed to Sam that Coach could have given him a heads-up. But the man's philosophy had always been you learned more by doing than talking, so he'd apparently just thrown Sam in the deep end and expected him to swim.

"Okay," he said, turning his attention back to the players. "We're getting on a bus for an away game Friday night. That means we only have a couple of practices together and I need everybody to show up tomorrow afternoon ready to work. For now I want to know what you guys think I should know about the Eagles and what I have to do in order to be the guy you need on the sidelines."

The boys talked for almost an hour, walking him through a typical practice. He could tell by what they stressed what mattered to them, and he took a lot of notes. Nothing earth-shattering, but he hoped it would subconsciously reinforce in the boys' heads that no matter who was standing on the side-lines, they knew what they were doing and they did it well.

When they ran out of steam, and PJ's stomach growled so loudly it actually drowned out the sound of his voice, Sam decided to call it a night.

"Now that we've got the talking out of the way," he said, "I expect you guys to be ready to work tomorrow. I want to see what you can do when you're not playing a team of old guys."

They were laughing as they filed out of the room, so he wasn't surprised when Jen smiled at him. "That went well."

"Thanks. They're a solid team. They could probably do just fine even if nobody was on the sidelines in a goofy polo shirt."

"It's not goofy."

The words sounded automatic, but when her gaze traveled

from his face and down to his waist, he could tell she thought he looked pretty damn good in it. Too bad he wasn't her type *at all*, though.

"I should have talked to you about Shawn Riley before the meeting," she said when she was done admiring the fit of his goofy polo shirt. "Or Coach should have. Got a few minutes?"

"I'm starving, actually. And it's late. You hungry? We can go over to the House of Pizza and you can fill me in on anything I need to know while we eat."

Her eyes widened, but then she looked at the clock on the wall and sighed. "I am hungry. Half the team probably went straight to the pizza house from here, though. We wouldn't be able to talk."

"O'Rourke's?" He wasn't sure why he didn't just tell her he'd stop by her office tomorrow before practice.

"Okay. I have to go back to my office for a few minutes, but I can meet you there in twenty minutes or so?"

"Sounds like a plan."

Sam watched her go and then picked up his clipboard. He needed to go back to Coach's office and grab the massive binder that served as the playbook. And he should call Mrs. McDonnell and let her know he wouldn't be joining them for dinner because he'd be with Jen Cooper.

But only in a professional capacity, of course.

04

Jen hesitated outside the entrance to O'Rourke's Family Restaurant. She'd seen Sam's truck parked across the street, so she knew he was already inside. And once she went in and sat down with him, there'd be no putting that juicy tidbit of fruit back on the grapevine.

Hell, the way this town worked, there was a good chance she'd get a text message from Kelly or Gretchen before her food even arrived.

She'd just have to make it firmly known to anybody who asked that it was a meeting to talk about the football players and it happened to take place in a restaurant because they were hungry. Nothing more. Leaving wasn't an option because she'd told him she'd meet him here, and the last thing she wanted was for him to think she couldn't face being alone with him.

When she'd said hello to Cassandra Jones, who owned the restaurant with her husband, Jen walked to the table in the back where Sam was. He stood when she approached, and she appreciated the show of old-school manners. It was sweet, and she smiled at him as they both sat down.

She noticed a few people looking their way and tried to ignore them. People would say whatever they'd say. But then she wondered if Kelsey would hear about this and think she'd been lying about calling dibs on Sam. Which, naturally, made her think about licking his neck again.

Snatching up the menu, she opened it and intensely studied the offerings, even though they probably hadn't made any changes in the last five years or so. By the time their server took their orders for burgers and fries, with soda for him and iced tea for her, she'd managed to pull it together.

"I'm glad you suggested this," she said. "I wanted to have a chance to talk to you about Shawn, but I didn't realize how hungry I was until you mentioned dinner."

"I didn't think the meeting would go quite that long, or I would have had a snack beforehand. Or ordered pizza for everybody."

"I had a couple of cookies in the break room. There are usually cookies or brownies or something in there on any given day. If it's a big platter and not labeled, it's usually safe to snack on. Just, whatever you do, don't ever eat anything in a plastic dish with a green lid."

"Science projects?"

She laughed. "Mr. Hammond's lunches. He's one of the science teachers, but he's forbidden from using the break room fridge for projects. There was an incident about two years before I started there. He's a pretty laid-back guy, unless you touch the food his wife packed for him."

"She must be a helluva cook."

"Rumor has it she writes him sexy notes and tapes them to the bottom of the lid, but it's just a rumor."

They talked about the school staff, laughing at some of their funny quirks and reminiscing about the teachers who they'd had in high school who were still there. Jen got lost in the conversation and was surprised when their server interrupted them with their meals. She would have liked to keep talking because she loved the sound of Sam's laugh, but they were hungry enough to focus on eating.

"So," he said once they'd put a big enough dent in their burgers to take the edge off. "You seem very involved with the team for a guidance counselor."

"I'm very involved with *all* of the students once they hit sixth grade. My office is in the high school, but two mornings a week, I'm at the middle school. Sometimes more if the kids or parents make appointments with me. The elementary school has a part-time guidance counselor they share with a couple of other small schools in the area, since the needs are different."

"I was surprised when I heard you'd be at the meeting today."

"I know those students more than any other member of the staff except Coach. I try to touch base with each of them at least once a week. There's a lot of pressure when it comes to playing sports. And trying to balance that with academics along with responsibilities at home can be hard on them."

"Especially when things are tough in the community and at home."

"Exactly. And I have to stay on them pretty constantly about their futures. It's easy for teenagers to think an athletic scholarship is their ticket out of a small town, especially when they play for a really good team. But the reality is that this school barely registers on the collegiate sports radar. Some of them are good enough so they might get some scholarship money, but the likelihood of going pro is very slim. I have to keep them focused on what they'll be happy doing five days a week until they're sixty-something years old."

"Must be hard to find the balance between realistic and discouraging."

"It is, but I try to err on the side of encouraging them to dream big. Anyway, that's why I'm so involved with the team. And we all wanted to see how they took to having you step in for Coach, which went well. But I won't be following you around, looking over your shoulder the entire time, if that's what you're worried about."

"I'm not worried at all. It was just an observation. I don't remember the guidance counselor ever talking to us back when I was on the team."

"I don't remember ever talking to the woman at all."

"I don't imagine you really needed her much."

She frowned, trying to figure out what he meant by that. "Every student should have a good relationship with the guidance counselor."

"You had a pretty sweet upbringing, though. A dad that wore a suit to his job at the bank. Your mom baked stuff for fund-raisers. His-and-hers sedans in the two-car garage."

She arched her eyebrow at him. "I'm not going to say I didn't have a nice childhood, because I did, but that didn't make me less entitled to academic and career counseling."

"You're right. Old jealousies, I guess."

Part of her wanted to dig around in what he'd said and see just how deep that resentment went. But he looked a little embarrassed and she let it go. "The guidance counselor we had is one of the reasons I do it. And a big reason I came home when she finally retired. She was lazy as hell and kids slipped through the cracks. When you're in a small town like this, it's so important to help the kids see the bigger picture and prepare them to go find their way."

He tilted his head, smiling at her. "You're pretty passionate about your job."

For some reason, she felt her face flush, even though she certainly wasn't ashamed to love what she did. "I am."

"So tell me about my quarterback."

"When Shawn was little, he had some pretty serious speech issues and he was bullied about it. Even, unfortunately, by some members of his family. The pattern you'll see, of Shawn hanging back and letting Hunter run the room, was established back in elementary school."

Sam sighed and leaned back in his chair. "Does Shawn think he's going to play college ball? It's not very likely he'll find a school that'll let him bring Hunter with him everywhere he goes."

"It's not that bad, really. Around second grade, they were finally able to get some decent speech services for Shawn, and by the time they started middle school, he was age-typical. If you get him alone, without the other guys to do the talking, you'll see he does just fine when he has to make his own way."

"You made it sound like I should tiptoe around him a bit."

She took a sip of her iced tea and shrugged. "He left his

speech delays behind, but it's not as easy to leave behind the effects of being bullied, especially by people you're supposed to trust."

"I know."

Startled by his flat tone, Jen set her glass down. Of course he did. Probably nobody in Stewart Mills knew more than Sam how much childhood betrayals left a mark. But she also knew he wouldn't appreciate her turning the conversation to *his* younger years. "I don't even know if he's aware of it, but he gets angry if an adult male he doesn't know well pushes him to talk in front of other people. From what I've gathered . . . I . . . Crap. I'm not sure what to do here."

"Technically, I'm a member of the high school staff. Kelly rushed the background check through the day after she called me, and I'm on the books as a substitute." His eyes were serious as he gave her a sad smile. "I don't gossip. And the last thing I want to do is make this harder on *any* of the boys by triggering something ugly."

Jen knew in her gut that if there was anybody she could trust to look out for Shawn Riley's best interests, it would be Sam. And he was not only right about being a staff member, but Shawn's speech issues weren't really a secret. Half the town could probably tell him the story.

"Shawn was raised by a single mother. She had to work a lot of hours, so there was no choice but to depend on her father and her brothers to help out with Shawn. I gather they were disgusted by his speech delay and would make him talk so they could laugh at him. He was made fun of at school and then his grandfather and uncles would mock him at home."

Jen watched Sam struggle to maintain a professional

demeanor. But his eyes narrowed slightly and the muscles in his jaw flexed. The fingers of his right hand curled into a fist for a moment before he flattened his palm on the table.

After a moment, he inhaled deeply and then spoke quietly. "Okay."

"The more he gets to know you, the more he'll step out of Hunter's shadow."

"That must be why I really don't remember him from Eagles Fest. There are some kids with big personalities on the team. And I remember thinking they had a good quarterback during the alumni game, but I don't remember talking to him."

"I know he played, but he missed some of the other stuff. He works a lot of hours to sock money away in the summer so his mom could quit her second job."

"Sounds like a good kid."

Jen picked up a fry and dragged it through the ketchup, making squiggles on her plate. "There's more."

"I'm starting to wonder why Coach didn't tell me all of this."

"Coach doesn't talk about his players," Jen said. "Unless it has to do with academic eligibility or he thinks there's a dangerous behavior happening, he keeps everything to himself."

"We always knew we could trust him. Even I learned to trust him, but it took a while."

"And that brings us back to Shawn Riley. He plays football because of you."

She wasn't surprised when his brow furrowed in confusion. "Because of me? The kid doesn't even know me."

"No, but he knows *of* you. It's a small town. People know

you were . . . that you had a rough childhood. He told me once that he chose to be like you and seek out the male role models and team bond that made you stronger."

Sam gave a short, self-deprecating laugh. "Does the story include the part where I only showed up because the alternative was jail?"

"I know that part, but I don't know if the kids do." She knew that part because he'd talked about the brick-throwing incident the night she'd seen him walking and picked him up.

And taken him parking.

She hadn't *meant* to take him parking, in the making-out sense of the word. It was simply a pretty spot with plenty of privacy for conversations. And other things.

Before her mind could cough up a highlight reel of the *other things*, Jen popped the French fry into her mouth. After swallowing that, she downed some iced tea and then dared to meet Sam's gaze again.

He was grinning.

"What?" she asked, assuming she had ketchup on her mouth or something.

"Nothing." But she could see he was highly amused about something and simply stared at him until he broke. "*You* were thinking about it this time."

"Was not."

He laughed, causing several women in the place to turn to watch him. "Yeah, you were. You must really suck at poker."

She did, but she wasn't about to admit that to him. "So we both think about it. Pretty sure that's normal."

"I think about it a lot," he said in a low voice that made her breath catch. "Good thing I'm not your type or we'd probably end up doing more than thinking about it."

Even as heat curled through her body, she caught the slight edge to his voice. Being perceptive was a big part of why she was good at her job, and he didn't like that she'd said that earlier. Or rather that she'd claimed they weren't *each other's* types, but that's not what he said.

Before she could say anything, not that she had any idea how to respond to that, Sam pulled out his cell phone and looked at the time. "I hate to eat and run, but I'm supposed to go see my mother. She's kind of a night owl, I guess."

"Oh, you're going to see her now?"

"Down, Miss Guidance Counselor." He gave her a wry grin. "Just a quick visit to say hi in person. We talked a few times after I went back to Texas. I'm trying, and that's enough."

Considering the stories she'd heard about Sam Leavitt's parents when they were growing up, she admired the effort. "You know where to find me if you want to talk."

He cocked his brow at her. "Like last time?"

Damn her lack of a poker face. *Yes, please.* "No."

Chuckling, he stood and took out his wallet. She wasn't surprised when he insisted on paying for her dinner, but she did win the battle to leave the tip.

"See you tomorrow," he said casually as they stepped out onto the sidewalk.

"Good night."

The autumn night had definitely taken a chilly turn, so Jen hurried to her car. But as she opened the door, she looked over her shoulder to where Sam had parked. He was watching her and when their eyes met, the heat in his gaze chased the chill away.

After a few seconds, she took a deep breath and slid into the driver's seat. Every time she looked at Sam, it got a little bit harder to convince herself he wasn't her type. And he was going to be in town just long enough to cause her a lot of sleepless nights.

S am drove down a dirt road on the outskirts of town, his fingers tight on the steering wheel. He remembered the road from his teen years, since it ended at a river that had a tree perfect for a rope swing.

There was a small cluster of tiny houses, which had started out as camps back in the day, about a quarter of a mile shy of the river. Over time the camps had been converted into year-round homes and at some point a guy had bought them and used them as cheap rental properties. His mom's house was a lot smaller and shabbier than the house Sam had grown up in, but at least looking at the outside didn't make him want to vomit. If his mother still lived in that other house, this visit wouldn't be happening.

She opened the door as he reached the step, and gave him a smile that he managed to return, despite the anxiety humming through him. "I wasn't sure you'd come."

"I told you I would."

Sheila Leavitt was tall, like he was, but very thin. Her dark hair showed a lot of gray, and it was pulled into a low ponytail. Lines framed her dark eyes, and he could see the toll her life had taken on her skin. But her eyes were clear and she stood straight, with her shoulders back.

She pushed the screen door open and then backed up so he could enter. He'd come here earlier in the summer, when Mrs. McDonnell had told him his mother had been sober for a while, but he hadn't gone inside. She'd stood in the dooryard and cried and apologized. He'd softened enough to give her his email address. Eventually, once he was back in Texas, they moved to the telephone, though only a few calls he kept short.

When his mom stepped away, he breathed a sigh of relief. All day his mind had bounced between worrying about the football meeting and wondering if he could tolerate his mother hugging him. She hadn't hugged him as a child, but he knew how much she wanted to repair what little relationship they'd had.

But she was content to gesture to a well-worn couch. "Have a seat. It's a little messy, but it's mostly clutter. And a little messy is a good thing, I guess. I clean when I feel shaky, so the place needing to be picked up means I've had a string of good days. Sometimes even weeks."

"What does that mean? A good day. A day you don't drink?"

She shook her head. "I haven't had a drink in almost three years. A good day is just a day the cravings don't drive me crazy and I'm mostly content."

Mostly content. It made him sad that a good day for her was a day she was mostly content. Despite the past, he wanted her to be happy.

He *wanted* a relationship with his mother. He wouldn't have kept in touch if he didn't and, before he'd driven all the way from Texas for a second time, he'd done some soul-searching on the subject. If he came back here again, he was going to have to make peace with his past, and that meant making peace with her once and for all before he went back west.

But it was hard. This woman's earnest eyes and shaky smile tugged at him, and he felt a weird urge to wrap his arms around her and soothe some of her anxiety. As much as he'd worried about her hugging him, he couldn't help thinking about hugging her now that they were together.

The past was like a bad horror movie playing in the back of his mind, though, and he could feel the buckle of his old man's belt striking between his shoulder blades. And he could still see his mother turning away, bringing the bottle of cheap booze to her mouth so she could drink herself into oblivion. When the alcohol and muscle fatigue screwed up his father's aim and the buckle caught Sam in the head, making him cry out, she'd take the bottle in the bedroom and close the door.

"I can't change it," she said quietly, and he realized he'd been staring at her. Considering where his thoughts had gone, he shuddered to imagine how hard his expression had been. "I tried to drink away the guilt and shame for years, and I finally had to accept that I can't change anything that already happened. All I can do is be better and be strong today, and then try to be even better and stronger tomorrow."

"One day at a time," he said softly. "I'm trying. I'm here because I'm willing to try. That's all I can do."

"One day at a time," she repeated back to him.

"I know more about alcoholism and abuse and addiction and shit than I did then. I read a lot of books over the years. When I finally went to the community college, they had mental health services and I talked to some people." He'd missed having Coach and the guys but, no matter how illogical it was, he'd felt like reaching out to Stewart Mills would put his mother back in his life, and he hadn't been ready. He'd had to turn his back on everybody to feel like he'd turned his back on her.

"I'm glad. That you tried to work through your feelings, I mean."

"I know I need to forgive you for not protecting me." He paused, pressing his mouth together because he was afraid his bottom lip would actually quiver. "And I know that you can't change what happened."

"You know you need to, but *can* you?" He noticed her hands were shaking and, when she saw him looking, she clasped her fingers together.

"I wouldn't be here if I didn't think I can. Eventually."

"One day at a time," she whispered. Then she smiled again. "Do you want something to drink? Or to eat?"

"No, thanks. I just had a burger at O'Rourke's with Jen Cooper."

"Really? She works at the school, doesn't she? Runs around with Coach McDonnell's daughter and Gretchen Walker?"

"Yeah, she's the guidance counselor. She wanted to talk to me about a couple of the players and I was so hungry, so we moved the meeting to the restaurant."

"Oh. So it wasn't like a date?"

He couldn't tell if she thought that was good or bad, and he also couldn't tell if she'd heard about what he and Jen had gotten up to out by the dam. He didn't think so, though. For his mom to have heard, enough people would know so Coach would be one of them. And he definitely would have said something.

"Nope, not a date," he said. "Strictly professional."

"I've run into her a few times in town. She seems very nice. And she's very pretty."

"She is, to both."

"It's funny that you ran around with Chase and Alex when you were in high school, and now they're engaged to Jen's friends."

He didn't need a map to see where she was heading with that. "That is funny. But we just wanted to discuss work and eat at the same time."

"Oh." She actually looked disappointed.

Silence stretched out between them until it was uncomfortable, and Sam shifted on the couch. "Does me coming here make it harder for you not to drink? You said guilt and shame made you drink. Does seeing me bring that back in some way?"

"It does bring it back and it feels horrible, but I won't drink, because losing you again would be more horrible. I know if you come here and I'm not sober, you'll never come back." She paused, but he didn't say anything. He certainly wouldn't lie and deny it. "And if I don't drink, I can see you and be a part of the life you have now."

"I have one more question. Has he ever come back?"

"No." She shook her head. "After a few years, the people from the state helped me go through the divorce process so I could get assistance. I haven't heard from him since . . . that night."

The night Sam fought back. The night he was finally big enough and strong enough to take the belt away from his old man. It was also the night his mother finally dropped the bottle and tried to intercede. She'd begged Sam not to hurt his father because he'd only make it worse.

The old man had taken off. He got picked up and spent the night in the drunk tank and left town as soon as they let him out. Sam might have taken off, too, but he knew if he took off, his mother would drink herself to death within days. It was the rage at himself for not hating her enough to do it anyway that made him drink for the first time.

Two years later, it was Coach looking him in the eye at the police station and telling him he believed in him that made him drink for the last time.

"I want to know about your life *now*," he told his mom. "I want to know where you work and what kind of movies you watch and your favorite television shows."

A genuine, happy smile lit up her face and Sam let himself bask in the warmth of it. Today they were both better and stronger. It was enough.

05

Jen heard her phone's text message tone dinging and knew it was either Kelly or Gretchen. Her alarm clock went off at six in the morning and it was fifteen minutes after, which meant one of her friends had given her enough time to pee and stumble to the coffee brewer before texting.

Her friends had no way of knowing she'd tossed and turned half the damn night, trying not to think about Sam and sex and failing miserably, or that she'd already hit snooze once and had intended to hit it again.

But it was Friday and she liked her job, so she threw back the covers and sat up. After scrubbing her face with her hands and shoving her hair out of her eyes, she picked up her cell phone and unhooked it from the charging cable.

WTH? Spill.

It was a group text started by Kelly, and Jen guessed Gretchen had already seen it and was waiting for a reply. Even though the Walker farm hadn't had cows to milk in years, they still did the "early to bed and ungodly early to rise" thing.

She typed a response. Had a biz meeting.

After tossing the phone on the bed, she went into the bathroom for a few minutes and wasn't surprised to hear it dinging when she came back out. She grabbed it on her way to the kitchen and read their responses while waiting for her coffee to brew.

Biz meeting? Please. That was Kelly.

Gretchen started her message with a monkey emoji. Monkey business? Then there were more monkeys and a banana.

Jen rolled her eyes. Since Alex would be traveling at times, he'd bought his fiancée her first smartphone so texting would be easier for her and they could video chat. Jen wasn't sure if Gretchen had mastered video chatting yet, but she was sure as hell enjoying the emojis.

No bananas involved. Then she sent the cheeseburger emoji.

I'm disappointed, Kelly texted.

Gretchen sent a sad face. Jen responded with the coffee cup and alarm clock emojis.

Then she set the phone down so she could add sugar and milk to her coffee. It was too early in the morning for group texts and pictograms. Her friends seemed to have taken the hint, so she watched the news while she drank the first cup. Then she showered and made another.

She'd just finished drying her hair when she heard the phone go off again. Assuming it was Gretchen or Kelly, she

took the extra couple of minutes to put on the tinted sun-
screen she wore every day and a little lip gloss.

It wasn't Kelly or Gretchen. It was Sam's name that
popped up. They'd all exchanged info during Eagles Fest,
since the three women were essentially in charge and the
three guys were among the guests of honor. She didn't want
to think too hard about why she hadn't deleted his info when
he went back to Texas.

Mrs. McD wants to know if there's a bake sale for
homecoming.

Under that text bubble was another, sent a few seconds
after the first. Sorry. Good morning.

Crap. Homecoming was right around the corner and
her to-do list for it was epic. She has enough going on with
Coach.

Nonsense. There was a pause and then another bubble
popped up. That was her comment, not mine.

Jen laughed and took the last sip of her rapidly cooling
coffee. She really should be leaving for school. I think the
kids would riot if there was no bake sale.

After a few seconds, her screen indicated he was typing
and she washed out her cup while she waited. She'll make
mini chocolate chip muffins.

Sounds good.

Will there be pistachio bars? Then a second bubble. That
was me, not Mrs. McD. She said she keeps forgetting to ask
you about the bake sale and you get up early so she'd call

you except she's cooking so I said I'd text. In case you were wondering.

You can text me anytime. As soon as she hit send, she decided that sounded too flirty. She needed a distraction. There are always pistachio bars. And brownies. The good chewy, fudgy kind.

I'll bring a gallon of milk with me.

She really had to go or she was going to be late for her first appointment. You know you have to attend all the homecoming stuff, right? Coach.

Lucky me. Is there a schedule somewhere?

I'm on my way in so I'll make a note to check if there's a final version and drop it by practice.

Thanks. See you then.

She sent him a smiley face emoji and then felt stupid, so she grabbed her bag and went to work. During the short drive, she tried not to think about the fact she'd found an excuse to see him. She could have given him the link to the school's website and told him where to find it. Or she could have taped it to his office door.

Instead she'd offered to bring it to him personally, which meant she'd get to talk to him for a few minutes, and she felt a flutter of anticipation. At the rate she was going, if she didn't get a handle on this crush, it was only a matter of time before she was sending Gretchen and Kelly little monkey emojis.

Sam stood in front of the mirror, staring at his reflection and wondering what the hell he'd gotten himself into.

He liked his life simple, if a little rough around the edges. A hard day's work followed by an ice-cold soda or two in his camp chair before falling asleep in front of the television. An occasional night on the town. Calluses and worn denim and sweat.

The man in the mirror looked like the kind of guy people expected big things from. Freshly showered and clean-shaven, Sam was wearing the blue polo shirt with the Stewart Mills Eagles logo that had been Coach's uniform for decades. And khakis. He'd bought and was wearing his first pair of khakis. No matter how ill prepared he felt on the inside, he couldn't deny that on the outside, he looked like a high school football coach.

It was weird.

He went downstairs to say good-bye to Coach and Mrs. McDonnell. There was still time to kill before practice, but he wanted to swing by and look at the apartment Kelly had lined up for him. And he didn't think there were enough hours in the day, even when he got up at the crack of dawn with his hosts, to memorize Coach's playbook binder.

"You heading out?" he heard Coach call from the recliner, no doubt alerted by the sound of his feet on the stairs.

"I am. Do you need anything while I'm running around town?" Sam frowned, not liking Coach's color today. Sometimes if he didn't sleep well, it would give his skin a grayish pallor, so maybe that's all it was.

"Nope. Helen just left to go to the pharmacy. They're

going to change one of my medications because it's making me sick during the night."

"Hopefully that'll work. I can hang around until she gets back."

"I don't need a damn babysitter," Coach snapped.

"Good, because running herd on teenagers is hard enough without adding babysitting to the mix. I just meant I'd keep you company."

Coach sighed. "I appreciate that, son, but to be honest I'd really like to have *no* company for the hour or whatever it'll take for Helen to run her errands. I'm tired of having people fuss over me."

Sam didn't want to leave him alone. He was right about that. But he could also understand Coach wanting a break from being watched like they were afraid he'd go heels up at any second. "You have the phone?"

Coach showed him the handset to the cordless landline, which was tucked next to his thigh. "I have the phone, a glass of water and the television remote. All I need now is some peace and quiet."

"You better still be alive when Mrs. McDonnell gets back or she'll never let me hear the end of it."

Coach chuckled. "I wouldn't do that to you. Oh, and one more thing before you go. You're going to need this."

When Coach held out the silver whistle on the blue nylon cord, Sam felt himself balk and couldn't make his feet move toward the recliner. It wasn't just a whistle. It was *Coach's* whistle.

"Don't be making that face," Coach said. "I'll take it back from you when I'm ready."

Sam swallowed hard. "It means a lot to me that you called me."

"Not as much as the fact you came means to me."

A few hours later, Sam stood on the sidelines, watching the team run through some plays. Dan, the school custodian and new dad, had shown up a little late, but his mother-in-law had flown in from somewhere out west and he'd have more free time for a couple of weeks. Him being there to direct the action gave Sam a chance to stand back and watch the boys at work.

Jen had been right about Shawn Riley. When the quarterback was on the field, he was like a totally different kid. Still quiet, but with an air of confidence everybody on his team could feel.

When Dan called for a water break, Sam caught Shawn's attention and called him over. "You look good out there, kid."

"Thanks."

"You may have noticed the coaching staff's a bit of a shit show right now." He was surprised when the quarterback chuckled. "I'm doing my best to nail down the playbook because I can't depend on knowing who else will be with me on the sidelines, but Coach has a way of making football on paper look like advanced geometry."

"I've got no problem with calling audibles on the line."

Sam gave him an approving look. "I didn't think you would."

Back when he'd played ball, it had been important to Coach that the players out on the field could think for themselves. No amount of experience would sharpen a player's instincts if he looked to the sidelines for directions on every single play.

"So you and I will figure it out as we go along, then," he said.

"Yup."

"Okay. Back to work."

While the team hydrated and took a breather, Sam ran through some of the things he'd noticed while watching. He had a short list of things he thought they could improve on, but he also complimented them on some plays they'd executed really well.

When they went back onto the field, Sam got a little more hands on. He moved around, focusing on different parts of the line with each snap. They were definitely one of Coach McDonnell's teams, he thought with pride as he watched them. There was some laughter and some friendly trash-talking, but when push came to shove, these guys lifted each other up rather than putting each other down.

As he watched, Hunter Cass broke a tackle and headed for the end zone. It was a hell of a run, but the kid playing safety ran him down just shy of the red zone. Cass hadn't done anything wrong—he didn't try any fancy moves or try to showboat too soon. The other kid outran him.

Stewart Mills didn't have a track team, but Sam made a note to talk it over with Coach. The male body went through a lot of muscle changes in the teenage years, and they might need to back off some of his weight training and focus on his speed this year.

Hunter bent over, resting his hands on his knees and panting. Sam grabbed a towel and started toward him. "You trying out to be our new *jogging* back, Cass?"

The kid lifted his head enough to glare at him. "That's so funny. Really."

"It was when Coach McDonnell yelled it at Chase Sanders back in the day." Sam paused, and then chuckled as he tossed the towel to him. "Yup. Still is."

Hunter straightened, still trying to catch his breath, and looked at some spot past Sam. "Your girlfriend's coming."

Frowning, Sam turned and saw Jen making her way toward them, a sheet of paper in her hand. "You feel like running laps until you puke, Cass?"

"Isn't she?"

"Miss Cooper and I are friends, not that it's any of your business."

Hunter gave him a thumbs-up. "Hey, Miss Cooper."

"Hi, Hunter."

When the kid walked off to rejoin the team, Sam turned to Jen, wondering what if any of that conversation she'd heard. He was fairly sure she couldn't have heard the girl-friend remark, but the part about them being friends might clue her in to the fact they were the subject of gossip.

Not that that would be a surprise in Stewart Mills.

"Basically your entire weekend next week is shot," she said, handing him the sheet. "The parade starts at seven on Friday night, but it takes an unbelievable amount of time to get ready for it. Then there's the bonfire. The game Saturday afternoon, and then the dance."

"Okay, wait. So everybody's going to be out until all hours of the night, and then they play the biggest home game of the year. And *then* they dance?"

Jen laughed. "It's been this way for as long as there's

been a Stewart Mills High. You rode in the parade and then did who knows what with who knows who at the bonfire until the wee hours. Then you played—and won all four years, if I remember correctly—and then danced."

"I was like seventeen at the time. And we lost the homecoming game my freshman year."

"I was still at the middle school when you were a freshman. And you guys weren't all together on varsity yet, were you?"

"No. It was about halfway through my sophomore year season that we got our shit together."

They wandered back to the benches, keeping an eye on the practice drills. Sam noticed Dan kept his cell phone in his hand at all times and checked the screen frequently, but he wasn't about to give him a hard time about it. Having a new baby *and* his mother-in-law at home had to be hard on the nerves.

"They look pretty good," Jen said after a while. "It's interesting to see them out there without Coach. They must like you."

"Thanks, but I don't think it has much to do with me. I'm not sure these kids need anybody on the sidelines at all."

"I don't know about that. Blow the whistle." When the boys all looked, she pointed at the freshman safety—Danny something, Sam thought—and then beckoned him over. "You can't keep up with the wide receiver if he's looking forward and you're looking behind you."

"I gotta play the ball, Miss Cooper. If I don't know where the ball is and I touch him, that's a penalty."

"You're practically running backward, so you're not going fast enough to touch him at all. You need to watch *him*. He knows where the ball is supposed to be thrown and if he's still got his head down, running flat out, he's not there yet, so neither are you. You'll learn to spot when he's getting ready to make his move and *that's* where the ball is."

"Yes, ma'am." The kid put his helmet back on and trotted out to his teammates.

Sam looked at Jen, who shrugged. "When you spend most of your life hanging out at Coach's house, you learn things."

"That's incredibly sexy."

Her cheeks turned pink and she rolled her eyes at him as she turned to face the school. "If you could not make me blush in front of two dozen teenage boys, that'd be great."

He loved how easy it was to make her blush. Actually, he loved how easy it was for *him* to make her blush. She was always pretty calm and unflappable around other people, but he could unnerve her with just a look and he liked that.

"This dance thing," he said. "I have to chaperone, right?"

"Yes. You don't have to dress up or anything, though. What you're wearing would be fine."

"I don't care about the dress code. Do chaperones get to dance?"

She laughed. "Are you going to get out on the dance floor and bust some moves?"

"God no." He took a step closer to her, so she had to look up to see his face. "I want to dance with you."

Her lips parted slightly and then she gave him a saucy smile. "I'll have to check my dance card. It might be full."

"I'll bring an eraser."

Jen jumped a little when Dan blew the whistle three times, signaling the end of practice. "I need to get back to my office. I think my to-do list is self-populating when I leave it unattended for too long."

"See you later."

The team was leaving the field, so Sam didn't allow himself the pleasure of watching Jen make the walk back to the school doors. It didn't matter. All he had to do was close his eyes to summon the sexy sway of her hips as she walked.

"Good practice, Coach," Shawn said as he jogged by.

"You too," he called after him.

Dan took off right away, but it was almost a half hour before the last of the players left the locker room. Once everybody was gone, he locked the door to the office and killed the lights in the gym before stepping out into the lobby area.

He stopped in front of the tall glass case and stared at the trophy—the first football championship for the Stewart Mills Eagles football team. It dominated the others from the top shelf, and had a framed team photo next to it. Several newspaper clippings were mounted to the glass behind them. But he didn't see the pictures.

All he saw was the trophy.

Jen purposely stayed in her office until practice had been over long enough so she was sure everybody associated with the football team—especially the coach—had left the building. Since a truck restocking the vending machines had messed up the parking situation that morning, she was parked in the big lot, and cutting through the gym lobby was the fastest way to get to her car.

She stopped short, though, when she saw Sam standing silently in the middle of it, staring at the trophy case. "Sam?"

For a few seconds, she wondered if something was wrong with him because he gave no indication he'd heard her. Then he gave an almost imperceptible shake of his head. "I can't do this."

It would be a lot easier to throw out a chipper *of course you can* and go about her business, but something rough in his voice froze her in place. "It looked like you guys were having a great practice today. What is it that you don't think you can do?"

Because he was staring at the trophy, she was guessing he meant coaching the team. But he could also mean something else, like trying to heal his relationship with his mother or being back in Stewart Mills. Or seeing *her* every day, even. Just because he was looking at the trophy case didn't mean he was talking about sports.

"I don't know," he said, shaking his head.

"Yeah, you do. It's just you and me here, Sam, and you know I'm a good listener."

He turned then and looked at her, his dark gaze locking with hers. The last time she'd given him a shoulder to lean on, she'd ended the night leaned over the hood of her car and, judging by the sizzle in that look, he was thinking the same damn thing.

Then the heat faded and he turned back to the trophy case. "I can't be to these boys what Coach was to me."

"They don't need you to be Coach McDonnell. They still have him. But now they have you, too. Another man in their lives who believes in them and wants to see them succeed."

"Fighting to win that trophy saved my life."

She went and stood next to him, facing the trophy case. "No. Having a positive male role model and good friends changed your life. You saved yourself by letting them in."

"What if I let these kids down?"

"You can't compare the impact Coach and the Eagles had on you with what you're doing now. These kids aren't you, Sam. They all struggle in different ways and some have it tougher than others, but none of them have gone through what you did. Hell, some of them are only on the team because there's nothing better to do."

"You can't tell me it doesn't mean anything when you and Gretchen and Kelly worked your asses off with Eagles Fest to fund the team."

"I would never say it doesn't mean anything. I'm just saying it means different things to different kids and you might be projecting what it meant to *you* onto the kids, which is putting too much pressure on yourself for no reason." She turned to face him and put her hand on his arm. "You know I've been watching and I promise you're doing a great job. They're lucky to have you, Sam."

"I'm being stupid."

"It's never stupid to care. You've had a lot going on. Coming back here the first time. Seeing your mom. Then getting the call Coach had a heart attack and coming back. It's a lot and it stirs things up inside. That's all."

He smiled down at her, setting the nervous butterflies off. "There *has* been a lot."

"You just need to relax."

"Talking to you relaxes me." His voice was low, with a husky tone to it that made her realize she still had her hand on his arm. She let it drop, but he grabbed her wrist and tugged her closer. "I could use a hug."

Big mistake, she thought. *Big.* But she didn't seem to have any willpower when it came to him. When he looped his arm around her shoulders and pulled her close, she didn't resist. Closing her eyes, she wrapped her arms around his waist and pressed her hands against his back.

"Feel better?" she asked.

"You feel amazing." His hand slid up to the back of her neck.

"That's not what I meant."

When he used his other hand to tip her chin up, she opened her eyes. His expression was soft, but there was no missing the underlying heat. "I keep thinking that someday I'm going to crawl into bed and close my eyes and *not* think about that night."

"Sometimes I hope that day comes, but I like thinking about that night," she confessed.

He ran his thumb over her bottom lip. "I didn't kiss you that night."

"We kind of fast-forwarded to the getting naked part." Every nerve in her body seemed zeroed in on the sensation of his thumb stroking her mouth.

"Let's rewind a little bit."

He lowered his mouth to hers, lowering his thumb so his lips could take its place. She leaned into him and her fingers curled, gathering the fabric of his shirt into her fists as he kissed her.

When his tongue dipped between her lips, she opened to him. His hand slid up the back of her neck, into her hair, and she sighed. Nothing existed in her world anymore except Sam's mouth and his hands.

He kissed her—one hand fisted in her hair and the other cupping her ass—until they were both breathless and their bodies were pressed together. Then he broke it off, exhaling a shaky breath.

"God, woman. You make me forget everything."

The words washed over her like a glass of ice water, leaving her confused and uncertain of what was happening. The first time they'd been together, he'd been upset by seeing his mother. Tonight, besieged by doubts and memories of the past, he'd reached for her again. *You make me forget everything.*

"I'm not some kind of comfort object you can reach for when you're feeling crappy."

"What? I didn't mean . . ." He scowled, taking a small step back. "Is that what you think is going on?"

"I don't know. I know it seems like when you're feeling low emotionally, we end up with our hands on each other."

"Or," he said, arching his eyebrow, "maybe when I'm feeling emotionally low is the only time you soften up enough to forget I'm not your type."

"That's not . . . soften up? What the hell does that mean?"

"I . . . hell, I don't know." He scrubbed a hand over his jaw. "I don't know what's happening. What I *do* know is that we could win the football championship and I could have the trophy in one hand and the keys to a new Corvette they want to give me for being Coach of the Year in the other, and then they could interrupt me to tell me I won the lottery, and if I saw you in the crowd, I would *still* want my hands on you."

She took a second to sort through that in her head and then smiled. "That sounds like quite a daydream you've got going on."

"I'm just saying, even if I was on an emotional high, I would still want you. And when I said you make me forget everything, I meant the fact we're in the middle of a high school hallway, so this comfort object theory of yours is bullshit."

"Okay, let's say it's bullshit. You still have a lot going on."

For a few seconds, she thought he might argue with her. But he sighed and put a little more space between them. "You're right, I guess."

There was something in his eyes that made her want to explain more—to try to make him understand why she was keeping him at arm's length. She wasn't totally sure she understood it herself, so trying to verbalize it would probably end in disaster.

Before she could try, they heard the squeak of sneakers on the waxed floor and moved apart. It was Ronnie, and he looked frustrated.

"Hey, Coach. My car won't start and everybody's gone. They let me in the office door because your truck's still out there so you must still be in here."

"I am," he said.

"I should go," Jen said quickly, and Sam gave her an inscrutable look. "I'm not good at cars not starting, so good luck."

She practically ran to the exit and across the parking lot.

06

Carrying two bags and a few boxes up a flight of stairs wasn't so bad, but it made Sam keenly aware that he was going to spend at least the next few weeks, if not a couple of months, with very few possessions to call his own.

But the one-bedroom apartment over the insurance office had been available for immediate move-in and it met all of his requirements for a residence—no long-term commitment, a bathroom, and an outlet for the coffee machine. And the previous tenant had abandoned the couch—for good reason—so he had something to sit on.

The primary reason he'd jumped at it, though, was that he'd wanted to get out of the McDonnell house as quickly as possible.

He didn't think there was another woman in the world who could make a person feel as welcome and comfortable in her home as Mrs. McDonnell. But with that came a need to fuss over her guest and Sam knew she had enough on her plate with Coach's health. No matter how much Sam told her he could cook for himself and do his share of cleaning up, she wouldn't hear of it.

He wanted her to worry about two people—Coach and herself.

Then there was the fact he'd lived alone since he left Stewart Mills after high school, and he wasn't very good at living his life on somebody else's schedule or remembering to put on pants before coffee in the morning.

When he went down for the last box, he left the apartment door propped open. Unlike most of the apartments over downtown businesses, he didn't have an interior staircase with a second door at street level. There was a small parking lot behind the insurance company, and an exterior set of stairs led up to a deck just big enough to allow him to open the screen door without knocking himself off.

After hours, the lot was only for residents, but during the day people who couldn't parallel park worth a damn used it when they had errands on the main street. As he climbed into the bed of his truck to grab the last box, Sam noticed a small car doing a slow roll past him.

He looked at the driver and couldn't hold back the grimace. Edna Beecher. The Wicked Witch of Stewart Mills. Nobody knew exactly how old she was since she seemed to predate every other living person in town, but she didn't seem to be slowing down any.

She thrived on being in everybody's business and, if she didn't like what she saw, she threatened to call the FBI. Half the time, she *did* call them, and Sam could only imagine what they thought of her. She'd even called them on Alex recently because he was taking pictures of the teenage boys. The fact that he was a photographer chronicling the football team didn't even slow her down.

Edna glared at him as she slowly drove past, and he thought for a minute she might stop and roll down her window to give him a hard time. But she didn't. Many years ago, she'd insinuated that Sam's father hadn't run off, but had been "taken care of." At the time, Sam had simply smiled and refused to rise to the bait and, ever since, she'd given him a wide berth. She'd watch and glare and let him see she was there, but she didn't verbally harass him like she did other residents.

"She's watching you," he heard a voice say, and he turned to see Paul Decker standing on the other side of his truck.

Deck was a big tree trunk of a guy and he'd been the heart of the Eagles defensive line back in the day. Now he owned and operated Decker's Wreckers and had a wife and two boys. He was also holding what looked like a pie carrier, and Cheryl Decker was no slouch in the kitchen.

"Tell me that's for me."

"Yeah. The wife heard you were moving—like literally heard you were carrying a box up the stairs—and whipped it up. It's still hot."

Sam dragged the box down to the tailgate and jumped to the ground. Then he hefted it and nodded for Deck to follow him up the stairs. "I don't know if I have plates, but I know I've got two spoons."

After setting the box in the corner of the combination living room and everything but the bathroom, Sam turned to take the pie from Deck, but the big man had stopped in the doorway.

"Interesting design scheme," he said.

Sam looked around his temporary new home. Besides an ugly, brown couch, there were two collapsible camp chairs he'd picked up at the hardware store, facing where the television would go if he had one. A folding camp table was between the chairs so he and a guest had a place to set their drinks. A couple of duffel bags and some boxes rounded out the look.

"Easy to clean," he said.

"I guess I'll stand. That couch looks like it wants to bust a spring up my ass. And those chairs, man. Best-case scenario is the chair collapsing under me so I land on my ass."

Sam laughed. "What the hell is the worst-case scenario?"

"Me walking around with a chair stuck on my ass because I'm wedged in so bad even you can't pull it off."

"I've got a bed coming tomorrow. Had to call and order it over the phone, so I hope it's as comfortable as it looked online. And I might hit the secondhand shop today and see if they have a decent TV."

"You're living large, my friend." Deck set the pie on the counter and pulled off the lid while Sam grabbed a couple of spoons out of a box with *coffee* written on it in big, bold letters. "It's good to have you back again."

"It's good to *be* back. For a while."

"How the boys doing?"

"They're good. They miss Coach, but Mrs. McDonnell said maybe this weekend they can stop by and visit him for a little while. Away game tomorrow night, and I can't decide how I feel about it. On the one hand, I'd like to coach my first game in front of people who already know I have no idea what I'm doing. On the other hand, if I screw it up too badly, maybe having a bunch of strangers in the bleachers wouldn't suck."

"Trust me, if you screw it up, we'll all know before the bus even rolls back into town."

"Funny. You know, you can stop in and give me some advice anytime."

Deck winced, then dug his spoon into the hot blueberry pie. "I filled in for Coach once a few years back when a stomach flu wiped out the coaching staff. It was a disaster. It seems I'm a big softie and I'm incapable of telling people what to do, especially kids."

"I've spent some time with your boys and it seems like you keep them in line. They're good kids."

"I'll tell Cheryl you said so, since she's the one who does the actual keeping in line." He put a big spoonful of pie in his mouth, closing his eyes as he savored it. "Speaking of Cheryl . . ."

And here it comes, Sam thought, going to the fridge to grab a couple of waters since he hadn't bought milk yet. Someday he was going to have a conversation with somebody in Stewart Mills that didn't circle around to Jen Cooper. And it was a crying shame to have hot blueberry pie without milk.

"Heard you had a nice dinner with Jen at O'Rourke's night before last," Deck finished.

"I don't know about a nice dinner, but we grabbed a couple of burgers."

"They make good burgers."

"True. Anyway, yes, Jen and I grabbed a bite to eat while we talked about team stuff."

"And?"

Sam shrugged. "And we talked about team stuff."

"Cheryl's going to be disappointed."

If she knew she was missing out on the details of a

smoking-hot kiss in the gym foyer, she'd be *really* disappointed. "Your wife's not alone. I swear, Stewart Mills needs a movie theater or something."

They made a hell of a dent in the pie before Sam put the lid back on the dish and set it in the fridge. "I can't believe we ate half a pie for breakfast. Hell, I can't believe your wife *baked* a pie first thing in the morning. You're a lucky man."

"Nothing luckier than watching your wife bake pies meant to be given away."

Sam put his hand on his stomach and groaned. "Okay, *I'm* a lucky man. At least there's practice after school so I can work off some calories."

"Yeah, it's a helluva workout, standing there blowing that whistle."

"Asshole. Watch it or I'll shove you into a chair and leave you there."

Hot kisses, blueberry pie and trash talk with an old friend. For this moment, at least, it sure was good to be back.

At least once a month during the school year, and sometimes during the summer break, Jen met Kelly at O'Rourke's for a meeting. It wasn't really business, since their discussions were off the books, but they both considered the unofficial meetings a core part of their jobs.

Today they were meeting for a late breakfast because Kelly had the day off and was expecting Chase to get home in the early afternoon. He was still commuting back and forth to New Jersey to wrap up some business he had going on before Eagles Fest had brought him back to Stewart Mills and Kelly for good. Jen had told the office she had an off-site appointment and would be late getting in, and she'd taped a note for students on her door before she left the night before.

It was the last thing she'd done before ending up in the gym atrium, kissing Sam.

"How's the new school year going?" Kelly asked once they had coffees on the table and their breakfast orders in.

"So far, so good." She rapped her knuckles lightly on the table, even though it probably wasn't real wood.

"I know you've been focused on the football team quite a bit, for which my dad and I can't thank you enough, but how are things going at the middle school?"

"Not too bad. I'm dealing with a few kids who aren't handling the step up in academics very well. And a couple of parents who are really overreaching for their kids. It's a huge adjustment."

"And Em?"

Jen smiled. She and Kelly knew each other so well they could usually communicate without using names in public. But the restaurant was almost empty and they both had a soft spot for twelve-year-old Emily Jenkins. Her mother had passed from cancer about two years back, and the little girl and her father really went through a rough spot. It had culminated in the police being called when Emily shoplifted feminine pads from the convenience store because she knew money was tight and was too embarrassed to ask her dad for them.

Luckily the police officer who responded, Dylan Clark, had called Kelly in and the situation was quietly resolved. Jen spent some time working with both of them—especially stressing to Mr. Jenkins that his girl was heading into puberty and didn't have a mom, so he needed to get comfortable with awkward conversations pretty quickly—and she checked in with Emily on a regular basis.

"They're doing really well," she said. "And now they have a little basket on the kitchen counter where they can leave notes to each other. She's at that age where father-and-daughter talks can be awkward and make each other uncomfortable, so they write notes back and forth. She said at first it was mostly hard things, like her needing to go bra shopping or talking about her mom, but now they share funny stories and jokes, too. Her grades are good and her teachers say she's bouncing back."

"I'm so glad." Kelly leaned back against the booth. "That's one of the things I love about being part of a small-town police force, especially in my hometown. We have a better chance of helping people *before* things get too bad."

"Speaking of, anything on Spruce Street?" Jen had gotten a tip over the summer that one of the high school students might be involved in a drug situation, though she hadn't been given specifics.

Kelly shook her head. "Nope. We've been patrolling and we even got an undercover from the county task force to go in as a strange face and look around. Nothing at school?"

"Nothing." Besides the random locker checks that were a regular part of the school policy, they'd been keeping a close eye on the student. "I'm starting to wonder if that little tip was somebody just looking to cause trouble. Maybe they thought we'd bust down the door first and ask questions later."

"Maybe." Kelly brought up another name and they went through the list of kids they'd had concerns about before or were keeping an eye on now.

The list was a lot shorter than it had been earlier in the year, which Jen was thankful for. Stewart Mills had been a mess for a while. When the economy tanked, families were stressed—some of them beyond the breaking point—and the kids started acting out. More drinking and more petty crimes. And then they took away football.

Things were looking up now, though, and by the time their breakfast came, they'd run out of problems to talk about. Just a few minutes after the server left their plates, Kelly frowned and leaned over to see past Jen. "What the hell?"

Jen turned in her seat to see Sam walking toward them with Coach McDonnell. Her stomach knotted at the thought of the guys joining them because Kelly would definitely notice her staring at Sam Leavitt's mouth the entire time. But Cassandra peeled off and set two menus on a table over by the wall, so she blew out a sigh of relief.

"Does Mom know you're here?" Kelly asked, standing to kiss her father's cheek.

"She does."

Kelly narrowed her eyes. "And she doesn't care?"

Sam laughed. "She called me and told me if I didn't get him out of the house, she was going to put a pillow over his face and count to five hundred."

"That sounds like Mom. I thought you were moving this morning."

"That didn't take long." He rubbed his stomach, which drew Jen's gaze to where his shirt hid abs she'd like to run her hands over again. "It took longer to eat a quarter of the fresh blueberry pie Deck showed up with. Hell of a breakfast."

Jen snorted. "Only Cheryl could whip up a pie in time for it to be breakfast."

"She must use frozen crusts," Kelly said.

"She must."

Sam shrugged. "I don't know, but it was good."

"Shut up," Coach barked. "I'm allowed to have scrambled egg whites, dry toast with some jelly and decaf with skim milk."

They all winced. You knew it was serious when you had to have skim milk in your coffee. Jen took a sip of her own coffee to avoid looking at Sam, and then felt guilty because hers was pale from the extra half-and-half cups she'd dumped into it.

"Helen even called Cassandra before I left to make sure I didn't try to sneak a hash omelet by her," Coach grumbled.

Kelly shook her head. "Trust me, every single resident of Stewart Mills knows you're not allowed to have a hash omelet. Sam, are you ready for your first away game tonight?"

"I don't really have a choice. I think we're ready, though."

"We'll let you girls get back to your meeting," Coach said. "Looking at your plates is just pissing me off even more about having to eat scrambled egg whites and skim milk."

Once they were out of earshot, Kelly leaned across the table. "Okay, what happened?"

"What do you mean?"

"You and Sam wouldn't look at each other. And there was tension. Like a rubber-band-about-to-snap kind of tension."

"You're imagining things."

"And you're lying."

Jen pulled out her phone and pulled up her texting app. We kissed in the gym atrium after practice last night. She hit send and waited for Kelly's phone to ding.

Her friend's eyebrows rose when she read the message. Then she looked at Jen. "And?"

"That's it."

She texted again. It ended a little awkwardly and we left separately.

Why are we texting?

Because he's sitting right there.

"Way over there," Kelly said out loud.

"Not far enough."

"Are you going to the game tonight?"

Jen shook her head. "It's an hour and a half drive each way. I wish there were more schools in our competition class with football teams because the travel's crazy."

"It's an expensive sport, which we know all too well."

"Are you going?"

"No. Chase isn't going to want to drive all the way from New Jersey and then add another three hours on top of that to watch the game. If it was closer, maybe. And I have to work tomorrow."

The Stewart Mills police force had been reduced to the chief, some support people and two officers—Kelly and Dylan Clark. That meant Kelly had to work a lot of weekends, even if Chase was in town.

"Chase knows Sam is back, right?"

"Of course. And Gretchen told me Alex should be back tomorrow morning, so Chase said he might organize a guys' night out while I'm at work."

"It's too bad you have to work or we could do a girls' night out at the same time." As soon as she said the words, she thought about Kelsey Jordan's observation that it seemed logical for her—as the third of the female best friends—to hook up with the third of the male trio.

"You could hang out at Gretchen's and I can swing by about break time. Maybe Gram'll make us up some macaroni salad."

Even though she was actually in the process of eating a meal, Jen's mouth watered at the thought of Ida Walker's famous macaroni salad. "You should text Gretchen."

Ten minutes later, it was a plan, macaroni salad and all. Kelly grinned and put her phone away. "This is perfect. Maybe we should do this once a month. Send our guys out to the pizza house while we invade the farm and eat Gram's cooking."

Our guys. Even Kelly was subconsciously falling prey to the assumption. *Whatever*, Jen said to herself. They could think whatever they wanted as long as there was macaroni salad involved.

During the almost ninety-minute drive to another high school in their division, Sam had thought hell was being trapped on a school bus full of pumped-up teenage boys. But being trapped on a school bus full of teenage boys who'd played hard in the rain and lost by a missed field goal was so much worse.

Sitting up front, across the aisle from Dan and Joel, Sam listened to the chatter behind him and with every passing mile got more pissed off. Some of the players had stuck earbuds in their ears, cranked the music and checked out. But too many of them were rehashing the game and there was a lot more blame than he'd expected from this group.

"What kind of loser can't kick a football twenty-three yards?"

"It was pouring, asshole."

Sam heard rumblings about a fumble that happened in the third quarter, and a lot of crap being said about the defense not containing the run. Dissecting a game was one thing. But the guys were angry and they were taking it out on each other.

"If you can't catch one of the slowest running backs in the state, maybe you should try out for the girls' softball team next year," he heard Hunter Cass snarl at somebody.

Sam stood and turned to face the rest of the bus, putting a hand on the back of the seat to keep his balance. "Hey! What the hell is going on?"

Silence fell immediately and they all looked at him with guilty eyes. The few that had earbuds in took them out and he had everybody's attention.

"We have to win for Coach," Hunter said, the anger in his voice tempered by sadness. "We *have* to."

Sam understood the sentiment and probably would have felt the same way back when he was in high school. They were feeling the pressure of not letting down a guy they respected and loved. He got it. But Sam was the adult in this situation and keeping these kids on track was as much—if not more— his job than just being the guy on the sidelines calling plays.

"You *have* to win for Coach?" he challenged, sweeping them all with a questioning look.

"Coach doesn't expect us to win every game," Shawn said. He didn't raise his voice but, as always, the other guys gave him their full attention. He stood and leaned against the window so he could see his teammates. "He expects us to give every game our best."

When he fell silent and the quiet stretched out, Sam risked pushing him for more. This was the leadership he wanted to see from the kid. "And?"

"And he'd rather we lose as a team than win because we're tearing each other down." Shawn looked at Sam for a few seconds, and then turned back to his teammates. "We lost. We've lost before and we didn't turn on each other. The only difference is that we wanted to win to honor Coach, but that isn't how we do it. We honor Coach McDonnell by being the team he's taught us to be."

Life should come with a soundtrack, Sam thought, because the moment really needed a swell of dramatic music. "That's the truth, guys. I know what Coach means to you. I don't think anybody knows better than me what he means to you guys. Hell, here I am, a decade and a half later, and I still want to make him proud."

"You made him proud," Hunter said. "You won the championship."

"Yeah, we did. We won the championship and the town went wild. A parade. That damn shrine in the lobby. They renamed Coach's street to Eagles Lane. But I know in my heart if we'd fallen short that day, the town would have been disappointed, but Coach would still have been proud."

There was no response to that, but a lot of them were nodding and they all looked thoughtful. That was probably enough for now. He gave a quick nod of thanks to Shawn and then sat down. After blowing out a frustrated breath, he took out his phone.

You busy? He hit send before he could change his mind.

Jen responded almost immediately. No. Everything okay?

Lost by 3.

I heard. How are they taking it?

What he really wanted to do was call her. He missed the sound of her voice. That gave him pause, though, because maybe she'd been right. Here he was having a rough night again and his first instinct was to reach out to Jen.

He didn't believe that made her any kind of comfort object he was using to make himself feel better, though. She was simply the person he wanted to turn to when he was having a rough day. Maybe he didn't have a lot of experience with healthy relationships, but he was pretty sure that was supposed to be a good thing.

Well, a good thing if they were actually going to *have* a relationship. But he wasn't going to be in New Hampshire long enough to make that kind of commitment, and he wasn't staying. She wouldn't leave here. Even if he was her type, which he wasn't, it was a moot point.

Not well. He debated on how much he wanted to type, then added to the text. Blame and anger and some harsh words for each other. But I stepped in and then Shawn took over. Gave them a pep talk.

Good. A moment later another text followed. I'm sorry this was your first game with them. Are you okay?

He wasn't sure about okay, but he felt better now. I'm okay. And they'll bounce back. Just wanted you to know they had a rough night.

Are you home yet?

No, we're on the bus. He wondered why she asked. Did she want to see him?

Too bad. Sometimes talking on the phone is easier than texting.

So much for wanting to see him. But texting was okay, too. At least she was talking to him. After the awkwardness between them at O'Rourke's that morning, he was afraid he'd blown it. Blown what, he wasn't sure, since he wasn't even sure what they were doing, but he knew he didn't want her avoiding him.

He realized he should respond to her text. I'll let them have the weekend to calm down and do some thinking and we'll regroup. If I think they're still off heading into homecoming, I'll bring Coach into it.

That's a good plan. Touch base with me Monday if you think there are any particular issues.

Okay. Have a good weekend.

Good night.

He put his phone away and sighed. *Touch base with me on Monday* . . . If that wasn't all business, he wasn't sure what was. For a woman whose job it was to help teenagers and their parents navigate high school and get ready for college, she sure had a way of messing with a man's mind.

07

Sam met Alex and Chase at the Stewart Mills House of Pizza on Saturday night, more than ready to talk to men who weren't flailing their way through adolescence. They'd invited Deck, but he'd already committed to getting a sitter and taking Cheryl to the city to watch a movie, so it was just the three of them.

He'd thought about calling Mrs. McDonnell and getting permission to bring Coach, but he changed his mind before he made the call. As much as he loved Coach, that would be kind of like taking your dad along on a guys' night. You still have a good time, but you can't talk about anything you wouldn't want your mom—or in his case, Mrs. McDonnell—to know.

He was the last to arrive, so the first thing they did was

order two pizzas and a basket of fries. Sam grabbed a soda, while Alex and Chase ordered a pitcher of beer.

The young man working the counter gave Chase a nervous look. "I, uh . . . your girlfriend called. Officer McDonnell, I mean. She said one pitcher has to last you the whole night and then you have to switch to soda."

Sam didn't even try to disguise his snort of laughter with a cough. While his two cohorts were probably too drunk to remember it, the last time they'd had multiple pitchers of beer was during Eagles Fest. They'd decided to break into the high school to see the trophy they'd won a decade and a half before, and Officer McDonnell had busted them.

Chase shook his head at the pizza guy. "I think that's a serious abuse of power on her part. The police department can't dictate the beverage choices of citizens unless laws are broken."

"Officer McDonnell is also sponsoring my half marathon next month," the guy continued.

"Bribery." Alex slapped Chase on the back. "She's good."

They brought their drinks to a table and made themselves comfortable. The place was close to full, which wasn't surprising for a Saturday night. While a lot of people preferred takeout, there was only so much to do in Stewart Mills, and the pizza house had two arcade games in a side room.

They talked about the football team for a while, before Sam finally held up a hand. "You know what? I've had enough football for this week. They're good. Coach is good. Everything's good."

"How's the plumbing business going?" Chase suggested. "I know he's had somebody coming up from the city, but I wasn't sure if you'd be helping out."

"I'm an electrician, not a plumber." Sam laughed. "And I'm hoping to avoid getting roped into anything that requires going back to school again."

"I'd make a joke about not knowing plumbers went to school," Chase said, "but plumber jokes are only funny if there's a plumber in the room."

"What's going on with you?" Sam asked. "How much longer do you have in New Jersey?"

"Not much longer, actually. I'm hoping to have everything wrapped up by Thanksgiving." He smiled, and it was the smile of a man who was pretty damn happy with his life. "Then I'll be home and Kelly and I can get started on our future."

Sam looked from Chase to Alex. "You guys aren't going to get sucked into some goofy double wedding thing, are you?"

"No," they said together.

"Besides," Alex said, "you know if Gretchen and Kelly have their way, it'll be a goofy *triple* wedding."

"Three best friends marrying three best friends," Chase said. "Trust me, I've heard it."

"So have I," Sam said. "It's not going to happen."

And he really hoped nobody was sitting close enough to hear them. The volume level was pretty high, though, since the jukebox was on and everybody was trying to talk over it. He didn't see any faces that set off gossip alarm bells, and nobody seemed to be paying attention to them, anyway.

Chase leaned closer. "I don't get it. I've heard the chemistry between you guys like literally sparks."

"Who the hell did you hear that from?"

"People."

"I can't handle somebody like Jen in my life right now."

Alex snorted. "You mean somebody attractive, intelligent, good with kids and—judging by the look you get on your face every time you talk about her—somebody who you'd like to see naked on a regular basis?"

"I mean somebody who totally has her shit together."

"The horror," Chase said.

"I'm serious. She comes from a normal family. She has a great job and, from what I've heard, a nice house. She doesn't have any baggage and she deserves a guy who's like her, you know? Like a teacher or an accountant or something. They'll have perfect little kids who are smart and pretty like them."

"You're an idiot," Alex said.

Chase held up a hand. "Not that I disagree with Alex on that fundamental point, but I do kind of get where you're coming from. You guys know when I came here for Eagles Fest, my life was a mess. My business partner took off with our money, not that there was much left of it. And my girlfriend left me for some other guy. I basically had no business and no place to live."

"You have a nice truck, though," Sam said.

"Never underestimate having a good truck," Chase agreed. "Anyway. Kelly wanted her life all neat and tidy and I was a total shit show and in the end it didn't matter because—"

"If you say love conquers all, I'm throwing something at you," Sam interrupted.

"I was going to say because I'm great in the sack."

"Sure. And none of it matters because as soon as Coach takes his whistle back, I'm getting in my truck and going back to Texas."

"Coach Leavitt," the pizza guy yelled from behind the counter. "Your pizzas are ready!"

Sam heard the name, and he let it sink in for a few seconds. The boys on the team had called him that a couple of times, but that seemed different somehow. When he was in the Eagles polo shirt with the whistle around his neck, he was the substitute coach and it made sense.

But hearing it out in public, from a guy he didn't know, touched him. It was nice to have an identity in his hometown that had absolutely nothing to do with his parents. Even when people talked about the championship football team, his role as quarterback was more often than not tied to his childhood because it made for a feel-good story.

They dug into the pizza and fries, catching up while they ate. Alex told them about a project he was considering, taking photos of a recently renovated ski area for their promotional campaigns.

"Advertising pictures?" Chase asked. "No offense, but isn't that kind of a step down for you?"

"I don't consider commercial work a step down. A lot of photographers have to balance their art and needing to pay the bills. And I certainly wasn't working for free before, awards or no awards. Besides, being home with Gretchen and Gram is more important to me."

"And Cocoa," Chase added, and Alex gave him a high five.

Sam popped a fry into his mouth, chuckling. He hadn't had the pleasure of meeting the chocolate Lab yet, but he'd heard a lot about her.

Chase looked around at their fellow customers. "I wonder if we can talk somebody at one of the other tables into getting us another pitcher of beer."

_____

Jen was late getting to Gretchen's, and she hoped like hell the others hadn't eaten all the macaroni salad. Her mom had called, though, and it had been a while since they talked, so she didn't send her to voice mail.

All was well with the Cooper family. It still struck Jen as ironic that her parents fell in love with the southwestern corner of the state when she went off to college in Keene. They'd made the move her junior year since her brother was accepted to a college only an hour from hers, and then she'd turned around and gotten the job back in Stewart Mills.

Her brother was married now, with two small children, and her parents had bought an antiques store instead of finding office jobs in their prior fields. They were all content, except for missing Jen. She hadn't gotten down to visit as often as she usually did during the summer break because of Eagles Fest.

Once she was finally off the phone, she drove to the Walker farm at maybe just a few miles over the speed limit, and parked behind Gretchen's truck. Kelly's cruiser was in the drive, too, and Jen hoped she hadn't been there long.

They were laughing when she walked into the kitchen after high-fiving Cocoa on her way through the living room. "What's so funny?"

"Jen! You made it." Gram left whatever she was doing at the counter and walked over to give her a hug.

Ida Walker was like a grandmother to all three of them and since Jen's family had moved, she and Mrs. McDonnell usually filled in when Jen needed maternal advice or love in person.

"Sorry I'm late," she said. "My mom called."

"How's she doing?"

"Really well. They all are."

"We already ate all the macaroni salad," Kelly said. She was in uniform, sitting at the table across from Gretchen.

Jen stopped halfway across the kitchen. "No, you did not."

"Kelly Ann McDonnell," Gram chided. "Since you're being mean, you can serve everybody. Cocoa and I are going to go watch some television and let you girls visit."

"How's your dad?" Gretchen asked once they each had a bowl of macaroni salad, and Kelly rolled her eyes.

"He's driving my mother crazy, so she's driving *me* crazy. He's the worst patient ever."

"I was going to call and see if he wanted to go on some pumpkin deliveries with me just to ride in the truck and see some people, but I think he would have tried to take over the unloading for me because watching me work wouldn't sit well with him."

"He doesn't seem to grasp that his personality is the reason Mom has such a tight leash on him. If we could trust that he'd settle for being out of the house, she probably wouldn't mind. But you're right. He'd jump into whatever was going on and probably end up back in the hospital."

"That sounds like Coach," Gretchen said.

Jen held up a forkful of macaroni salad. "I almost feel sorry for the guys, having to make do with pizza while we have this."

"I'm glad they'll all be here for homecoming," Kelly said. "It only seems fair since they're a big reason we even get to *have* it this year. Plus, I love seeing them together. I feel like we're all a big family coming back together, the way it's supposed to be. We even have the guys convinced we want a double wedding."

Gretchen laughed. "Actually, we have them convinced we're after a triple wedding."

"Don't even start," Jen said with a sigh.

She couldn't even imagine what Sam would think if the other two guys started talking about a triple wedding. Since she'd so often heard the assumption she'd hook up with Sam, she had to assume he'd heard it, too. But—sex on the hood of the car notwithstanding—they hadn't managed a kiss without it being awkward after. Marriage was too big a jump even if he wasn't planning to leave town again.

"We're not even having a double wedding, so it's just a joke to mess with their heads," Kelly said. "Besides, one of us just wants to go to the town hall."

Jen looked at Gretchen, but she was surprised when she nodded her head back toward Kelly. "You're kidding."

Kelly shrugged. "You know I'm way too practical to spend who knows how many thousands of dollars on a party."

"Not a party. Your wedding."

"The marriage part is a legal document. The wedding itself is just a party to celebrate the legal document."

"What about Coach and your mom? Will they be disappointed?"

"We did the whole thing the first time, with the gown and the walking me down the aisle and the tears. It didn't stick. I'd rather hit town hall, have a barbecue in the backyard and then spend that money on something else."

Jen shook her head. "I would have guessed it was you, Gretchen, who'd want to skip the gown and the flowers."

She shrugged. "Remember when you guys dressed me up to go to that fancy function with Alex? I kind of liked that. Not all the time, but one princess day would be fun."

"It would be awesome," Jen agreed. "But based on your day-to-day fashion sense, Kelly and I get to pick our own bridesmaid dresses."

Kelly laughed. "Does the feed store have a formalwear section?"

"Hey! I'm a farmer. Leave me alone."

"What kind of wedding do you want, Jen?" Kelly asked. "When you find Mr. Right, of course. Who I think you've found but are pretending you haven't for reasons you can't seem to articulate."

"Really?" Jen gave her a look. "If and when I get married, I'll do the dress and flowers and fancy cake thing, but on a reasonable scale. My mom would be disappointed if she missed out on any of the mother-of-the-bride glory."

"Remember when we were young and would talk about the weddings we'd have someday?" Kelly said.

Gretchen snorted. "I think there have been royal coronations with less pageantry than we had planned."

Jen remembered the many hours they'd spent as teenagers talking about their future weddings. And their future husbands. Her Prince Charming always wore nice sweaters and could quote book passages and knew how wine tastings worked. She wasn't sure why the wine tasting mattered, except that she'd seen them on TV and they looked very sophisticated.

But now when she thought about her future, she couldn't help but picture the man with rough hands and the faded T-shirts. His book quotes were plays from the football playbook and he didn't drink because his childhood had been a nightmare.

No, Sam wasn't a man she would ever have daydreamed about actually marrying when she was younger. The adult her, though, spent so much time daydreaming—and night dreaming—about him, she wasn't sure she thought about anything *but* him anymore.

"Earth to Jen."

Startled out of her thoughts, she looked at Kelly. "What?"

"I asked what you're wearing to the homecoming dance."

"I don't know yet. I'll just grab something out of my closet." Something that was tasteful, but would still knock Sam's socks off. "It's not really about us, anyway. We're just the invisible chaperones. Half the staff members there will be in jeans."

"I'll be in uniform," Kelly said, not sounding happy about it. "But maybe I'll throw on some glittery lip gloss."

They laughed, and then Kelly's cell phone chimed. She looked at the screen and grimaced. "Time to get back to work. Somebody just rode an ATV down the main street."

"By the time you get there, whoever it is will be out in the woods again," Jen said.

"Yeah, but I can get a description and we'll have an excuse to remind people they can't do that. You guys don't talk about anything interesting after I leave, okay?"

Gretchen stood and started gathering the empty dishes. "We'll probably talk about *you*."

"Yeah, right. Knowing you two, you'll end up talking about work stuff. Thanks for wrangling us some macaroni salad from Gram, Gretchen. And Jen, I'll call you this week about the final float count for the parade."

It wasn't long after Kelly left that Jen caught Gretchen trying to stifle a yawn. "Gee, and I haven't even started talking about work yet."

"Sorry. Alex was away so we've been . . . catching up. But it's not like I can start sleeping half the day away because I have a guy now, so I'm pretty tired."

"I don't think many people guessed you guys would end up together."

"The farm girl and fancy, world-traveling photojournalist? I sure as hell didn't see it coming." Gretchen gave her a serious look. "What's holding you guys back?"

"There is no us guys, Gretchen, and you know it. We barely spoke to each other after that night at the dam, and he left without saying good-bye. As soon as Coach is ready to return to the field, he'll take off again."

Gretchen shrugged. "Maybe you need to stop worrying about what will happen in a few weeks and just go with the right now."

"Just go with what? We're not doing anything."

"And that's the problem. Neither of you can think straight from wanting to have sex again, so why fight it?"

"Because I'm thirty now and I want to start having a family soon, so I'm looking for forever, not just fun for now."

"I'm sorry, was there a line of potential husbands outside your door that I missed?" Gretchen snorted. "If a possible Mr. Right shows up, then maybe you reconsider your priorities. But for now, having orgasms isn't a bad thing to put at the top of the list. A little monkey business never hurt anybody."

"You just want me to text you monkey emojis."

"Hey, life's more fun with monkey emojis. And orgasms."

There really wasn't any denying that.

08

By Tuesday, the upheaval from Friday night's loss seemed to have passed and Sam thought they were having a pretty good practice. Rather than talking about last week, they turned their focus to Saturday's homecoming game. They'd be playing a rival and they didn't need any urging to work hard.

About halfway through the practice, he spotted Alex standing by the bleachers, snapping photos of the team. Sam knew he liked to take pictures for the yearbook and sometimes even for the local weekly paper. But mostly Sam thought he just liked capturing random moments in people's lives.

He waved Alex over, and saw that Cocoa was with him. Sam lifted his hand when the dog gave him a high five. "Hey, Cocoa, it's nice to meet you. Field trip today?"

"Family trip to town," Alex said. "Gram has an appointment with the doctor and then they came up with a list of things they needed to get and . . . it became a thing, so Cocoa and I came, too."

The chocolate Lab had run onto the field, and practice was interrupted while the players greeted her, most of them getting high fives. It was funny how one energetic dog could turn a team of focused athletes into little boys, and the two adults watched them for a few minutes.

"She'd make a great mascot," Sam said. "It would be fun to make her a little Eagles T-shirt for the parade."

"Sounds fun until you picture her jumping on and off the float so she can high-five every damn person lining the sidewalks."

"Yeah, we don't need a mascot." When Cocoa went for a second high five from PJ, Sam shook his head. "You guys really need to teach that dog another trick."

Alex lifted the camera. "Cocoa! Say cheese!"

The Lab immediately sat and lifted her jaw, turning her head slightly to the side as if she was an English monarch or old French general posing for a portrait. The shutter fired and then Alex yelled, "Good girl, Cocoa!"

"I was thinking fetch or play dead, but posing for formal portraits is a good skill for a dog to have, too."

Alex laughed. "She did it while I was taking a shot of her with Gretchen and it was so funny we made a big fuss. She loves to be the center of attention, so she's worked hard on it."

"How's Mrs. Walker doing? You said she's seeing the doctor."

"Just a checkup. Her blood pressure's been a lot better, so they might adjust her medications again. How's Coach?"

"He's good. They're doing some more tests on him this week because they're afraid there might be more damage than they thought, but it's not like an emergency thing. I was over there Sunday helping out with some of the yard chores and he was pissed as hell he was only allowed to sit on the porch and supervise."

"He's not the kind of guy who likes sitting much. He must be driving Mrs. McDonnell crazy."

"That's an understatement. But they're going to talk to the doctor about him taking part in the homecoming festivities, so that would be a big help. She's absolutely forbidden him to come to the school, though. He wanted to just watch the practice, but you know how that would go."

"It won't be easy for him to sit in the stands for Saturday's game. That would probably be more stressful than just letting him coach the damn game."

"I did mention that to Mrs. McDonnell and she gave me the look. He's on his own."

Sam heard a cell phone text tone and Alex pulled his phone out of his pocket. After reading the message, he sighed. "Gretchen and her emojis. I swear, sometimes I have no idea what she's talking about. But I think she's telling me they're done at the doctor's."

"You guys will be in town Friday for the parade, right?"

"Wouldn't miss it."

They shook hands and Cocoa gave Sam a good-bye high five. Once they were gone, Sam blew the whistle and gestured for the guys to get back to what they were supposed to be doing.

The weather was unseasonably hot, so there was a lot of running to and from the bench for water, but a scuffle over there caught Sam's eye. There was some pushing and shoving and, for a second, he thought maybe the ghost of Friday's loss had reared its ugly head again.

Then he saw Cody Dodge shove Hunter Cass. "You sat on my kid, you asshole!"

Oh, shit. He broke into a jog and got there in time to keep Hunter from retaliating for the shoving. "What the hell's going on here?"

"He sat on my kid, dude."

"What the hell was your pumpkin doing on the bench?" Hunter asked.

"What was I supposed to do with it? Leave it in my locker?"

"Okay," Sam said. "We'll get another one and—"

"You can't get another one," PJ interjected. "Mrs. Fournier says we're supposed to treat the pumpkins like real babies and you can't just get another baby if you sit on the one you have and squash it."

Sam had hated health class in high school and he hated it now. "Cody didn't squash it, though. It's not his fault."

"It doesn't matter. Cody and Mara are responsible for anything and everything that happens to the pumpkin. If it was a real baby, they wouldn't leave it somewhere it could get sat on. Well, Cody might. And Ronnie would probably lose his kid."

Ronnie laughed. "My mom said she's having tracking chips put in any grandchildren I give her."

"They don't put tracking chips in babies, dumb-ass," Hunter said.

"They put chips in dogs when they're little puppies. I think they can put them in babies."

"Maybe they should neuter you like a dog so nobody has to worry about it."

Sam put the whistle in his mouth and blew it so hard the kids winced and covered their ears. "Nobody's getting neutered. Let's focus on the pumpkin problem."

"I'm totally going to flunk health now and I won't be able to play because Cass is an asshole."

"Enough," Sam barked. "It was an accident. And you're not going to flunk health. One bad grade isn't enough to fail you."

The guys all looked at Cody and then away, shifting nervously. So the kid wasn't very good at health class. Great.

"Maybe you can ask Miss Cooper for help," PJ said. "She likes you and Mrs. Fournier doesn't seem to hate her too much. If it's presented as more about his grades affecting his future and less about playing football, Mrs. Fournier might go easier on him."

Sam had to agree with that. "I'll ask her to plead our case."

"Dude, Mara's going to kill me," Cody said. "She's been on the high honor roll like her entire life and if she gets a bad grade in health, she'll never talk to me again."

"Maybe you can go out to the Walker farm and get another one and nobody will ever know. Except Coach Leavitt, but he won't tell. Right?"

"I, uh . . ." He wasn't sure how far solidarity with his team was supposed to go. He should have their backs, but turning a blind eye to academic cheating seemed like a stretch.

"The pumpkins are marked and documented," PJ said. Apparently he was the resident expert on the health class pumpkin project, Sam thought. "You'd never get away with it. Plus Mara did the face and none of us can do painting like this."

PJ held up a piece of broken pumpkin, showing them the cute face she'd painted on it. He was probably right. "You need to tell Mara what happened and tell her we're going to try to make it right with Mrs. Fournier. In the meantime, are there any other pumpkin babies here?"

One of the freshmen raised his hand, but he'd put his pumpkin in a box and tucked it next to the bench's leg. Others explained they'd worked out their schedules with their project partners so they didn't have custody during football practices or games.

"And a lot of us already took health," Hunter said. "Cody's grandma had Miss Cooper rearrange some of his classes so he wouldn't be there with us. He's easily distracted or something."

"Shut up, dude. I guess I should text Mara."

Shawn decided to pipe up. "You don't text somebody their kid got sat on."

Sam sighed as a whole new argument broke out. As much as he liked the football aspect of this temporary job, he was starting to see why Coach McDonnell had a heart attack.

Jen scanned the newsletter on her computer screen for what felt like the thousandth time, looking for any last-second corrections. The letter, intended for the families of juniors and seniors and detailing timelines and deadlines for the college process, was done from a template she'd made several years back, but she had to double-check all the dates and check the links to online resources.

Once she was satisfied it was correct, she sent it to the printer. She'd take a box of Stewart Mills High School guidance department envelopes home and stuff them while watching TV so she could drop them in the mail within the next couple of days. She'd also send the notice by email, but there were too many families without reliable Internet service to depend solely on it.

Then she opened her calendar and pulled up the school district calendar and the sports calendar. Trying to find a day for the financial aid fair was like trying to throw a dart into the eye of a needle.

By far the biggest part of her job and the part she gave the most energy to—besides trying to keep her students emotionally and physically healthy—was the financial aid process. There weren't a lot of resources in the northern part of the state and there definitely wasn't a lot of money. Statistically, there were more parents who hadn't gone to college than in the southern part of the state, too, so a lot of them didn't even know where to start. College financing was a vitally important but totally scary and confusing process for many of the school system's families.

She'd known that when she came back to Stewart Mills to take the job, and she'd rolled up her sleeves that first year. She made a list of everybody she could think of who could help parents and students through the maze of paperwork necessary. Experts from nonprofits. Volunteer students from some of the state colleges who got credit for helping. Some of the experts focused on the admissions process. Some talked about scholarships and student loans. Jen had her own library of books in the office that families could borrow, and she gave every senior a personalized list of at least five scholarships they might qualify for and made appointments to help them do the paperwork.

Don and Cassandra Jones donated dinner for everybody who made the drive north to help Jen out with the financial aid fair, and the turnout was often a pleasant surprise. This year she had two dates that could accommodate all of the volunteers on her wish list, and now she had to figure out which day worked with the high school's schedule. She should have already nailed it down, but she was running a little behind because she'd waited for the organization that helped with the federal forms to confirm their availability.

It was a headache, but she didn't spend seven years convincing her students they could do anything in life if they worked hard enough only to have them succumb to frustration or hopelessness at the end and give up.

A knock on the doorjamb made her look up, and she smiled when she saw Sam standing in the doorway. "Hey, is practice over early?"

"There was a tragic accident involving a pumpkin baby today." He shifted his weight from one foot to the other. "I was hoping you could maybe intercede with the health teacher for us."

"I don't know. I'm sure the health teacher is going to question whether or not football practice is the best place for a baby and I can't say I disagree with her."

"Really, Jen? It's just a pumpkin."

Jen smiled when he cocked an eyebrow at her. "It seems to me you shouldn't have any trouble breaking it to Mrs. Fournier, then, if it's just a pumpkin."

"Dammit, I'm not going to go in there and tell the woman that Cass sat on Dodge's baby. That's weird."

"So you think *I'll* go in there and tell her Hunter sat on Cody's ugly pumpkin baby?"

"It wasn't really ugly, actually. Cody's partner is good at art and it had a funny little baby face with big blue eyes. It was kind of cute." Jen only counted to eight before Sam groaned and ran a hand over his face. "This is ridiculous. This entire town is ridiculous and now that I'm back, it's infecting me, too."

"Has anybody broken the news to Mara yet?"

"Mara? Oh, is that the pumpkin's mama?" When she nodded, he shrugged. "Cody was going to text her, but Shawn told him that wasn't the kind of news you broke by text message. So he decided to put it on Facebook. Then there was a huge fight over whether a text message and Facebook were essentially the same thing. PJ said neither was acceptable. But Ronnie said he found out his grandmother died on Facebook and she was a real person, not a pumpkin, so it was okay."

"Wow. What did they decide?"

"I have no idea. They were still arguing about it when I walked away."

Jen laughed, able to picture his frustration. "I hate to tell you this, but Mrs. Fournier's a hard-ass when it comes to the eggs. Or pumpkins. The babies. You must remember that."

"I remember." He tilted his head, smiling a little. "I remember wishing you were a little older so you could have been in my health class and been my egg's mom."

"You did not," she said, shaking her head. "You barely noticed me."

"You had such a perfect family, so I knew you'd be a great mom."

"We're not our parents," she reminded him firmly. "And no family is perfect."

"No, but it looked perfect to me."

"Who was your egg's mother? Did you get a good grade?"

"I forget her name. And we got a good grade because she made me lie about my involvement. She never let me touch the egg except to set it on my desk in health class once in a while for appearance's sake."

Jen snorted. "Control freak much?"

"She was afraid I'd lose my temper and smash it."

Her inner guidance counselor heard the underlying hurt—old as it was—in his tone and wanted to soothe it. The rest of her wanted the name so she could find out if the woman still lived in town and kick her in the kneecap or key a curse word into her car door.

His chuckle surprised her. "You're cute when you want to slay my dragons."

"Did that show on my face?" He nodded. Of course it did. "Cute, though? Not fierce?"

"More like fiercely cute."

She rolled her eyes. "Whatever. For the record, I would totally pick you to share an ugly pumpkin baby with me if we weren't actually adults."

"That might be the nicest thing anybody's ever said to me."

She was going to laugh, but he started walking around her desk. "What are you doing?"

"Stand up."

"No."

He laughed. "Just for a second."

"What are you doing?"

She'd barely stood when Sam cupped the back of her head. His mouth covered hers and she braced her hands against his shoulders as heat rushed through her body. She slid her hands down his chest and he moaned against her lips.

He devoured her, kissing her until she wanted to peel his shirt up over his head and then wrap her legs around his waist. But when she felt the urge to sweep everything off her desk and shove him down on it, she broke off the kiss.

"Shit. I can't do this," she said, her voice soft and breathless. "We're in my office. The door's not even closed, for crap's sake."

He ran his hand over his hair and blew out a breath. "I got carried away. Maybe I should go to the locker room and take a cold shower now."

"Or just picture the lecture Mrs. Fournier would give us right now."

Sam actually shuddered, and she didn't blame him. "She scares me."

"I'll talk to her tomorrow about Cody and Mara's pumpkin. Maybe I can get them a replacement baby in the spirit of homecoming or something."

"Thanks, Jen."

"I expect you to throw me some good candy from the float Friday night."

Sam paused at the doorway and looked back at her. "And I expect you to save me a dance Saturday night."

09

By the time Sam was supposed to report to the homecoming parade floats Friday evening, he was exhausted. It had been a long week and looking at the schedule Jen had given him didn't prepare him for just how much energy would be expended. And this was only the second event, if he counted the pep rally.

Hell, his ears were still ringing from being trapped in the gym earlier in the day. Back when he'd been the star quarterback and the screaming and hollering was for him and his teammates, he hadn't minded so much. Now, though, each class competing to see who had the most school spirit had left him cranky and hitting the school nurse up for acetaminophen.

The staging area for the parade was so full of people he couldn't help but wonder if there was anybody left in town to actually line the sidewalks and wave to them. He knew from the Eagles Fest parade that once it was time to roll, there would be no messing around. Part of their route through town required them to stop traffic on one of the busiest roads in the state, which connected the highway with pretty much every other place in the northern part of New Hampshire. Stewart Mills parades had to be short and move fast so traffic could start flowing again.

The siren on the police chief's SUV sounded twice, which was the signal to get their asses on the floats and hold on. There was only the one cruiser, since Kelly and Dylan were in charge of stopping traffic, and then the ambulance and a couple of the volunteer firefighters from the area would turn on the flashing lights in their pickups. Deck always had his wrecker decorated for the occasion, and then the floats. Each class, from the freshmen to the seniors, had one, and they'd be judged for school spirit. And then the parade ended with the football team. The starters and seniors were usually on the float with Coach, and the rest of the team threw candy from the two pickup trucks following.

Coach had refused the offer to ride in a convertible. "I'll be on the float with my boys or I'll just stay home and watch more *Pawn Stars* repeats."

They'd finally compromised by putting a folding camp chair on the float so if he got tired, he could choose to sit for a while. Or, more accurately, if Mrs. McDonnell thought he was getting tired, he could be forced to sit.

"Whatever you do, don't fall off," Sam said once he'd climbed onto the float. "I swore to your wife I wouldn't let anything happen to you. Plus, the ambulance is *in* the parade and we'd probably run over half the town trying to get it out of line."

Coach snorted and then pointed to a big basket that was decorated with blue and gold ribbons and had an Eagles T-shirt draped over the top. "What's that basket for?"

"That's the nursery." When Coach just waited, Sam rolled his eyes. "I guess the girls decided that, since the guys on the team get to ride on the big float, they could bring the pumpkin babies with them. And, after the tragic accident involving Cody's pumpkin, we had to come up with a way to keep the babies safe during football activities, so we have a nursery. And we have to keep it covered because direct sun can do unpleasant things to a harvested pumpkin's life span. I think they only have another two weeks of parenthood or so to go."

"Maybe this summer we should have a festival to raise funds to bring our health class into this century," Coach mumbled.

"You won't feel that way when you're trying to run a practice and there's a basket full of crying robot babies on the bench."

"I was thinking more along the lines of giving up on saddling the kids with inanimate objects they toss on the counter and ignore as soon as they get home and actually giving them knowledge instead."

"I think there are some words nobody wants to hear Mrs. Fournier say out loud."

The siren sounded a second time, which meant traffic was stopped and it was time to move. They'd leave the staging area, drive through town and pull into the funeral home's parking area, which abutted the field where the bonfire would be lit.

The players were ready when the float lurched into motion, their hands full of cheap candy to toss to the crowd. The energy level was high and the mood was exceptionally good because the town had come so close to losing this, so Sam definitely didn't have to prompt the kids to smile and wave.

About a third of the way through the route, he spotted Jen standing with Gretchen, Alex and Chase. He'd invited the guys onto the float but they said they'd had their fifteen minutes during the Eagles Fest parade and wanted to be spectators. The spotlight was back on the team, where it belonged.

Jen's cheeks were pink with excitement and the chill of the night air, and she waved at every float as it went by. When she spotted the football float, her gaze locked with his immediately and he smiled. Then he waved for her to come closer and reached into his pocket for the 3 Musketeers bar he'd bought because Mrs. McDonnell remembered they were Jen's favorite candy.

When he held it up to show her, she laughed and put out her hands. Luckily he hadn't lost all of his throwing skills and she caught it without it touching the ground.

Thank you, she mouthed, holding the candy bar to her chest.

He winked and then gave his attention back to the parade. Every so often he'd blow the whistle and the boys would do their team chant while the spectators cheered. The reaction to Coach McDonnell waving was just as loud. And when Sam spotted his mother in the crowd, hanging toward the back, he waved to her. Her face lit up as she waved back, and the pride on her face warmed him.

As tired as he'd been before, he was almost sorry when they made the turn into the funeral home's lot. Seeing everybody in Stewart Mills in such high spirits and cheering on their high school kids made him feel pretty damn good.

As soon as the trucks were in park, there was a mass

stampede toward the bonfire field, but Sam stayed with Coach. He'd opted to skip the bonfire—probably at the very strong urging of Mrs. McDonnell—and was waiting for his wife to pick him up so they could head home. Rather than admit he'd be tired and didn't feel up to the event, he'd said he wanted Sam to have his night in the spotlight.

"What's going on with you and Jen Cooper?" Coach asked him once they were alone.

"What do you mean?"

"Seems like something's going on."

"Because I tossed her a candy bar? Throwing candy's what you do when you're on a parade float." Playing dumb was only going to fend Coach off for so long, but Sam wasn't sure how much he wanted to say. The man was the first person he'd turn to when he needed advice on almost anything, but Coach would also feel free to give his own feelings on the matter, and Sam didn't have room in his head for anybody else right now.

"When a man takes the time to find out a woman's favorite candy bar and then goes out and buys one, keeps it in his pocket and then looks for her in the crowd so he can toss it to her in front of half the damn town, it's a little more than throwing some parade candy her way."

"She got Cody Dodge out of a jam with Mrs. Fournier."

"I heard about that. And since I see my wife's car coming up the road, I'll pretend you're not yanking my chain."

Mrs. McDonnell pulled the car up alongside the float and got out. Sam saw the worry on her face as she got out, and then saw it fade into a smile when she saw Coach. He thought about how scary that phone call from the hospital must have been for her and how much fear she'd carried around since then.

But Coach looked good and he looped his arm around his wife's shoulders. "Did you get me some good candy?"

"Rumor has it Jen got the good candy," she responded with a pointed look at Sam. "But I got you a few Tootsie Rolls because you love them and you can cheat a little bit on your diet."

Since Mrs. McDonnell had been near the start of the parade route with some friends of hers and nowhere near Jen and the rest of them, word about the 3 Musketeers bar had certainly spread like lightning. She might have suspected what Sam planned to do when he asked her about Jen's favorite candy, but knowing Jen had gotten it meant people had noticed and found it worth talking about.

"I'm going to go home with my wife and eat some candy," Coach said, slapping Sam's shoulder. "You have fun at the bonfire."

"You better hurry if you want anything from the bake sale," Mrs. McDonnell said.

He wanted a pistachio bar, dammit.

Once the McDonnells' car pulled out of the lot, he did a final sweep of the float to make sure none of the guys had left garbage or cell phones or jackets behind. They hadn't. But Sam spotted the basket of pumpkin babies and groaned.

Apparently he was babysitting tonight.

Jen nudged Gretchen when she saw Sam walking toward them carrying a basket decorated with blue and gold ribbons. "I can't believe they stuck him with the pumpkins."

"It could be worse. He could be carrying around a basket of putrid eggs. He doesn't look very happy, though."

"I bet the boys those pumpkins belong to are dodging him." Jen chuckled. "It's dark and almost everybody's wearing blue and gold, so finding a few kids who are deliberately avoiding him won't go well."

"Have you seen Cody?" Sam asked when he reached them.

"Nope," Gretchen said, "but I see Alex, so I'll catch you later."

"Babysitting pumpkins isn't in my job description." He scowled, glancing around at the crowd. "Making them run laps *is*, so they're going to be some kind of sorry."

"Here, I rescued this for you." She extended the napkin with the pistachio bar on it. "I'm glad you're here because it's not easy carrying around a pudding and whipped cream treat on a cookie crust."

Sam's face lit up when he saw the treat, and he took it from her. "Thanks. So you rescued it? Was it stuck in a tree?"

"It was the last one."

"You're kidding."

"They go fast."

He took a bite of the end and closed his eyes to savor it. She watched the pleasure flit across his face and almost moaned when the tip of his tongue flicked over his lip to get a smudge of whipped cream. "No wonder they go fast. It's delicious."

"She doesn't make them often, either, so people are trained to grab them first."

He extended the bar, folding the napkin back a little. "Here, have a bite."

Though she didn't get the appeal of pistachio bars quite as strongly as the rest of the town, he made the offer so sweetly, she couldn't resist. She took a bite and then smiled when he devoured the rest of the bar.

"They *are* good," she agreed. "I was going to get a brownie, but I ate my candy bar instead. Did you know those are my favorite?"

He grinned and her skin practically tingled in response. "I might have done some research."

"Thank you." She wanted to thank him by grabbing his face and kissing him until they passed out, but standing in a field surrounded by the entire high school student body was not the place.

"It's freaking cold out here tonight," he said, looking around. "What's the holdup on the bonfire?"

"There was a tie between the sophomore and junior class floats, so they're trying to figure out how to decide which class president gets to hold the torch. I think it was going to a coin toss."

Suddenly there was a whooshing sound and the crowd cheered as the bonfire erupted in flames. The fire reflected in Sam's eyes, and Jen decided she'd rather watch that way than to turn and face the actual fire.

"I always enjoyed the bonfire back in high school," he said quietly. "I hated the dance, but the bonfire was my favorite part of football besides the actual games."

"You know, if you really don't want to go to the dance, you don't have to. Kelly's dad doesn't always go."

He looked at her, the flames dancing in his eyes. "I'm going. And you're going to dance with me."

"Oh I am, am I?" she challenged, expecting him to smile. If anything the smolder grew more intense. "Yeah, you are."

"That'll certainly give people something to talk about." Especially if they once again lost track of their surroundings after they had their hands on each other.

"They're talking already."

So he knew they'd been the subject of a lot of speculation. Of course he did. He'd not only grown up in Stewart Mills, but his family had definitely been whispered about behind hands and closed doors.

"Coach!" They both turned when they heard Ronnie's voice.

"Probably got lost trying to find the huge bonfire," Sam muttered, and Jen laughed.

When the players demanded Sam's attention, Jen gave him a little wave and went to wander around. Every year, the eighth graders at the middle school sold hot chocolate at homecoming to help fund their annual class trip, and she stopped there first.

Sipping the warm drink, she made her way around the crowd. Every few minutes somebody would talk to her, but she didn't stand still long. Even with adults present, teenagers had a way of getting themselves in trouble. The fire department kept a close eye on the bonfire, starting even before it was lit, which was why the truck wasn't in the parade. The kids knew that the rules were the same as if they were on school property. And at any given time, a staff member could inspect beverage bottles or cups and make sure they hadn't been spiked in any way. Very rarely did they have a problem, but she suspected that was due more to vigilance than the nature of their high school students.

The entire time she walked around, she caught herself scanning the crowd for Sam. Sometimes she heard his voice or his laugh and she'd have to fight the urge to turn away from whoever was talking to her to find him. She knew he would stay until the end. At about ten, they would start knocking the fire down and letting it die on its own. A little before eleven, the guys from the fire department would douse it and, using rakes, make sure it was fully out. Sam would be on hand to threaten the players with grueling workouts if they didn't go straight home and go to bed so they'd be rested for the big game.

"Hey."

She'd been watching the fire and hadn't noticed Sam coming up beside her. "Hey, you. Having fun?"

"It was a lot more fun when I was seventeen, to be honest. And less stressful."

Because he was talking quietly, he was standing close enough to her so part of his body was tucked behind hers and it was tempting to lean back against him. "I've had to deal with a few minor issues, but nothing involving the players. Coach has always been very strict with them and one year he benched half the starting offensive line because they filled soda bottles with alcohol before the bonfire."

"I've been volunteered to drive three kids home because their parents didn't want to stay the whole time." He sighed. "Oh well. It's one night, I guess. I know Chase is still here because Kelly is, but I haven't seen Alex and Gretchen in a while."

"They already left. Gretchen wasn't feeling so hot."

When he put his hand on the small of her back, Jen sighed. Staring into the flames, she accepted the inevitable. Very soon, she and Sam Leavitt were going to fall into bed together if for no other reason than they couldn't *not* do it anymore.

She didn't know what it meant or where—if anywhere— it would lead except her in his rearview mirror as he left town, but it was time for her to just go with the right now.

10

The atmosphere on Saturday afternoon was electric and Sam paced the sidelines, absorbing the energy of the team and the crowd. It was almost as potent a feeling as when he ran out onto the field himself a decade and a half ago.

Dan and Joel were on the sidelines with him, along with Deck. Decker wasn't really a coach, of course, but they didn't want the other schools to know just how thin their coaching staff was stretched. Especially this one, being a longtime rival. Sam had beat the other team for homecoming back in the day and, while he couldn't be sure, he thought one of their assistant coaches had been across the line of scrimmage from him.

Coach was in the stands with Mrs. McDonnell, who'd already made it quite clear she'd have him removed from school property if he got too worked up. Jen, Alex and

Gretchen were sitting with them. Chase was supposed to be sitting with them, too, but he kept wandering down the stands to talk to Kelly, who was in uniform and technically on duty.

The noise and trying to keep the team from getting too nerved up kept Sam from being able to dwell too much on the amount of pressure he was feeling, which was probably a good thing. And he felt optimistic about their chances. They'd had excellent practices, the weather was nice and the kids were in good spirits. He'd been worried the pressure building over the week would bring the tension from last Friday back, but it hadn't.

Because it was homecoming, they'd done a big entrance, with each player's name booming through the big speakers. He'd even had to run onto the field himself, waving to a screaming crowd, which had amused him while at the same time tying his stomach in knots. Now he stood, watching his team go through their pregame routines. Some of the kids liked to chat and fiddle with their equipment, while others were quiet and focused.

His cell phone vibrated in his pocket, and he pulled it out to see a text message from Gretchen. It was all in emojis—a football, a thumbs-up and some kind of party horn blowing confetti—and he laughed. After sending back a happy face, he looked up at the stands in time to see Gretchen glance down at her phone. After a second, she lifted her head and gave him a wave.

Sam couldn't stop himself from shifting his gaze to her right, where Jen sat. Their eyes met and the smile she gave him settled his nerves in a way none of the pep talks he'd given himself in the mirror that morning had. Then her lips moved. *Good luck.*

He waved to her, and then realized everybody would look to see who he was waving at. Thank goodness Coach and Mrs. McDonnell were sitting in front of her, Gretchen and Alex, so most people would assume he was waving to them. When Coach gave him a thumbs-up, he grinned. Even Coach, apparently.

It didn't take long for the mood to shift once the game started, though. Their opponents were not only very good, but their guys were bigger, on average. And older, from what Sam had been told, with a lot of seniors on the team.

The Eagles defense played well, keeping it a two-touchdown game, but with the game ticking down toward halftime, their offense had yet to put any points on the board. Sam paced the sideline, working the playbook and trying to keep the boys' heads in the game.

He didn't allow himself to look up into the stands for Coach McDonnell. He knew he wouldn't see disappointment there because his boys were playing good, clean football, but there might be some frustration and Sam was struggling enough with his confidence without piling the weight of Coach's emotions onto himself. And he didn't want to wonder if the older man disagreeing with any of his plays was putting stress on Coach's heart.

Dammit. He should have argued harder against Coach being there at all.

"Hey, Coach," he heard PJ say and, because he'd been thinking about Coach McDonnell, it took Sam a few seconds to realize the kid was talking to him.

"What's up, PJ?"

"I know Sloan likes the outside," he said, referring to Parker Sloan, the Eagles wide receiver, "but the guy they have defending him has a real hard time cutting to his left. I think if you have Sloan go out and then cut hard left across to the middle, he can get at least a yard of separation and probably more."

"You think so?" He looked out at his offense, visualizing the play. If the wide receiver could pull off the move and Riley could get him the ball, he'd have a pretty clear shot at the end zone.

"I'm sure enough of it so I think you should burn a time-out."

PJ was a good cornerback, but he'd bragged in the past about his ability to read the field being his real skill, and how that was why he was Coach McDonnell's secret weapon. Sam signaled to the ref and waved for the guys to hurry off the field.

"Your show, son," he said to PJ, who grinned before pulling the offensive line into a tight huddle. Sam had no doubt the kid would achieve his dreams of coaching football someday. He was a natural.

As he watched, the other guys started nodding, and then Shawn Riley grinned. "Save it for third down. They'll expect me to hand it off to Cass and their secondary isn't as responsive."

The guys looked to Sam and he gave a sharp nod. His quarterback was no slouch in the observation department, either, and every time he saw them play, he became more certain they didn't even need him.

With his stomach tied in knots, he glanced at the clock and then watched his offense take the field again. It was going to be tight, but they could get something on the scoreboard before the half, even if they had to settle for a field goal.

An incomplete pass stopped the clock. Then Sloan caught a short pass and was forced out of bounds short of the first down, stopping the clock again. Third down, with two yards to go, Sam thought. It couldn't have been more perfect.

Hunter Cass took his spot on the line, eyeing the defensive players across from him as if looking for their weakest link. He was good at digging in and bullying his way through for short yardage, and everybody would expect him to get the ball.

As Sam watched, his body practically shaking with tension, Riley took the snap and fell back. Sloan exploded off the line, racing across the grass with a defender on his heels. Suddenly he cut to his left, toward the middle of the field. The defender followed, but he was slow turning to his weak side, just as PJ had said he would be, leaving Sloan open.

Riley's pass was a bullet right into his hands, and then the wide receiver was gone, closing the distance to the end zone at a speed that made Sam remember the sensation of the field under his cleats. Being quarterback, he'd never gotten to sprint down the field like Sloan, but he'd had a few good runs back in the day.

When Sloan broke the plane, falling across the goal line in a tangle of defensive players, the crowd roared and Sam got his hand up in time to accept a triumphant high five from PJ.

"Touchdown, Eagles!" The guy running the PA system could barely be heard over the crowd, but the stands quieted as the boys took their positions for kicking the extra point.

Despite still being down by seven points, the team was in good spirits as they went into the locker room for halftime. Being a small school with limited space and funding, they used the girls' locker for home games, letting their visitors use theirs. They'd been doing it for so many years, nobody thought anything of it.

His phone vibrated and he pulled it out to see a text message from Coach. You're doing great.

You going to come give us all a pep talk?

After a few seconds, the response came through. Nope. The boys look good out there and so do you.

Thanks, Coach.

No, thank YOU, Coach.

Emotion balled up in Sam's throat and he ran his thumb over the words before slipping the phone back into his pocket. Here he was, a grown man, and a few words from Coach McDonnell still felt like a warm, strong hand on his shoulder, letting him know he was doing okay.

Dan, Joel and Decker talked with the boys while they dissected the first half and took care of any issues with their gear or equipment. Sam watched, keeping an eye on the time, until it was almost time for the second half. Then he gave them a short pep talk, letting them know they were doing a great job and they just needed to keep on executing their plays and any other encouraging words that popped into his head.

"You're playing a good game," he said, wrapping it up. "Just keep doing what you're doing."

The Eagles fans in the stands welcomed them back to the field with raucous cheering, and Sam settled in for the third quarter. He knew his team and they had a tendency to start losing steam toward the end of the third before digging deep and playing hard in the fourth and final quarter. He needed to keep them from slacking off too much.

As the game went on, Sam forgot everything but the team and the playbook. He didn't think of Coach or Jen or anybody else. All of his focus was on the field as the time on the clock seemed to race by and, despite playing hard, they were down by three when their opponents' offense took the field for what would probably be the last time.

On second and two, their quarterback went long and Sam's stomach sank as he watched the ball sail through the air. Their receiver had his head down, running hard, with Danny Bartolo right on his heels. And then the receiver's body language changed as he prepared to turn into the catch, and Danny turned first. Arms up, he plucked the ball out of the air and brought down the interception.

And then he started running. The screaming of the crowd echoed through Sam's head as he jogged down the sideline, watching the freshman cut around defenders and sucking in a breath every time an Eagle tackled a guy about to take the kid down.

When Danny Bartolo crossed the line into the end zone, Sam held up his arms like everybody else. He turned, looking down the field for any flags that might signal a penalty was going to take this moment away.

"Touchdown, Eagles," the man with the microphone shouted over the crowd.

Sam watched the boys celebrating in the end zone for a few seconds before waving them over. They had to kick the extra point and the other team was going to get another chance with the ball. They couldn't win with a field goal and there shouldn't be enough time for their opponents to get it down the field for a touchdown, but he needed his team to stay in the game until the final whistle blew.

One kickoff and two unsuccessful plays later, the score was final and Sam found himself in a crowd of celebrating teenagers. There was a lot of backslapping and high fives, and then Decker hugged him so hard he was afraid his ribs would break.

"You won the homecoming game," Deck said, shaking his head.

"We did," Sam reminded him. "But mostly they did. Thanks for being here with me, though. You might not be bossy enough to be a head coach, but you sure know how to give sideline pep talks."

Then Coach was there and Sam wasn't surprised when that handshake become a hug. "We did it, Coach."

"You sure did, son." Then Coach pulled back and grinned at him. "Well, you won homecoming, anyway. Still plenty of games left to play."

Sam groaned and made a mental note to buy some antacids next time he was at the store because there was a good chance he was going to need them.

This team had the potential to win the championship and, if there was a God, Coach would be back on the sidelines before that game because Sam wasn't sure his nerves could handle that kind of pressure.

Jen looked at her reflection in the full-length mirror, trying to decide if the anxiety making her cheeks flush and her stomach dance was coming from excitement and anticipation, or if it was her subconscious mind's way of telling her she was on the road to making a big mistake.

If she went to the dance, she was going to end up dancing with Sam. And if she danced with Sam, she was going home with him. Or he was going home with her. She wasn't sure whose bed they'd end up in, but they were going to get naked together somewhere.

There was really no reason not to, she told herself. It wasn't as if she had to keep worrying about whether or not they'd be compatible in the future because Sam was going back to Texas. He wasn't offering her forever, and love and marriage weren't on the table. What was the harm in having a little fun before he left?

It wasn't easy having a casual fling in a town as small as Stewart Mills. Most of the single guys, she'd known her entire life and there wasn't exactly an element of mystery there. And once you were seen out with a man, it was only a matter of time—a very *short* time—before every person you met on the street seemed to greet you by sneaking a peek at your left ring finger.

Jen hadn't dressed up for the dance tonight. Unlike the Winter Carnival dance, homecoming wasn't semiformal, though a lot of the girls would change into pretty dresses simply because there weren't a lot of opportunities to dress up in Stewart Mills. Jen had chosen black leggings with a long tunic sweater that matched her eyes, along with low-heeled boots that hugged her calves.

It was dressy without looking like she was there for the party. She was chaperoning from the shadows. And the outfit was warm enough for the weather without being too warm for the gym. And it was pretty but practical. The fact that it made her look taller and thinner had nothing to do with the choice, she thought before rolling her eyes at herself.

The low-key outfit didn't mean she hadn't spent a lot of time getting ready, though. After the game, she'd treated herself to a nice long soak in a bubble bath. And she'd shaved her legs, just in case, before putting on one of the few matching lace bra-and-panty sets she owned. Though she didn't think it showed on the outside, she was definitely a woman planning to end her night naked with a man.

Her cell phone chimed and she walked to the bedside table, where it was charging. She'd taken so many pictures during the game, she'd worn the battery down and eventually given up. Since Alex Murphy was two seats over, taking professional-quality photos with his fancy camera, she'd decided to just beg copies from him.

Do you want us to pick you up on our way into town? The text message from Gretchen ended with a tractor emoji, which confused Jen until another message came through. There's no pickup truck emoji and I like the tractor better than the little cars.

Laughing, Jen typed in a response. I wasn't sure if you were planning a hayride to the homecoming dance.

That would be fun.

Not really, Jen thought. And even though she sometimes rode into town with Gretchen if they were going to the same event, she would pass tonight. Not only would she have to explain why she wasn't leaving with them if she *did* go home with Sam, but she wanted her own car. Her parents had drilled into her as soon as she had her license that she should never have to depend on a man to give her a ride home from a date in case it took a bad turn and, even though it was Sam and they'd be right in town, it was a habit that had stuck with her.

Thanks, but I'll take my car in case I stay to help clean up.

Somebody from the custodial staff usually went in with the student council members on Sunday to clean up after the dance because it ended so late, but she hoped Gretchen wouldn't think too much about what she'd said.

Okay. See you there. That was followed by an emoji of a woman dancing in a red dress and then a happy face. At least she didn't mention the monkey emojis this time.

Usually the only adults at the dance were the coaching staff and some of the school staff, acting as chaperones, and either Kelly or Dylan Clark in street clothes. But because Gretchen, Alex and Chase had been so vital in helping Eagles Fest save the team, they'd been asked to attend. Jen always went, and of course Sam was the interim coach so . . . there they went doing the best-friends-pairing-off thing again.

There would be no stopping the gossip if she and Sam spent the night together, but there was gossip already and they hadn't even done anything yet. If you were going to do the time, you may as well do the crime, right?

Only, on the other hand, she wanted to keep the speculation to a minimum because she didn't need the people of Stewart Mills thinking she was heartbroken when Sam went back to Texas. She felt as though she was damned if she did and damned if she didn't.

Sighing, Jen unplugged the phone and tucked it into the pocket of her sweater. The pockets—one for her phone and one for her car's key fob—were another reason she loved the sweater so much, since she could lock her purse in the trunk and not worry about keeping track of it at the dance.

As soon as she walked into the gymnasium, decorated in more blue and gold than the eye could handle by the homecoming committee, she spotted Sam. He was with Shawn Riley and Danny Bartolo, both of whom were still in their game jerseys, though they'd changed into jeans. She knew from experience that the entire team would be dressed the same way.

Sam was wearing a blue Eagles polo and khakis, as he had been earlier, but when she got close enough, she realized he'd changed from the ones he'd been wearing on the sideline into a clean set. And judging by the spicy scent and the smooth jaw, he'd showered and shaved, too.

Like a guy who hoped to end the night naked with a woman.

Jen sighed. Or maybe like a guy who hadn't wanted to spend the evening in the clothes he'd worn while moving up and down the sideline in a nervous sweat.

"Hey, Miss Cooper," Shawn said.

"Hi, guys." She tried not to blush at the way Sam's head jerked around when the quarterback said her name. "Great game today."

"Thanks."

"My first interception," Danny said. "You were totally right, Miss Cooper."

She remembered the day she'd called him over to the

sideline to point out that he was too busy trying to track the ball to keep up with receivers. "You were amazing, Danny. You all were."

The lights dimmed slightly as more students arrived, and she winced as whoever was manning the sound system hit play. It was very loud and she wondered if there had always been so much bass thumping in the music. Maybe she was just getting too old for this high school dance thing.

But she didn't feel old when she caught Sam looking at her in her peripheral vision. She knew the cut and soft yarn of the tunic not only hugged her body just right but, when combined with the leggings and boots, made her legs look longer and pretty damn good, if she did say so herself.

Across the gym, she saw Chase and Kelly walk in. Chase was wearing the same faded Eagles T-shirt from high school he'd worn for Eagles Fest and the game—claiming it was good luck—and she had changed from her uniform into black jeans and a dressy top. Coach's daughter might be technically off duty, but she was still Officer McDonnell and if there was a problem, she'd deal with it. The school administration and police chief had decided years ago they didn't need a uniformed officer at the dances considering how many members of the staff were usually in attendance, and they hadn't regretted the decision so far.

They waved to her from across the gym and then a few minutes later, Alex and Gretchen walked in. It was getting crowded, but she didn't mind too much. She always enjoyed seeing the students out of the classroom, laughing and having a good time. Especially tonight, when the win had their spirits high. Like any high school, there were cliques and they had their share of angst and drama at Stewart Mills High, but tonight everybody just wanted to celebrate.

"Is the music too loud or did I get really old without knowing it?" Sam shouted near her ear.

She turned to face him, noticing the boys he'd been talking to had wandered off and they were as alone as possible in a full gymnasium.

II

It was surreal, being at a high school dance with Jen. The echo of music and loud teen voices in the Stewart Mills High gym took him back a decade and a half, to the senior prom. He'd gone stag with a few friends, but not because he couldn't get a date. While he'd avoided long-term relationships, he'd dated several cheerleaders that year. But he didn't want to admit he couldn't afford a tux rental and a corsage and the traditional dinner at O'Rourke's before the prom, so he'd pretended he was too cool to dance with just one girl.

But he wasn't that teenage boy trying to make something of himself anymore. And Jen wasn't a cheerleader looking to impress her clique by hooking up with a bad-boy quarterback. They were adults, and she smelled delicious, and right now she was looking up at him with amusement curving her lips.

"At least you're not lugging around a basket of pumpkins tonight," she said, and he laughed.

"I was going to ask the guys what they did with them, but then I decided if I didn't ask, I wouldn't be forced into the position of choosing between being a responsible member of the school staff—even if I'm a temporary one—and being a guy who doesn't give a rat's ass about pumpkin babies."

"Somehow I don't see you reporting your team's lack of pumpkin-parenting responsibility to Mrs. Fournier."

He nudged her arm with his elbow. "You think this is funny, don't you?"

"A little bit, yeah." Her eyes were warm and glimmered in the dimmed lighting punctuated by two ancient disco balls that had been suspended from the basketball hoops at school dances for as long as he could remember. "But they know there's a zero percent chance of Mrs. Fournier showing up tonight. And they won the homecoming game, so I'm going to pretend this conversation never happened."

When the others—which is how he thought of their paired-off friends—came over, Sam accepted their congratulations, along with quick hugs from Kelly and Gretchen. He wasn't much of a hugger, but theirs didn't bother him too much.

After a few minutes of chitchat, the women wandered off to grab some punch and do a circuit of the gym, leaving the guys to talk and keep an eye on the dance floor. Sam wasn't surprised when Alex reached into his pocket and pulled out a small, but very expensive-looking, digital camera. He couldn't remember a time the guy didn't have a camera within reach, even in high school, except for when they were on the football field.

"This brings back some memories," Chase said, looking around the gym.

"Yeah," Sam agreed. He caught Danny Bartolo's eye and scowled. The safety was getting a little too frisky with his girlfriend for so early in the night. "It doesn't seem like anything's changed, except now I know why the chaperones watched us like hawks."

Alex laughed, lifting his camera to take a shot of a group of players huddled around the refreshment table, their heads thrown back in laughter. "I swear they look twelve years old to me, but when it was us, I felt like I was all grown up and knew everything."

Both guys agreed, and then Chase nodded at Alex's camera. "School dance photographer. That doesn't bother you? Going from globe-trotting, award-winning photojournalist to taking pictures for the Eagles yearbook?"

Alex didn't even hesitate before shaking his head. "I saw the globe. Won the awards. Made the money. It was awesome for a while. But what's even more awesome is walking through the pumpkin field with Gretchen and Cocoa. And taking pictures of the sweaters Gram knit so she can sell them on the Internet. You guys should learn how to knit, by the way. That woman's raking it in."

Sam looked at his hands, huge and callused, and chuckled. "Yeah, I don't think so."

"And I do more than take pictures for the yearbook, not that there's anything wrong with that. I've done a couple of assignments, plus I do some freelance work and I've gotten more than a few calls from the news stations down south. It's a long drive for a camera crew and if they want more than user-submitted cell phone pictures for a story, it's easier for them to call me."

"Not cheaper, though," Sam said.

Alex shrugged. "My rate's been adjusted quite a bit. And the cut in pay is worth it because it also cuts down on travel that keeps me away from the farm, and from Gretchen."

Even though he was supposed to be watching the teenagers and enforcing some vague rules about how much and which parts of their bodies could be touching while they danced, Sam found himself searching the crowd until he spotted Jen.

She was still with Kelly and Gretchen, and they looked up to no good with their heads close together as they talked, and smiles curving their lips. He couldn't help but wonder what they were talking about, but it could be anything.

Then Gretchen pulled out her cell phone and showed them something on the screen. All three of them laughed and Sam felt himself grin in response, even from across the gym. He loved watching Jen with her friends, when she was relaxed and unguarded.

"You should ask her to dance," Chase said, giving his arm a bump.

"What?" Thank goodness he wasn't the blushing kind, because he knew he'd been busted staring at Jen, but he didn't have to admit it.

"You should ask Jen to dance. You know you want to."

"I'm here to chaperone, not dance to songs I've never heard." It wasn't a denial, so it wasn't a lie.

"Even if anybody cared, which they don't, you're the coach. You get to have a dance when you win the homecoming game."

He didn't want to feel like he was in a spotlight if he danced with Jen. In his mind, they'd be able to find a dark and quiet corner when a slow song came on, and just sway a little as he held her in his arms. It wasn't meant to be some kind of victory lap for an audience.

Luckily, a few of the boys approached and Sam didn't have to respond to Chase's pushiness. They were a good distraction, since everybody was in a great mood after the win, and students wandered in and out of conversation with them as they watched over the dancing crowd. No matter how much he tried not to think about her too much, Sam always seemed to have a general awareness of where Jen was, just like he had at the bonfire.

And more than once he caught her looking back at him. Every time their eyes met, he felt the punch of desire and anticipation in his gut. He wanted her. She wanted him. And they already knew just how good their hands felt on each other, so he wasn't going to be able to play this game very much longer.

Several times over the night, he almost approached her about the dance he'd promised she would save for him, but he kept losing his nerve. Seeing her surrounded by so many students and some of the staff, he couldn't help but think about how being connected to him might affect her in the community.

But when he saw her off to one side, tossing empty punch cups into one of the big garbage cans they'd borrowed from the cafeteria, and the music slowed into what would probably be one of the last ballads of the night, he lifted his chin and started toward her.

He wasn't that Leavitt boy anymore. He'd been welcomed

back to Stewart Mills with nothing but warmth and appreciation and, for tonight at least, he was damn near a hero. Nobody in the gym would think any less of her if she danced with him.

And, hell, half the town and most of his football team thought they were dating already, anyway.

"You promised me a dance," he told her, taking a plastic cup out of her hand and tossing it in the garbage can.

"I thought maybe you forgot," she said, smiling. "Or changed your mind."

"Not a chance." He didn't lead her out onto the dance floor with the kids, but pulled her close—if not as close as he would have liked—and still holding one of her hands, put his other on her hip. "Even if being in this gym makes me remember high school and how nerve-wracking it was to ask a girl to dance."

She laughed as they swayed in time to the music. "I don't know if I believe you were ever nervous about asking a girl to dance with you."

"Every time. One, because, as you can probably tell, I'm not very good at it. And because I maybe had a little bit harder of a time accepting no than other guys. Like maybe I jumped to conclusions about why she didn't want to dance with me and felt shitty about myself, instead of shrugging it off because maybe she just didn't want to dance with me." When her expression changed and he realized she was going to go all guidance counselor on him, he dropped her into a sudden dip. She squealed and dug her nails into his arms, which made him chuckle before he pulled her upright again. "Did you think I was going to drop you?"

"Not deliberately." She laughed, shaking her head. "I admit it took my breath away for a second."

"You take my breath away." The words came out of his mouth of their own accord but, when her eyes softened and her cheeks heated, he couldn't bring himself to regret them. And whether he should have said it or not, it was the truth.

The hand she'd been resting on his shoulder crept up to cup his neck. "I'd been asking myself for like the last hour if I should remind you I was supposed to save you a dance."

"Sometimes it takes me a little while to work around to things," he said.

"Yes, it does." She raised an eyebrow at him. "And sometimes it doesn't."

He knew she was talking about that night at the dam, and his body reacted immediately to the memory. That had been one of the sweetest nights of his life, even bookended by the turmoil of being back in Stewart Mills. But he knew being able to take his time with Jen's body would be even sweeter.

He brushed his lips over her cheek and then whispered in her ear. "I want you to come home with me tonight."

"I was thinking maybe you'd come home with *me* instead. Since I'm not right in the middle of downtown and I have a garage, we'd have a little more privacy."

So nobody would know she was running around with that Leavitt boy? It was stupid, he knew, since she was currently in his arms in front of half the town. But old feelings ran deep and he couldn't stop the old insecurities from rising to the surface.

But he was slowly learning they were his feelings, not the

feelings of the person who'd triggered them in him, and he took a second to shove those feelings back before responding. "Your place works. I just want you. In a bed this time."

She smiled. "We do release stress very well together."

"Yeah." He felt a need to make sure there wouldn't be any misunderstandings, but he wasn't sure how to say it. "I, uh . . . you're just in this for the fun, right? Casual."

She arched an eyebrow, her mouth twisted in a wry smile. "And temporary? Yes, I know you're only in town for a little while and we're just enjoying each other while you're here."

That's what he wanted to hear. "Good. Because I intend to enjoy the hell out of you."

Her face flamed and the hand cupping his neck curled so her fingernails pressed into his skin. If this song didn't end soon, he was going to embarrass himself.

"Just a few more songs and we'll start throwing everybody out."

"Can't I just blow the whistle and dismiss everybody early?"

She laughed as the song came to an end and he was forced to let her go. "No. Go hang out with the guys so I can finish cleaning up and we can leave."

"You don't have to clean up everything, do you?"

"No, thank God. The custodian and some of the student council members will clean up tomorrow. But we don't like to leave punch and stuff out overnight because it's gross and sticky in the morning."

"Need help?"

"Gretchen and Kelly will give me a hand. Seriously, go find Chase and Alex. I can't think straight with you standing so close to me."

He grinned before walking away, liking the sound of that. A few more songs, he told himself. Then he didn't care if he had to sweep everything left in the gym into a giant trash bag. They were leaving.

Jen unlocked her door and led Sam into her house, her pulse pounding in anticipation. Sam kicked off his shoes on the mat, as she did, and then he hung his coat over the back of a kitchen chair.

"It's pretty," he said. "It suits you."

"Thanks." She loved her little house. And right now, she really loved the fact she was a neat person, in general, so there were no embarrassing housekeeping failures to worry about. She'd even put clean sheets on the bed that morning, just in case she brought Sam home with her.

He stepped up behind her and she shivered when he brushed her hair to one side and kissed her neck. "That was the longest school dance I've ever been to."

"It sure felt that way."

"Maybe you should show me the rest of the house."

She laughed. "That was subtle."

"I can't think about anything but getting you naked right now."

That worked for her. She took his hand and led him through the living room without slowing down. "This is the living room. Couch. Television. Living room stuff."

Then she led him into her bedroom. It was as uncluttered as the rest of the house, with a pale blue color scheme and pale wooden furniture. "And this is my bedroom."

"I was expecting more lace."

Laughing, she turned to face him. "Really? Sorry to disappoint you, but I save the lace for my bra and panties."

He made an appreciative sound deep in his throat. "Then I hope the tour's not over yet."

Jen reached up and cupped the back of his neck to pull his head down. She wanted his mouth. She pressed her lips to his, not surprised when he took control, deepening the kiss with a hunger that sent a shiver of anticipation and pleasure down her spine.

He might not have kissed her that night out at the dam, but he sure didn't mind now. He kissed her until her knees were weak and she couldn't stand having clothes between them anymore.

She yanked the blue polo shirt out of his pants and then broke off the kiss so she could pull it up and over his head. Tossing it aside, she took a few seconds to run her hands over his naked chest.

When she reached down and unbuttoned the khaki pants, he sucked in a breath. Rather than lower his zipper, she stood on her toes to lick the hollow at the base of his throat before running her tongue up over his Adam's apple to his jaw. "Dibs."

"What?"

"Nothing. Just talking to myself."

"Did you say *dibs*?"

"Long story." When she started slowly and carefully working his zipper down, pulling it away from his erection, Sam made a sound that started as a moan before his lips parted and it became a shuddering exhale. "Do you want to hear it?"

His chuckle was strained. "Only if you can multitask really well."

Clearly impatient, he took over stripping out of his clothes, so Jen did the same. She saw him take a condom from his pocket and toss it on her bedside table before dropping his pants on the floor. Leaving on the bra and panties since, judging by the smoldering look in his eye, he was clearly enjoying the lace, she stripped off the rest.

"God, you're beautiful," he said in a husky voice and when he looked at her like that, she couldn't help but believe him.

"So are you," she said, not surprised when he scoffed. But he was. Tall and solidly built, with a broad chest. And he was naked, so she took a few extra seconds to appreciate the full view.

"Come here," he said, grabbing her hand and pulling her close.

He kissed her again, his mouth hungry and demanding. His thumbs brushed over her nipples, the sensation making her pulse race despite the lace covering them. Without taking his lips from hers, he turned her and started backing her toward the bed. When her knees hit the mattress, he lifted her and set her in the center.

She ran her hands over his shoulders as he joined her, covering her body with his. "You do look good in my bed, Sam Leavitt."

"And you feel good in my hands. Undo the bra."

She tucked her arms behind her, which arched her back and thrust her breasts upward. As soon as the clasp released, his mouth was there. He ran his tongue over her nipple and then blew on the moistened flesh so she shivered. She slid the straps down her arms until Sam grabbed it and pulled it off totally.

He turned his attention to her other breast, nipping gently

at the nipple before circling the taut nub with his tongue. Jen ran her hands over his shoulders and arms, loving the feel of his taut muscles under her touch.

Sam lifted his head and kissed her again, dipping his tongue between her lips as he slid his hand down her stomach and under the waistband of the lace panties.

Her hips moved, rocking against his hand as he stroked her sensitive flesh. She savored the pleasure, moaning as he worked two fingers into her. When he lowered his head to her breast, rolling his tongue over her nipple, she skimmed her fingernails up his spine to keep from digging her nails into his back.

"I want you now," she said, her breath catching in her throat.

He caught her bottom lip between his teeth, biting down before answering. "Don't you want to come first?"

"Not this way. I really want you inside me, Sam. Now."

"Your house, your rules," he said, kissing her before pulling away to put on the condom.

She was so ready, and when he knelt between her thighs, she lifted her hips to make it easier for him. So close to orgasm, she growled as he took his sweet time, giving her just a little before pulling back and giving her just a little bit more.

He chuckled, reaching between their bodies to brush his thumb over her clit. Her body jerked and she balled the comforter into her fists. "Ever since that night at the dam, I haven't been able to forget how amazing you feel around my cock."

Knowing he'd thought about that night as much as she had inflamed her, and she thrust her hips upward, trying to force him to move. He only pressed down with the heel of his hand, holding her captive under his circling thumb.

"Why are you torturing me?"

"Because it feels good."

She couldn't take the teasing anymore. "You know what else feels good? Orgasms."

"You're not very patient when it comes to sex, are you?"

"Not when I've been waiting for this since you came back."

He pulled out of her completely and for a few seconds, Jen panicked, wondering if she'd said something wrong. But then he took her right leg and threw it over her left, forcing her to roll over. Grabbing her hips, he pulled her onto her knees.

"You want to come now, Jen?"

"Yes," she hissed, supporting her weight on her forearms.

He buried himself in her in one deep stroke, making her gasp. And then he drove hard, again and again. There was nothing gentle or teasing in him now, and it felt as if Jen's world blew apart as the orgasm tore through her.

Sam's fingers dug into her hips, almost painfully as his thrusts became faster and more erratic. Then he pushed deep inside her, almost still except for the pulsing of his body as he came.

Jen's arms gave out and she collapsed onto the comforter, managing to turn her face to the side so she wouldn't suffocate as she tried to catch her breath. He lowered himself over her, slightly to the side so he wasn't crushing her, and kissed her shoulder.

"That was so worth the wait," she said when she could finally talk again.

"You won't have to wait quite so long for the next one," he told her, his voice slightly muffled by her shoulder. "Maybe fifteen or twenty minutes. But I should warn you, I'm going to take my time."

She ran her fingers over his back, smiling when the muscles twitched under her touch. "Maybe."

"Challenge accepted," he said. "Maybe only ten minutes."

12

The sound of his cell phone chiming woke Sam and he rolled toward it. But instead of flinging his hand onto his nightstand to fumble for the phone, his arm landed on a warm lump. He opened his eyes in time to see Jen pull the covers up over her head with a groan.

He hadn't meant to fall asleep. Spending the night with her and waking up in her bed hadn't been part of the plan at all.

His phone chimed again and now he was awake enough to realize it was farther away than a bedside table. It had been in his coat pocket, which he'd draped over a chair. When he pushed back his share of the comforter and Jen immediately pulled it into her nest, he smiled. So she wasn't one of those chipper morning people.

He pulled on his boxer briefs before making his way to the

kitchen. After hitting the power button on the coffee brewer, he grabbed his coat and pulled his phone out. The text was from Cody Dodge, which surprised him, even though it wasn't as early as he'd first thought. They'd slept until almost nine.

Hey, Coach Leavitt. Do you have any free time for a talk today?

Just the fact the kid hadn't opened with *hey, dude* was cause for concern. I'm free. When and where?

Can I come to your place? At 10? I have to work at noon.

That left him time to get dressed and drink a cup of coffee before he'd have to leave, but at least he and Jen wouldn't have to dance around whether or not to have breakfast together. That was always followed by the awkwardness of spending the day together or parting ways. And it really didn't matter. Cody obviously needed a shoulder.

Sounds great. See you at 10.

He was setting two mugs of fresh coffee on the table when Jen walked into the kitchen. She'd thrown on a long T-shirt over a pair of stretchy pants that clung to her legs. And she wasn't wearing a bra, so he did his best to keep his eyes on her face. He had to go soon.

"Good morning," he said. "I hope you don't mind, but I helped myself."

"I smelled the coffee. Thanks."

There was nothing in her voice or her expression to give him a clue how she felt about him still being there. She hadn't thrown him out last night, but he remembered how limp she'd been against him, with her soft breathing, and guessed she'd nodded off as quickly as he had. And maybe he should have gotten dressed and left before she woke up fully, but that didn't seem right, either.

"I'm going to get dressed before I sit down," he said, and she nodded before pulling out a chair.

It only took him a few minutes to get dressed. He made a quick trip through her bathroom, borrowing her mouthwash, before going back to the kitchen. Jen set down her mug and smiled as he sat across from her.

"Sleep well?" she asked.

"I did, even though I didn't mean to."

"Did you mean to leave last night?"

He wasn't sure how to answer that. "I meant to take that cue from you, but we didn't make it that far."

"No, we didn't." She smiled again before taking another sip of her coffee. "Kind of nice to wake up to my coffee already made, though."

He turned her words over in his head, wondering if the word *though* implied her plan had been for him not to be there in the morning. But there was no point in overanalyzing it to death. "That was a text from Cody Dodge that made my phone go off. He wants to meet at my place at ten to talk about something."

Her brows furrowed as she sat straighter in her chair. "Really? Did he say about what?"

"No, but it seems a little out of character for him, so I told him I'd be there."

He watched her glance at the clock and then give a little nod. "It must be important."

"Do you have any thoughts on what it might be about?"

She stared into her coffee mug for a long moment before lifting her gaze back to his. "I'd rather let him tell you."

"You told me about Shawn Riley's issues," he reminded her.

"I did. But I also knew Shawn wouldn't tell you himself and you were in a position to really set him back. Cody's reached out to you. It's better if I don't interfere with that."

Sam bit down on his frustration. It had to be hard for her to protect the students' privacy in a small town like Stewart Mills, so he respected the way she found that balance. But at the same time, he didn't like to go into a talk with Cody blind. If he said the wrong thing, he could end up doing more harm than good.

"You can always call me after," Jen said. "You know, if you feel like whatever is on Cody's mind is too heavy for pep talks from his coach."

Sam knew from experience that pep talks from a coach could change a young man's life, but he was no Coach McDonnell. "Thanks."

She glanced at the clock again. "That doesn't leave you a lot of time."

He wasn't sure if that was a sign she was ready for him to leave or if she was actually concerned Cody would leave if Sam wasn't there when he arrived, and perhaps the opportunity to help the kid out would be missed. Either way, he took the hint and downed half the coffee, thankful it didn't brew hot enough to burn his throat.

"I'll drive fast," he said.

She laughed. "Just make sure you come to a complete stop at the stop signs."

"At least I've figured out where all the new ones are now." He got up and walked to the counter, where he downed the remainder of his coffee before rinsing his cup and setting it in the sink. "I guess I should run."

Jen stood, her hands still wrapped around her coffee mug in a way that prevented him from pulling her into his arms, and he wondered if it was a deliberate move on her part. "You'll let me know if whatever's going on with Cody is serious, right?"

"Of course." He pulled on his coat and walked to the door to shove his feet into his sneakers. "I enjoyed last night."

"The dance or after?"

She was watching him over the rim of her coffee mug, so he smiled and winked at her. "Both."

"Me, too."

Since she followed him to the door, Sam took the chance and stepped forward for a good-bye kiss. She leaned closer—tilting her face up—and when his lips touched hers, he realized spending one night with her hadn't quenched his desire for her. He hadn't gotten her out of his system by a long shot, and there was a good chance if she wasn't holding half a cup of coffee between them, he'd have his hands on her again.

But she was, so he reluctantly broke off the kiss and opened the door. "Thanks for the dance."

She was smiling, her eyes soft, when he walked out. He was careful not to rev the engine too much as he drove down her road, trying to avoid attracting attention, but he stepped on the gas as soon as he hit the main road. He wanted to clean up and put Jen out of his mind before Cody showed up so he could give him his full attention.

Sam had just enough time to rush through a shower and pull on clean clothes before he heard a knock on his door. He opened it to find Cody on the other side, looking downright subdued. "Hey, kid, come on in. You want a drink or something?"

"No thanks."

Rather than sit on the couch, which might make it hard for him to see Cody's face, Sam walked to the table and sat down. "Have a seat."

Cody sat and then proceeded to stare at his hands. It was so unlike him to be quiet, and it made Sam nervous as hell. Maybe the kid was in real trouble. "You're overthinking it, Cody. Just open your mouth and let the words fall out."

"If your dad contacted you, would you talk to him?"

Sam sat back against the chair, his mind suddenly empty of anything but the remembered fear of looking out the window one day and seeing Roland Leavitt standing in the dooryard. Over the years, the fear had faded but, right up until the day he left Stewart Mills, it had never totally gone away.

But he was looking at a teenage boy who suddenly looked a lot younger, and he drew in a deep breath. If this conversation was going to go to a hard place, he'd have to suck it up for the kid's sake. No matter how much he loathed talking about his old man.

"I won't lie to you," he said quietly. "No, I wouldn't, but that's me. Did your dad contact you?"

Cody nodded, his jaw clamped shut so tightly that Sam was surprised it didn't hurt. He waited, but the kid didn't say anything. Sam knew he lived with his grandmother, but he didn't know what had happened to his parents. Bill Dodge had been a little older than him, but he'd known him, of course. It was a small town.

"Cody, I know you live with your grandmother, but I don't know why. And even if I did, you're the only one who can decide if you respond to him or not."

"He's in prison." Cody's lower lip trembled for a few seconds, but then he gave his head a sharp shake, as if trying to gather himself. "He got addicted to drugs and things got really bad really fast. And then he took something and they were driving and he crashed, like three years ago. My mom died."

"Shit." He ran a hand over his hair, wanting nothing more at that moment than to call Jen for help. Or backup. Or something. Jen would be so much better at this. But Cody wasn't reaching out to an adult for advice. He was reaching out to a man who'd been alienated from a shitty dad as a teenager and might understand what he was going through. "I'm sorry, Cody."

"Thanks. I've been doing okay. My grandma's awesome and Miss Cooper helped me through a lot. And Coach. But sometimes I hate my father and you're the only one who knows what that feels like."

"It sucks, I know. And this is the first time he's contacted you?"

Cody shrugged. "He's written me letters. I read them all, but I never wrote back, though I know Grandma does. But he called and, I don't even know why, but I agreed to talk to him. Like, he was a really good dad until he broke his leg at work and started taking painkillers and then got into other drugs. And when I heard his voice . . . like that dad was the dad in my head."

He stopped talking, his eyes watering and his bottom lip trembling again. Sam got up to get the roll of paper towels as Cody swiped angrily at his eyes. After handing him a torn-off sheet and setting the roll on the table, he sat back down.

Sam cleared his throat. "You can cry here, son. It's a safe place."

Cody nodded, his face pressed into the paper towel as his shoulders shook for a few minutes. Then he blew his nose and took a second sheet to dry his eyes. "So I was talking to him and I missed him and then it was like *bam*, I remembered he killed my mom. And he only had a minute to talk, but he wants me to visit him."

"And you're torn."

"I don't know what to do. I miss my dad, but I miss my mom, too, which makes me so mad at my dad. I feel like I *have* to go because he *is* my dad, but it's like you said. You wouldn't talk to yours."

"First, you don't *have* to do anything." Sam got up again and poured them each a glass of water. "You have to take care of you. But my situation is different, Cody. My father was a drunk, mean son of a bitch filled with hate and anger my whole life. Your father was a good man who ended up on the slippery slope to addiction and fell. He's been in prison and he's clean now, so that dad you miss might be the dad he is again. But only you can decide if you want to give him the chance."

"Is it . . . is it disloyal to my mother's memory?" Cody ripped off another paper towel sheet and pressed it to his eyes.

"No, I don't think it is. Your mom loved you and I'm sure she loved the man your father was before he got sick, so seeing you both together and healthy would probably make her happy."

"You think so?" There was so much hope in Cody's cracking voice that Sam thought his heart might break. And he realized the kid probably just needed somebody to say it was okay to still love his dad even though he was in prison for the accident that killed his mother.

"I believe that." He didn't have a lot of experience with happy families, but he'd had the McDonnells. He knew that if, God forbid, they'd been in a similar situation, Mrs. McDonnell would want Coach and Kelly to find their way back to each other. "And your mom's gone, Cody. There's no good reason to go through life without your dad if you can forgive him and he can be the man he used to be."

"I'm afraid, though." Cody started shredding a paper towel, making a pile on the table.

"Of what?"

"I don't know. That sometimes I'll get angry or something and make him feel bad."

"I don't think you can say anything worse than what he's said to himself."

"What if it makes him want to do drugs again?"

Sam breathed in slowly through his nose and then released the breath. Trying to imagine what Jen would say in this situation, he leaned forward and propped his elbows on the table. "The only person responsible for your dad's sobriety is him. And you can always walk away if that's what you have to do. But there's going to be some hard stuff to work through. He's in a secure place and he probably has some kind of support group in there."

"So if I visit him at the prison, we can maybe get through some stuff while he's got help."

He sighed. "I'm trying really hard not to influence your decision. But yeah, if you *want* to rebuild your relationship with him, it might not hurt to start it while you have some automatic space and he can have a built-in support system. What does your grandmother think?"

Cody shrugged. "I know she wants me to see him, but she won't say so. Miss Cooper helped us, in the beginning. It was hard because Grandma's his mom, so we had to learn to respect that she would stand by him but that I didn't want to, you know?"

"So you know you'll have her support, then."

He nodded. "No matter what I decide, really."

"You can't beat that kind of love and support, kid. I hope you appreciate that."

"Oh, I do." Pushing back his chair, Cody gathered up the paper towels—including the mountain he'd shredded—and dumped them in the trash.

"It's not always going to be easy." Sam paused to take a drink of his water because his mouth felt dry all of a sudden. "I'm trying to work on my relationship with my mom while I'm here, and it's hard. And I think it's harder when you're trying to forgive a parent because they're supposed to take care of you no matter what and when they let you down . . ."

He let the sentence trail off, shaking his head. It still felt unnatural to him to talk about his relationship with his mother, and it was painful, too. Plus, he didn't want to scare the boy. The situations were different and as long as Bill Dodge stayed clean and had the patience to let his son work through his emotions, they had a chance at being happy again.

"I hope you and your mom work things out," Cody said. "And if you do, maybe you'll stick around instead of going back to Texas, right?"

Sam shook his head in sheer reflex. "I could never live here again. There's too much baggage. Too many memories."

Cody frowned. "That sucks. I gotta go get ready for work, but thanks for talking to me, Coach."

Sam smiled, knowing he'd probably said almost those exact same words to Coach McDonnell back in the day. "Anytime, Cody. And you can always talk to Jen—uh, Miss Cooper—about this, you know."

"I will, but I wanted to talk to somebody who understood, you know?"

"I know." Sam clapped him on the shoulder. "Keep me in the loop, okay?"

"I will." Cody opened the door, and then paused. "Thanks again, dude."

"No problem, dude," Sam said, just to be funny. Cody scowled before slowly shaking his head. "What? You say it constantly."

"Yeah, but I'm like . . . not old."

"Get out," Sam said, and then he laughed. "Being so not old, I guess you won't mind some extra laps at next practice."

"Gotta go!" He pulled the door closed behind him before Sam could say anything else.

His amusement faded and Sam dropped onto the couch, utterly exhausted. He had a hard enough time coping with his own emotional roller coaster. Riding one with a teenage boy? Not really in his wheelhouse.

But he thought he'd done okay. It was tempting to call Jen and recount the conversation so she could judge whether or not he'd handled it correctly, but he didn't. Mostly because he didn't want to betray Cody's confidence since there was no real threat to the boy.

And after spending the night in Jen's bed and then talking with Cody—including dragging some of his own emotional monsters out from under the bed—he felt vulnerable. And the last thing he could do was allow himself to be around Jen when he felt that way. She'd already accused him once of using her as some kind of comfort object.

But mostly it scared him, the way being with Jen made him feel . . . okay. It was as if being around her made life better in general, and that scared the hell out of him. He needed to fortify his defenses before he talked to her again so he could smile and keep it light. Fun. Sexy.

Temporary.

I could never live here again. There's too much baggage. Too many memories. Somehow that baggage didn't feel as heavy as it once had, though. Instead of lugging it around or tripping over it constantly, it was starting to feel like the baggage was in the basement. Taking up space, but not interfering with living his life. And the memories that popped first into his head now weren't from his childhood. He saw Jen laughing. His mom's smile. Breakfast with Coach and Mrs. McDonnell. A line of young men sitting on a bench, looking to him for leadership.

Not only was he unsure if he *could* fortify his crumbling defenses, but at this point, he wasn't sure if he should even try.

When Sam left, Jen watched him go until his truck was out of sight, and then took her coffee into the living room. She grabbed her phone before sitting on the couch and turning on the television.

Kelly had been right. Sex with Sam when they had time and privacy had been even more amazing than sex on the hood of her car. It was everything she had hoped it would be, and now she didn't know what to do about that.

She hadn't known what to do about Sam from the second his cell phone had awakened her, so she'd buried her head in the covers and put off facing him for as long as she could. Maybe it would have been easier if he'd pulled on his clothes and snuck out without even leaving a note, because then she could have at least told herself she was mad at him.

Instead, he'd made her coffee and kissed her good-bye. And the sight of him sitting across the table, drinking from one of her favorite coffee mugs, had triggered some seriously warm and fuzzy feelings about him. It was nice to have some-body to wake up and face the day with. She could too easily imagine them drinking coffee and making breakfast together before heading off to work. Then talking about their day while they made dinner, before curling up in front of the television for a while. Then they would go to bed and make love before falling asleep together like they had last night.

Until he went back to Texas.

Jen sighed and picked up her phone. The last thing she needed to be doing was spinning fantasies about blissful domesticity with a guy who was probably going to lay rubber leaving town as soon as Coach McDonnell could take his whistle back. He wasn't her type and he wasn't sticking around. She forced herself to remember how it had felt when he left town in July without even saying good-bye, and then drank some more of her coffee. Last night had been fun, but she needed to focus more on the orgasms and less on the warm and fuzzy feelings.

After tossing the remote control on the coffee table and brewing herself a second cup of coffee, Jen settled onto the couch and pulled up the never-ending group text with Kelly and Gretchen. Then, smiling because she couldn't help it, she sent a text message consisting only of the emoji of the little monkey covering his mouth.

OMG! Gretchen texted back, followed by a string of happy faces, party horns, cocktail glasses and more happy faces.

Then Kelly chimed in. High five! Was it worth all the drama?

Jen rolled her eyes at her screen. There hadn't been that much drama. Yes.

A snoring happy face emoji followed by a big red question mark came through, followed by another text from Kelly. Use your words, Gretchen.

You're no fun. Did you sleep together? Like sleep sleep?

Yes.

His place or yours? That was from Kelly.

Mine. More private, not that anything is a secret in this town.

At least Gram didn't tell everybody Sam bought condoms, like she did to Chase, Kelly typed.

Jen laughed at the memory of Gretchen's grandmother sharing that little bit of gossip with them. True. Maybe he brought them with him from Texas.

Is he still there? Gretchen asked.

No. He had to meet one of the football players this
morning, so he left after coffee. Which he made
for me.

KEEPER!

That was from Gretchen and made Jen wince. No. No
keeping. Just having fun before he goes back to Texas.

That sounds familiar. She could almost hear the laughter
behind Kelly's text. She'd been having fun with Chase before
he went back to New Jersey, too. Until they fell in love.

His baggage was a lot lighter than Sam's. Seriously.
Do NOT let me fall for this guy.

Gretchen responded first. No. Then a big heart emoji.
Got it.

Jen hoped so, because she was going to need her friends to
keep her on track. And she saw the irony of asking the two
women who were marrying Sam's best friends to keep her
from bringing it full circle by falling in love with him. But
when push came to shove, they'd realize he wasn't a good
forever prospect for her and keep her focused on the fun.

At least she hoped they would, because she might not be
able to do it herself. The first time Sam had returned to
Stewart Mills, he'd had a chip on his shoulder and it hadn't
surprised her when he ran the minute the festivities were
over. And when they'd dragged him back to town a second
time, she'd anticipated more of the same.

But he'd changed. Jen had watched him settle into Stewart Mills and, not only was he working on laying the ghosts of his past to rest and reconnecting with his mother, but she'd seen him with the boys on the team. He was a really great guy and the more time she spent with him, especially after homecoming and the night they'd spent together, the more she realized he wasn't such a bad catch, after all.

Another text from Kelly came through. Dinner tonight? Chase has to leave midafternoon.

Sunday dinners with Kelly weren't exactly a tradition, but one or both of her friends were usually available to keep her company when Chase had to go back to New Jersey. She did a lot better with the separation than Jen thought she would, but the first few hours after he left were usually lonely ones for her, so if Kelly wasn't on duty, she'd reach out to her friends.

Gretchen responded first. Sounds good. Gram and Alex can fend for themselves. I want to hear more about your monkey business.

Jen texted the monkey with his hands over his mouth again before returning to words. Dinner sounds good. I think I'll take a nap first, though. Didn't sleep much last night.

About damn time, Kelly texted, and then Gretchen wrapped it up with a smirking face and a thumbs-up.

Usually on Sundays, Jen would do some housekeeping or get her grocery shopping for the week out of the way, but she couldn't muster the ambition to get up and get in the shower. Instead, she put her feet up on the coffee table and started flipping through channels.

She hadn't been lying about the possibility of taking a nap. Sam had kept her up a lot later than her bedtime, not that she was complaining. And she was surprised she'd slept so well with him in her bed. Very seldom did she ever have overnight company, since there hadn't been many men she'd come to trust enough to bring them into her home. But her tiredness today came from the late hour, not restless sleep.

And she had a feeling she'd be doing a little tossing and turning tonight. She knew she'd be thinking about Sam and about sex and wishing he was there. Then she'd curse herself for wishing that because emotions couldn't have a place in their relationship. And since Sam hadn't mentioned being in touch when he'd left, she figured she'd see him again for the first time at school, and she'd spend some time worrying about how awkward that would be.

But right now she yawned and stretched, delighting in the sweet tenderness of her body after a night of delicious sex. As long as she could keep those warm and fuzzy fantasies at bay, her plan to have some fun with Sam while he was in town was off to a good start.

13

By the time Sam left for the high school on Monday afternoon, his stomach was a tight knot of nerves.

He'd screwed up and not texted Jen after Cody left his apartment the day before. Then his mother had called, her voice small and tentative, to see how he was doing. He'd known it wasn't easy for her to make the telephone call, so he'd talked to her about the football team and her job until the conversation became less stilted and more natural.

With each passing hour he didn't contact Jen, he became more convinced he shouldn't contact her right away. He'd kissed her good-bye and he was afraid calling or texting her too soon would make it appear as if he was pursuing a relationship. Like a *real* one.

Then he'd decided he was being an idiot. They were in a small town. They shared friends. They worked in the same building with the same group of kids. Communication between them was going to be an ongoing thing until Coach was back on the sideline, so there would be putting no distance between them.

He'd finally pulled out his phone and come up with a compromise that didn't make him panic at the idea of trying to guess how she might interpret his text. Letting her know, in broad terms, how things had gone with Cody was contact, but not overly personal.

Just wanted to let you know Cody's doing okay. He'll probably talk to you soon, but it's nothing bad. Then he waited.

Her response didn't take long. I'm glad to hear it. And I'm glad you could be there for him.

Of course. But he couldn't let it go at that. Are you busy right now?

I'm at Kelly's with Gretchen. We're waiting for pizza.
Do you need to talk?

Nope. He didn't even want to think about what she might be telling her best friends about their night together. I'll probably see you around the school tomorrow.

There was a long pause before she typed in, Probably.

He'd cursed himself for opening with Cody. While it had seemed like a natural way to break the post-morning-after communication awkwardness, the text message had kicked her into guidance counselor mode. She hadn't asked him if he wanted to get together. She'd asked if he needed to talk to her. Maybe it was a subtle difference, but it mattered to him.

After a restless night, he decided a good O'Rourke's

breakfast was what he needed to get through the day. But Chase was back in New Jersey and Alex was on his way to a community college to talk to them about teaching a photography course. Deck was too busy to close the garage for an hour, and he didn't want to ask Coach. That man could read his face too well and he didn't want deep conversation. Just an omelet and some football talk.

Instead, he ate a bowl of cereal standing at the counter and killed time with a run to the Laundromat until it was time to head to the high school.

He had Coach's keys to the doors, so he could have entered the school by the gymnasium. Once the final morning bell rang, all of the doors locked and visitors had to be buzzed in through the main entrance. But he needed to stop by the office and see if there was any mail for Coach McDonnell in his box. He got buzzed in and said hello to the administrative staff and, after dumping some flyers into the recycling bucket thoughtfully placed under the row of mailboxes, ended up with a few envelopes he'd drop by the coach's house later.

He did glance down the hallway that led to the guidance office. He couldn't help himself. But there was no sign of Jen.

"Hi, Coach."

He turned, realizing as he did that he was starting to answer to the word now, instead of looking around for Coach McDonnell. It was Miss Jordan, whose first name he couldn't remember. She was new, teaching social sciences, and he smiled. "Hey, how are you doing today?"

"Awesome. There's still some coffee cake left in the break room, and it's pretty good. Just so you know."

She was an attractive woman and when he'd first started at the school, he'd seen some interest in her expression. But hooking up with Jen was one thing. She knew who he was and where he came from. And she knew where he was going *back* to when Coach got the all clear to return to work. Miss Jordan knew none of that. And she was too young for him by more than a few years, he'd guess.

And then there was the fact he couldn't muster up any attraction to her when his body was busy being a radar antenna, waiting to catch a glimpse of Jen.

"Thanks," he said. "I just ate, but I'll keep it in mind."

"How's everything going with football?"

"Good. Everything's good, thanks." Movement caught his eye and he turned his head to see Jen through the floor-to-ceiling windows. She was at the far end of the hall, walking toward the office while taking a bite out of an apple and reading.

His body seemed to tighten in response to the sight of her, and he was grateful he wasn't a teenage boy anymore and could control what would have been an embarrassing reaction to have in the middle of the office. The envelopes in his hand weren't exactly math-book-sized.

"I need to get back to grading papers," Miss Jordan said, dragging his attention away from Jen. "See you around."

"Yeah. Have a good afternoon." After offering a small wave to the women behind the tall counter, he followed the social sciences teacher out into the hall, but slowed when she took a left turn.

Jen looked up from the paper as she neared the intersection of hallways in front of the office, as if she'd worked there for so long she had some kind of radar system that allowed her to read, walk and navigate all at the same time.

She paused when she saw him, but only for a second, and then she smiled. "Hi, Sam."

"Hey. I came to grab the mail for Coach. Heading to my glorified closet now."

That made her laugh, and the sound echoed against the cement walls of the empty hallway. "It *is* small. And you're bigger than Coach McDonnell, so it must feel like pretty tight quarters."

"I usually take the playbook and whatever else I need into the gym and sit on the bleachers. The gym teacher doesn't seem to mind and the kids mostly ignore me." Something about the way she nodded and her body language said she didn't really have time to stand around in the hallway and talk, so he mentally braced himself. "Are you doing anything later tonight?"

"I have some evening meetings, and I need to catch up on some work for the financial aid fair."

At least she hadn't told him she was washing her hair. "I should probably watch some game tapes, anyway. Maybe I can talk PJ into watching them with me. He's quite the strategist, that one."

She laughed. "Thankfully he uses his powers for good."

"So far, anyway. I guess I'll let you get back to what you were doing."

"Yeah." She smiled and started to turn, but then stopped. "What about Wednesday?"

He tried not to show how much he liked those three little words, just in case she didn't mean what he thought she did. "What about Wednesday?"

She shrugged one shoulder. "I don't know. I thought

maybe if you weren't doing anything, you could stop by after practice. I could feed you and we could . . . hang out."

He wanted very much to . . . hang out. "I'd like that."

Her smile was a lot warmer this time. "Great. I'll see you then, if I don't run into you before that."

He was about to say *can't wait*, but he didn't want to seem too eager. "Sounds good."

When she walked by him to open the office door, Sam forced himself to start walking. Going to her place for dinner and whatever hanging out meant to her sounded better than good. Even if hanging out just meant sitting on the couch with her, watching television. He'd take it.

And the realization that watching TV shows with Jen sounded like a wonderful evening to him, even if they didn't end up in her bedroom, was enough to make Sam take a right turn at the break room, in search of coffee cake.

By Wednesday afternoon, Jen had worked herself up to the point she was afraid she'd explode if something startled her.

It wasn't like her at all, to be the one who pushed for a second date. Or a second whatever it was. She didn't know what the rules were for fun flings, but she knew Sam well enough to know he might not put himself out there.

After having a meeting with a freshman whose grades had plummeted since she started at the high school, Jen sighed and rubbed her temples. She strongly suspected the girl was smoking marijuana, which, according to the grapevine, was readily available in her home. And for her grades to be dropping so badly, she not only was overdoing it, but there were probably underlying issues, as well. She was going to have to talk to the administration and Kelly and decide if they wanted to involve DCYF. She didn't know the girl's parents well enough to make an educated guess as to whether talking directly to them would make the situation better or worse for the student, but Kelly might.

She needed some sugar. She'd had more than enough caffeine, and she could really use food to settle her stomach and sop up some of the coffee sloshing around. After finishing up her notes on the meeting, Jen locked the file away in the cabinet and then headed for the break room, hoping there would be something sweet and home baked on the counter.

Kelsey Jordan was sitting on the love seat under the window with her shoes kicked off and her legs tucked under her. A stack of papers were on the arm of the love seat and when Jen walked in, she was marking the top sheet with a red pen.

"More papers to correct?" Jen asked when Kelsey looked up.

"Always. And between the fact I teach social sciences and we have to work on writing skills to up our standardized testing scores, it's not just correcting papers. It's wading through some of the worst handwriting I've ever seen in my life. If I didn't know better, I'd think every member of the sophomore class is going to be a doctor."

Jen laughed, even though she knew she wouldn't find it funny if she was the one who had to read all the papers. A lot of schools in the southern part of the state had moved to small, cheap laptops hooked virtually to clouds accessible by the students and the staff. Their work was online and, more importantly maybe, it was typed.

But Stewart Mills High had yet to be awarded a grant that would cover a computer for every high school student, and Jen had resisted previous attempts at teachers requesting homework assignments be done on a computer and printed. Besides limited Internet options in the area, there were too many households in Stewart Mills that had either no computer or none that could handle the most up-to-date software, and she wasn't in favor of anything that widened the gap between students who came from financial security and those who didn't.

Hopefully, nobody had told Kelsey that Jen was the one who'd fought for the kids to handwrite their papers until the school provided every student with a computer before she started working there. The young teacher might throw the red pen at her.

"Attack of the munchies?"

Jen nodded. "I've had so much coffee today my stomach's in knots. Is there anything good?"

"There are scones."

Ouch. Jen wasn't surprised Kelsey didn't actually answer the question she'd asked, since the wife of their assistant principal thought she was a lot better at making scones than she actually was. But if she was lucky, one of the scones would absorb some of the coffee in her stomach and help settle it. After setting one on a napkin and recovering the plate, she sat at the table.

As she took the first bite, she noticed Kelsey staring at her in a speculative way. Since her mouth was full and would be for a while thanks to the scone's density, she raised an eyebrow.

"So you and Coach Leavitt are finally a thing, huh?"

She almost inhaled the scone, which would have been bad because if she got a lump of that white cement lodged in her throat, it would probably take drain cleaner to dissolve it fast enough to save her. But she managed to finish chewing it and swallowed.

"What?"

The younger woman rolled her eyes. "Come on. I was at the homecoming bonfire. And the dance. And I saw him looking at you Monday, when you were coming to the office and hadn't seen him yet. You guys are totally a thing."

Her first instinct was to deny it, but Kelsey wasn't stupid and neither were a lot of other people in Stewart Mills. A denial would only make everybody more determined to be right. The gossip was already going around. She knew that, since she also wasn't stupid. But maybe she could control it and, at the very least, not deal with anybody feeling sorry for her when Sam left town again.

"Kind of a thing," Jen admitted. "It's casual. It's not serious or anything."

Kelsey nodded. "A fling with the hometown hero while he's around?"

Jen tried to imagine Sam's reaction to being called a hometown hero and it made her chuckle. "Something like that."

"Good for you." Kelsey sighed, but it was exaggerated and she smiled. "Even though you said you didn't have dibs on the coach, I was pretty sure you guys would hook up. I'm glad I didn't believe you and end up in something messy."

"Yeah, me, too." She didn't like the visual she got of Sam and Kelsey together, so she stuffed another chunk of scone in her mouth.

Kelsey turned her attention back to a paper, sighing again, though this one was genuine. Jen finished her scone and then, after saying good-bye to the teacher, went back to her office and tried to put the conversation out of her mind.

It wasn't easy. She wasn't sure how Sam would feel about her telling somebody outright they were an item, but she honestly felt it was the best way to handle it. Yes, they were a thing. A fun, temporary thing not even worth talking about. And no hugs or sympathetic glances when he got in his truck and blew out of town.

But for now she had to focus on her to-do list, which was staggering. She wanted to get home with enough time to check on the roast in the slow cooker and jump in the shower before football practice was over. If she knew one thing for certain, it was that hanging out didn't mean they were going to sit around and play gin rummy.

Thursday afternoon, Sam whistled as he made his way to his tiny office, feeling better than he had in a long time. Maybe better than he could ever remember feeling. He'd spent the previous evening with a woman who made him laugh and turned him inside out in all the best ways, and he'd come up with a great new trick play to run by PJ at practice.

Life was damn good. It was so good, in fact, that on the drive home from Jen's house—since he didn't spend the night due to it being a school night—he'd caught himself thinking about the weak job market in the area and wondering if he'd be able to find work if he stayed in town after Coach was cleared to take back the whistle.

He'd almost driven off the road when it truly sank in that he'd been considering staying. In Stewart Mills—the town he'd sworn he'd never even return to. He'd had a good reason for coming back both times, but the idea of calling the town home again should never have crossed his mind.

But once it did, he couldn't seem to shake the idea. And he'd awakened that morning with a sense of optimism about the future that wasn't familiar, but had him in a good mood.

He nodded to the gym teacher as he walked through the gymnasium to his office, sticking close to the wall so as not to disrupt the class. But when he got to the door, he saw a pink message slip taped to the whiteboard Coach McDonnell had screwed to the door so the guys could leave him a note if they stopped by when he wasn't around.

Sam's name was on it, so he pulled it free, scowling at the name and number written below it. He didn't recognize either, but the box was checked to indicate whoever it was would like a return call.

After closing the door of his claustrophobic office to cut out the noise, Sam glared for a few seconds at the big desk phone with its overabundance of buttons and lights before pulling out his cell phone.

The mystery caller answered on the third ring. "Hello?"

"Hi, this is Sam Leavitt from Stewart Mills. I got a message you called?"

"Sam! Neil Page." Sam's scowl deepened as the man explained who he was. The assistant coach of the team they'd beat for homecoming—the one he'd recognized as being part of the team Stewart Mills had beat back when Sam was quarterback.

"Was there a problem?" he asked when the man took a

breath. If he was calling to complain about the facilities or some imagined misconduct on the part of one of the Eagles, he was barking up the wrong tree.

"No problem at all. I actually wanted to talk to you about something, but with a forty-five-minute drive between us and the season in full swing, I'm not sure we can get together."

Sam was still waiting to find out *why* he wanted to get together and wished he'd get on with it. "Yeah, my schedule's pretty tight."

"I'd rather talk to you in person, but the phone will do. Do you have a few minutes now?"

He chuckled. "I called you, so I must."

"Good point. So here's the deal. Coach McDonnell's one of the most respected coaches in the state and high school football's a pretty close community, so we all know how tough it's been up there. You were one of his best. Hell, you even managed to steal my championship. But more importantly, seeing how the team is holding up after the rough year they've had is a testament to how good you are on the sidelines."

"Thanks." He didn't say anything else because he still couldn't see where the conversation was leading and he didn't like that.

"Our coach is retiring at the end of the school year," Neil continued. "Not many people know yet, so I'd rather you kept that under your hat. Especially with the team. Who knows how hooked up they all are on social media. But anyway, I've already been offered the position."

"Congratulations." Neil coached at a big regional school with a fat football budget, so he'd be sitting pretty.

"Thanks. I'm kind of . . . clinical. Strategy and conditioning and stuff like that. I need a head assistant coach who can really connect with the team and keep them on track, like you have with the Eagles. I know you came back to fill in for Coach McDonnell, but I'd like for you to consider coming and coaching with me next season. It's a paid position. You won't get rich, but the cost of living's pretty low around here."

Sam rocked back in his chair, trying to wrap his head around the fact he was being offered a job coaching football. His first instinct was to laugh at the guy, but he held it back and gave himself a few seconds to process it.

He had to admit he enjoyed coaching football a lot more than he'd anticipated. And forty-five minutes wasn't too far away. It was close enough to drive up on a Saturday and visit Coach and Mrs. McDonnell before hanging out with Alex and Chase. He could see his mom.

And Jen. They were having a fling—they'd both made that pretty clear—but he knew in his gut their connection went deeper than that. It wasn't just about the sex and if he didn't go back to Texas, they were going to have to figure that out.

"I don't know what to say," he said finally, in case Neil hadn't figured that out on his own. "This is unexpected."

"I know, but the good news is you have time to think about it because it's not something we're going to start giving too much time to until the season's over. But I wanted to touch base with you before Coach McDonnell is on his feet again and you head back to . . . somewhere down south, isn't it?"

"Texas." He blew out a breath. "And I'll think about it, but yeah, I'll need some time."

The transition from wanting to get the hell out of Stewart Mills to thinking maybe it wasn't so bad and then getting an offer that would land him nearby on a more permanent basis was too much, and his mind was reeling.

"If you want to get together and have a more in-depth conversation about our football program, just let me know. We could probably find a place halfway between us to grab a meal."

"I'll let you know."

When the call was over, Sam saved the number in his phone so he'd be able to find it again and then leaned back in his chair and closed his eyes.

Living in New Hampshire, coaching high school football. Not in a million years would he have imagined that as a possible future for himself. Yet here it was, his for the taking if he wanted it.

The old anger and resentment tried to rear their heads, but he forced them down. He was through letting his past dictate his future.

But even as he let that determination sweep over him, he decided he wasn't going to tell anybody about Neil's offer quite yet. It's what pretty much everybody in his life would want for him, and if he couldn't do it, he didn't want to let them down. Until he'd sorted through his feelings about staying in the state, he was going to keep it to himself.

How would Jen react? He couldn't help asking himself the question as he got up to open the door and let some air in, even if it came with the noise. Even if he moved forty-five minutes away, he'd still be in Stewart Mills a lot. Her best friends were marrying his best friends. They'd run into each other.

For a few seconds, he even allowed himself to imagine her going with him. It was a big school system, so maybe they could find a place for her. They could make a home together and . . .

The sense of longing was so intense it almost weakened his knees, so Sam slammed the door on those thoughts. He had to figure out—on his own—what the hell he was doing with his life before he could even think about sharing it with somebody else.

14

On Sunday morning, Sam drove to Eagles Lane and parked in Coach's driveway. Mrs. McDonnell had called him and offered him breakfast in exchange for going for a walk with her husband. The doctor wanted him walking more, but she had things to do and didn't like him walking alone. Sam also suspected the unusual amount of together time was starting to wear on them, though she'd never admit it.

He would have done it even without the bribe of a home-cooked meal, but he wasn't about to tell her that. Since he was expected, he knocked twice and then let himself in.

"We're in the kitchen," he heard Mrs. McDonnell call.

He followed the aromas of coffee and what he thought at first was bacon. But then he realized it wasn't *real* bacon and felt a pang of sympathy for Coach. After shaking the older man's hand, he kissed Mrs. McDonnell's cheek, moving quickly so he didn't interfere with her plating the food. "Good morning."

"Good morning, Sam. Perfect timing, as always. If you pour juice for everybody, I'll finish this up."

He hated orange juice, but he kept his mouth shut and poured three glasses. Kelly had told Chase, who'd told Sam that there had been an epic battle in the McDonnell household over coffee. Mrs. McDonnell wanted him to only drink decaffeinated, and Coach wanted none of that. He refused to drink it in the mornings and his wife had said it was decaf or nothing. He'd gone with nothing and there hadn't been a cup of real coffee brewed since then.

No wonder she was desperate to pawn him off on Sam.

He smiled his way through an omelet made with fake eggs, served with fake bacon and dry wheat toast. And he washed it down with the orange juice without even shuddering. Maybe he wouldn't be so quick to jump on invitations to breakfast at the McDonnell house during the remainder of his time there. Even if he took Neil up on the job offer, he'd be too far away for impromptu breakfast invitations and right now, that didn't look like such a bad thing.

"Thank you," he said to Mrs. McDonnell as he stood and started clearing the table. "It was delicious, as always."

"Liar," Coach mumbled into his napkin.

Mrs. McDonnell gave her husband a look. "Hush. You can't help make a boy into a good man like Sam and then call him names when he acts right."

Sam wisely kept his mouth shut and piled the dirty dishes on the counter. While there was an edge to it that was new, the McDonnells had bickered in the kitchen for as long as he'd known them. At first it had made him nervous because in his experience, spousal sniping led to drinking and yelling and hitting. But he'd learned very quickly there was genuine affection between the coach and his wife, even when they argued, and that Coach would throw himself in front of a logging truck before he lifted a hand to her.

"You guys go. Walk. Skip. Steal skateboards from some kids. I don't care what you do as long as you do it out of this house." Mrs. McDonnell waved a hand in Coach's direction. "And don't think I don't know you'll use every minute of it to complain about how awful it is having a wife who wants to keep you alive for a good long while yet."

Sam couldn't hold back the smile, so he turned his back and took his time rinsing the disgusting pulp out of the orange juice glasses. Once Coach had put on a coat and his shoes, Sam kissed Mrs. McDonnell's cheek again and went out into the chilly air. It was a little brisk, but there was no wind and the sun was warm. Once they started walking, they'd be warm enough.

"Do you have gloves?" he asked. "In case your hands—"

"Don't."

Sam dropped the subject and shoved his own hands into his coat pockets. He knew it had to be hard for Coach McDonnell. It didn't come naturally to him to be fussed over or to have to ask for help. And there was no sense in Sam trying to explain he'd scared them and they loved him and wanted him to be healthy. He knew that, too, but it wouldn't make it any easier to accept being coddled.

"Did you hear there's a buyer for the old mill?" Coach asked as they neared the end of the street.

"Somebody said there have been rumors of it off and on for a while."

"There has, but the rumors are true this time. I guess they make some kind of furniture kits. Modular desks or something that you custom order on the Internet, and then they make the pieces and send them to you to put together. Something like that, anyway."

Sam followed Coach's lead and they turned right toward the town square. He didn't think they'd make it that far, but it wasn't like they had any other destination in mind. "Sounds like the kind of thing that would be mostly automated."

"I guess it is to a point, but they said they'll be hiring at least thirty people at first, if not more. This is an expansion for them, so they're not bringing a big workforce with them."

"Every job helps."

"Amen to that." Coach nodded, tucking his hands in his coat pockets. "If it happens, it'll be a damn good thing for this town. Eagles Fest might have lifted everybody's spirits for a while, and it definitely helped keep the kids on track, but it's going to take solid employment to really make a difference."

Sam nodded, and then asked the question that was really on his mind. He'd been more introspective than usual since Neil's call, but he had a lot to work through. "Why did you have Kelly call me?"

"I told you, we didn't have any stability in the coaching staff and I didn't want them hiring somebody else while I was off my feet."

He shook his head. "I've seen this town pull together and you didn't need me. They wouldn't have replaced you. Hell, Kelly would have coached them herself if she had to."

"You're probably right about that." Coach snorted. "Those three girls can get anything done if they put their minds to it. But growing up with a dad who coaches football doesn't make you a coach."

"Neither does playing the game fourteen years ago. I don't think it's about you at all. I think it's about me. You wanted me back here and neither you nor Kelly was going to take no for an answer."

"I was afraid you wouldn't come back if you didn't have a damn good reason," Coach said after a long silence. "And I think you needed to come back and spend a little time in Stewart Mills."

"I hadn't come back for almost fifteen years and was doing just fine."

"You *think* you were."

Sam felt a rare flash of anger at the old man. Coach didn't know anything about his life in Texas. He had a good job and a place to call his own and he'd been doing just fine before Kelly emotionally blackmailed him into returning for Eagles Fest. And then he'd gone back to doing okay, more or less, until Kelly called him back for a second time. "What, because I don't have a wife and a bunch of kids, I'm broken somehow?"

Coach stopped walking and turned to give him a hard stare. "Not for a second have I ever thought you were broken, son. You know that."

The temper faded as quickly as it had come. "I do know that."

They started walking again, more slowly now. "When you came back here in July, stuff got stirred up inside of you. Like kicking over a log that's been sitting a long time. There's stuff under there and it scurried into the light. You weren't here long enough to deal with it, and you can never get that log back into the right spot with everything under it again."

Sam laughed, even though the truth in the other man's words made him a little uncomfortable. "That's one of the worst analogies ever, Coach."

"I couldn't come up with a good football-themed one. But you know what I mean."

Yeah, he did. "What are you hoping I'll find?"

Coach stopped walking and turned to face him again, but this time his expression was softer. "I hope you'll find whatever it is you're looking for."

Sam rolled his eyes. "Come on. That's corny even for a guy who's spent God knows how many years giving inspirational speeches to teenagers."

"Maybe so, but what I said will sit and stew in your subconscious for a while." As if Sam didn't have enough stewing in there already. "How long have we been walking?"

"I don't know. Maybe ten minutes?"

"Dammit. That's not enough. Let's keep going."

Sam shrugged and kept pace with him. "The stronger you get, the faster you can get back to running herd on your teenagers and I can get back to my actual job."

On the drive over, he'd recommitted to not telling anybody about the offer. Not even Coach. Or maybe *especially* not Coach. If Sam decided to stay, he had to know he was doing it only for himself. It felt like lying, but he needed a better handle on it before he let Coach in.

"You sound like you're in an awful hurry to leave town for a guy who's seeing an attractive, smart and all-around wonderful woman like Jen Cooper."

Sam's stomach dropped and he sighed deeply. "Me being

here is about you and the football team. It has nothing to do with Jen."

"But leaving will have something to do with Jen, one way or the other."

"I don't know what kind of medications they have you on, Coach, but you're talking in circles more than usual, and that's saying something."

"Just seems like starting a relationship with a woman when you're not planning on sticking around isn't a real stand-up thing to do."

"It is if she knows up front I'm not sticking around."

"So it's one of those casual things? Like friends with benefits or whatever you kids call it?"

"More or less." He did *not* want to talk about this with Coach.

"I guess we'll see about that."

Sam frowned. "What's that supposed to mean?"

"Nothing. Must be the medications addling my brain."

"Funny." Sam glanced sideways at him. "I know what this is. Chase fell in love with Kelly and Alex fell in love with Gretchen, so now the whole damn town is convinced I have to fall in love with Jen. Even you."

"Does have a nice symmetry to it, don't you think?" Coach snickered when Sam made a growling sound deep in his throat.

"That's not how it is." Or so he kept telling himself, in between those moments he wondered if that was true anymore.

Coach held up one hand. "I don't want the finer details on how it is. She's practically a daughter to me. Her and Gretchen, both. I won't interfere, but because of that relationship, I do want to say one thing."

Sam stopped when he did, forcing himself to look the other man in the eye. Whatever was coming, Coach was very serious about it. He knew the tone.

"Sound travels in old houses and I got the gist of what happened with you and Jen during Eagles Fest. And that's none of my business. But I also got the impression you left town without saying good-bye. Is that true?"

Sam swallowed hard and gave a sharp nod. "Yes, sir. But I—"

"You're a runner. Someday you're going to have to quit running. But if you decide to leave Stewart Mills, you stand up like a goddamn man and you tell that girl you're leaving. Maybe it'll hurt her or maybe it won't, but don't you run out on her."

"I won't."

"If you do, I'll fly down to Texas and kick your ass, do you hear me? I don't care if it kills me."

"We've been up-front with each other, Coach. We both know I'm not what she's looking for in a husband and this place is not what I'm looking for in a home." But he hadn't known she'd been hurt by his leaving without saying good-bye, and it bothered him. He honestly thought she'd been relieved to see him go. "I won't run out on her without saying good-bye."

"Good." Coach stared at him for another few seconds before nodding as if he'd seen the truth of Sam's intentions on his face. "I guess I'm ready to turn around now. If Helen won't let us back in the house yet, we can sit on the porch. Or sit in my car with the heat and the music on."

Sam turned, smiling at the mental image of the two of them sitting in a running vehicle in the driveway because

Mrs. McDonnell hadn't had enough husband-free time yet. "Just do me a favor?"

"What's that, son?"

"Can we just talk about sports now?"

As it turned out, Mrs. McDonnell didn't lock them out. But as soon as Coach and Sam were settled in the living room to warm up and finish their conversation about who had the best-conditioned athletes in the NFL, she grabbed her coat and keys and practically ran out of the house to do some errands.

But she stopped long enough to give her cranky husband a kiss before she left, and it warmed Sam's heart. This was what he'd always wanted and hadn't found, he thought. People thought he was single because his parents' marriage had scarred him. And maybe it had, both emotionally and physically, but he was single because he hadn't found what the McDonnells had yet.

And when Jen popped into his head, laughing and eyes shining, he deliberately mentioned an NFL coach known to be lax in discipline and conditioning just to annoy Coach. The ensuing debate would be heated enough to keep his thoughts in line. He hoped.

What are you up to right now?

Jen felt her pulse kick up a notch when she read the text message from Sam. Telling herself it was her body associating his name with orgasms and not an emotional reaction, she pulled up the on-screen keyboard to respond.

Nothing much. She'd been debating whether she needed enough staple items in the house to merit a trip down south to stock up in the bigger—cheaper—stores. If she did that, she could swing in and see her family for a while, since she bought perishables at the market in town. What are you up to?

I had breakfast with the McDs. Went for a walk with Coach. Then I went and had lunch with my mom.

She hadn't known he was doing that. How's your mom?

Good. It was a nice lunch. I invited her to O'Rourke's for supper Friday night since we have a Saturday game this week.

Jen smiled, even though she knew he couldn't see her. Healing his relationship with his mother was hugely important to Sam, even if he himself didn't recognize how much. So are you trying for a hat trick of free meals that you don't have to cook?

After a few seconds, he sent back three question marks.

Mrs. McD made you breakfast. Your mom made you lunch. Are you hoping I'll make you supper?

Oh. Actually I was hoping you'd want to take a drive. I'm sick of sitting and talking and eating and talking more and I like driving.

Taking me for a drive involves both sitting and talking. And I can't guarantee I won't bring a snack. She could almost hear his exasperated sigh.

It's different. Do you want to go for a ride with me?

Yes. When her phone rang in her hand a few seconds later, it startled her so much she almost dropped it. And Sam's name came up on the screen. "I said yes."

"I know, but I wanted to say something and I don't have the patience to type the words out on that tiny freaking keyboard."

Jen was tempted to point out his phone had the ability to transcribe his voice into texts, but she didn't bother. He hadn't lost his New England accent and picked up a Texas twang over the last decade and a half, but his accent was just weird enough now so he'd probably end up frustrated and smash the thing against a wall.

"What didn't you want to type?"

"I just wanted you to know that even though I had a long walk with Coach and then I saw my mom, I'm not asking you to go for a ride because of any comfort object crap. I've had a good day and I want to go for a little cruise and listen to the radio. And I'd rather do it with you with me. That's all."

"Okay. Then I'd love to take a ride with you."

An hour later, she was in the passenger seat of his truck, wishing it was summer so she could roll the window down and feel the wind in her hair. It was a little cold for that right now. But the radio was on and he was telling her about the new and definitely not improved breakfast menu at the McDonnell house.

"No coffee? Who doesn't have coffee for breakfast?"

He shook his head. "I drank orange juice. And not only did I drink orange juice, but it's the kind with all the little bits in it. I don't like bits."

Then he told her about the coffee war and she laughed at the idea of Coach McDonnell giving up coffee. Something would give, and it wouldn't take very long.

When Sam turned the truck up the road that led to the dam, Jen gave him a sideways, skeptical look. She wasn't sure what he had in mind, but there would be no reenacting of their July encounter with her on the hood of his truck. For one thing, he wasn't *that* tall. And for another, the difference between July and October was at least twenty degrees, if not more.

He pulled the truck into almost the exact same spot and put it in park. "Want to make out?"

"It's a little cold out there, don't you think?"

"Not out there. In here."

She laughed, because there was no way he was serious. "Aren't we a little old for that? And I'm not sure I've ever been flexible enough."

"Oh, we can find a way." He took off his seat belt and shifted in his seat before undoing his fly. Based on the bulge in his jeans, he was probably pretty uncomfortable, and Jen's mouth went dry.

"I bet we can."

"You need to get those jeans off first."

After unlatching her seat belt, she bent over and untied her boots. She had to loosen the laces and then brace the heels against the rubber floor of the truck to get them off. "This totally isn't fair. All you have to do is open the fly on your jeans and pull them down a little bit. I have to take mine off, which means taking my boots off. I need to start wearing skirts."

"I shouldn't have bought a truck with a center console," he said. "I can't get to you, so you're going to have to climb over here. Right onto my lap."

She gave him a *yeah right* look. "So in addition to the center console, you got the truck with the removable steering wheel?"

He frowned. "You get those jeans off and I'll figure out the logistics."

She finally got her boots and jeans off, along with her hoodie and shirt, though she left the bra and panties on because the idea of her bare ass on the seat of a pickup truck didn't appeal to her. She could just pull the lacy fabric out of the way once Sam had a plan.

He turned in his seat and reached for her, but just as he started pulling her toward him, there was a knock on his window. Jen's ass hit the seat with a jarring thump and she looked around Sam's head and saw Kelly glaring at him.

Trying not to laugh, Jen picked up the hoodie and pulled it on over the bra. She could put the shirt on later.

"Back up," Sam barked, and then he opened the door just enough to slide out. Jen wanted to point out that not opening the door all the way didn't make a lot of sense due to them being surrounded by windows, but she wasn't sure he'd appreciate the humor.

As Jen yanked her jeans up over her hips, she watched Sam's back as he seemed to sway back and forth. It took her a few seconds to realize he was doing it as Kelly tried to see around him. She probably wanted to talk to Jen, and he was blocking her view.

"What are you doing?" she heard Kelly demand.

"I'm trying to give her some privacy to get herself together."

Jen had to stifle a chuckle when Kelly threw up her hands. "Seriously? She and I have been best friends since kindergarten. I've seen her in her underwear more times than you have."

"I'm trying to catch up."

She heard Kelly snort. "Unless you plan on sticking around Stewart Mills for a good, long time, you're going to want to stock up on Red Bull and something for the chafing."

"Kelly!" Jen yelled, though dissolving into laughter probably took some of the sting out of the admonishment.

She shoved her feet into her boots without tying them and then, after taking a few seconds to zip up the hoodie, she got out. There was a good chance either she or Sam was going to pull a muscle or end up stuck somehow before either of them had an orgasm, anyway. And it was always nice to run into Kelly.

"You have an apartment," her uniformed best friend was saying to Sam, and then she pointed her finger at Jen as she came around the truck. "And *you* have a house with two bedrooms. Why, for the love of my sanity, are you not in one of them?"

"Seemed like a good day to take a drive," Sam said.

"This is not driving. This is parking." She turned to glare at Jen. "And public indecency."

"I should have let you do it," Kelly said. "And then been here when the rescue squad had to come because there's no way you were going to make that work with a guy this tall and a truck with a center console."

"I guess now we'll never know." Jen smiled and shrugged.

"Sure we will," Sam said. "We just need to try it when Deputy Killjoy here isn't on shift."

"Funny." Kelly shook her head. "Whatever. I'm going to O'Rourke's for a burger. I ended up on a traffic call and didn't get lunch."

"A burger sounds good," Jen said, and Sam nodded. "A

bacon cheeseburger, actually. Coitus interruptus cancels out calories in comfort foods. It's science."

Kelly snorted. "Let's go eat, then."

As Jen walked around the truck, she heard Sam talking to Kelly. "Can you turn the lights and siren on?"

"No, you're not getting a police escort to O'Rourke's."

"If I go first, then it's more like a police *chase* than a police escort."

"Get in your truck before I shoot all your tires out and leave you here while Jen and I go have burgers."

Jen took her hoodie off and put the shirt back on. Since they were going to a restaurant, the last thing she wanted was to get hot and take the sweatshirt off without remembering her shirt was on the floor of Sam's truck.

When he got in and slammed the door, she looked over at him. He was grinning. "I like her. She's funny."

"Hard to tell when she's kidding sometimes," Jen said.

"Well, she was kidding about my tires." When she didn't say anything, he raised his eyebrows. "Right?"

She shrugged, then laughed at his expression as he turned the truck around and followed Kelly's cruiser back into town.

When his mother opened her door on Friday evening and stepped outside, Sam tried to ignore the butterflies dancing in his stomach and smiled at her.

She'd obviously taken a lot of care with her appearance for this dinner, even if they were only going to O'Rourke's. She was wearing jeans, but she'd put a black cardigan on over a blouse, and she had a little makeup on. For a moment, he wondered if he should have offered to take her to a nicer restaurant in another town.

But he was glad he hadn't when she gave him a tentative smile. "Hi, Sam."

"Hi." The strain of being in a car together for more than a few minutes might have been too much. They were doing okay, but they both had to work at it. "You look lovely."

"Thank you."

He held open the door of his truck for her and then drove the short distance to O'Rourke's. She made small talk as he drove, mostly about a television show everybody seemed to be talking about. Sam hadn't seen it, but he'd heard the talk so he encouraged the conversation because it killed the silence.

He heard the whispers in O'Rourke's as he followed Cassandra and his mom to their table. It was to be expected, considering their history, but he admired the way his mom held her head high and didn't appear to let the buzz bother her.

After they were seated, everybody lost interest and went back to what they were doing. Sam asked for ice water and a decaf, and his mom asked for the same thing. Then they read the menu and eventually decided on a flat iron steak for him and the spaghetti for her.

"Tell me how the football is going," she said, and he noticed when she took a sip of her water that her hand was trembling slightly.

The tremor was almost imperceptible visually, but it touched him so deeply he took a sip of his own water to buy himself a moment to compose himself.

She wanted so badly for him to forgive her—to be her son again in a way that meant something. He could see it in her nerves and the way she looked at him. She knew how badly she'd failed him as a mother, and it was the fear of hoping and failing that made her hand shake.

He remembered his talk with Cody about his dad, and how he'd told the boy the situations were different because Roland Leavitt had been an abusive son of a bitch, but Bill Dodge had been sick. The drugs had changed him and cost them Cody's mom.

Sheila Leavitt had been sick, too. For her, it had been alcohol and fear, but the addiction had ruined Sam's childhood and cost her her son. And, like Bill, she knew she could never right the wrong, but maybe they could move forward from the past.

"The team's doing well," he said when he realized the silence had stretched on and she looked as if she feared he wasn't going to answer. As he expected, Neil's offer popped into his head again. Even though he'd been given time to think it over, he was going to need to make a decision soon or he'd drive himself crazy. "They're good kids."

"It's good you could come," she said. "For Coach McDonnell. I owe him everything, you know. Because he saved you . . . when I couldn't."

Sam ran his hand over his mouth, not looking directly at her. He *really* didn't want to do this here. "You had to save yourself first. And now you have and here we are."

"You have no idea how much I wish I could go back and do it all differently."

"You can't." He hadn't meant for the words to sound so harsh, but he couldn't miss the way she flinched. When he reached across the table and covered her hand with his, he could feel the tremor still. "You don't *have* to. We both made it out the other side and we're going forward from here, remember?"

She nodded, managing a smile that seemed more happy and less nervous reflex than her previous ones. "Together."

"Yes." He squeezed her hand before sitting straight in his chair again. It was tempting to tell her he had a chance to settle not far away, but it would be cruel to get her hopes up and then disappoint her. It was best, for now, to pretend nothing had changed. "Before I go back to Texas, I'm going to get you a better phone so we can talk and do videos and stuff, okay?"

She looked nervous again. "I'm doing okay, but I don't know if I can afford that."

"I'm going to add you to my plan."

"A family plan."

He understood why she said the words in such a quiet voice. It was a stupid thing most people probably took for granted, but for them to share the word *family*—even if it was just a cell phone plan—was profound. "Yeah. We'll have a family plan."

She was smiling when the server brought their dinner, which Sam was thankful for. Despite having covered some steep emotional ground, they weren't attracting attention and that's what he wanted. Not that he gave a damn what they said about him, but he just wanted a normal dinner with his mother.

"This is delicious," she said after taking her first bite.

"I don't think O'Rourke's has a subpar dish," he said. It certainly wasn't the steak. "I've been wondering about something. Have you ever thought about leaving Stewart Mills?"

She looked genuinely confused by the question. "Why would I do that? Where would I go?"

"You could go anywhere. Wouldn't it be nice to live

someplace where everybody doesn't know your past business? To have a clean slate with no history?"

"I admit I've thought about it a couple of times over the years. But it's scary, you know? It's not like I have a savings account, so I'd just be going out into the world hoping I can get enough work to keep me from living in my car. That kind of worry and stress isn't good for my sobriety."

"I can understand that."

"And everybody knowing my past isn't always a bad thing, believe it or not. I didn't have to answer questions about myself or explain why I don't have a husband or why I had pictures of a son I hadn't seen in fourteen years. And I can see how far I've come in the way this town treats me—the way they look at me and talk to me—and I draw some strength from it. Does that make sense?"

The first time he'd come back to Stewart Mills, he'd been hyperaware of the fact most of the people he ran into knew he'd grown up in a shitty home and gone bad himself for a while before joining the football team. Now they called him Coach Leavitt and knew he'd made a good life for himself and that he'd stood by the town when they needed him. They didn't know it was a lonely life, but he could understand his mom measuring how far she'd come by how the people of their hometown looked at her.

"It does make sense. And you have to do what's best for you and your sobriety."

"Right now, this is what's best for me. And looking forward. That's the best thing."

They lapsed into a comfortable silence while digging into their dinners, but then Sam wiped his mouth with a napkin and looked at his mother. "We have a game tomorrow at one, if you wanted to see the boys play. If you don't have to work, I mean."

"Really?" Her face lit up. "I have to work until one thirty, but I could see some of it. At least the second half."

"Only if you want to. And I'll be busy, of course. I might not see you."

"That's okay. I want to see you coach."

The light in her eyes dimmed a little, and he knew she was thinking about the fact he'd not only never invited her to watch him play football in high school, but he'd actually told her not to show up for his games. They were moving forward, though. "I think you'll have a good time. And we have some away games after that, so it'll be even colder by the time we play at home again."

"Will Jen Cooper be there?"

He could tell just by the way she asked the question that she had heard he and the guidance counselor were hooking up. "She usually is. There's not much else for Stewart Mills to do on a Saturday afternoon."

"I've always liked her. She's very pretty."

"Yes, she is."

She sighed, looking every bit the disappointed mother. "So the rumor you guys aren't serious about each other is true?"

"Judging by how good Coach McDonnell looks and the fact he had to slow down and wait for me when we went for a walk yesterday, it won't be much longer before I leave." Even if the position of assistant coach didn't start until the following summer, he'd want to move right away if he took the job. It would give him time to learn his way around the community. But he wanted to be influenced by his mother's emotions even less than by Coach's.

"Oh. Of course."

She hid her disappointment by concentrating on swirling spaghetti around her fork and taking a big bite. Sam cut off a piece of his steak, but his appetite had faded for some reason. Coach was going to be back on the sidelines, where he belonged.

And Sam was going to have to figure out where *he* belonged.

15

Jen clapped her hands together. Despite the blue wool mittens with the white and gold trim that Gretchen's grandmother had knit for all three of them, her hands were cold. Once the game started, excitement and cheering would warm them all up but, for right now, there were a bunch of people sitting in the cold, waiting for the game to start.

"It shouldn't be this cold yet," Gretchen said. "And why is football played in the cold, anyway. They should play it in the summer."

"There's no school in the summer," Kelly pointed out. "And if they played at that time of year, they'd probably all drop from heat exhaustion. As would we."

It was rare for the three of them to be out and about alone these days. But Chase had decided, with Kelly's blessing, to stay in New Jersey for the weekend. He was so close to wrapping up everything he needed to do, and they were both willing to sacrifice some together time now to get that much closer to him being able to call New Hampshire home for good.

And Alex had gotten a job taking some promotional shots for a new powersports shop opening about an hour north of them. They wanted professional pictures of their new building as well as some action shots of employees showing off their machines on their private test-drive circuit. He hadn't wanted to miss the game, but the money they offered was too good to pass up.

"You don't mind him working on the weekend?" Jen had asked when Gretchen told her she'd be at the game alone.

"I'm a farmer. We don't do weekends."

Jen had laughed, but she wasn't sure how Gretchen did it. Maybe it was spending every Monday through Friday in brick buildings with children, but Jen protected her weekends at all costs. Besides a few household chores and the occasional shopping run, Saturdays and Sundays were for fun.

Even if fun this time of year meant sitting on frigid aluminum stands, waiting to watch football. They'd put down a wool blanket, as most of the spectators had, but it would take a long time for body heat to warm the aluminum to the point the cold stopped radiating through the fabric.

Finally, the visiting team ran out onto the field. They all clapped politely while the parents and other fans who'd made the trip cheered for them. Then the Eagles were announced and everybody from Stewart Mills was on their feet, screaming.

Jen watched Sam jog alongside his team. Joel and Dan were behind him, and they all veered toward the home bench.

Sam looked focused, but more relaxed than he had at the homecoming game.

She watched him scan the crowd, wondering if the pressure he'd put on himself to fill Coach McDonnell's shoes still weighed on him, or if he'd figured out that he didn't need to do that. He just needed to be Coach Leavitt.

"Wave, Jen," Kelly hissed. "He's looking for you."

"No, he's not," she said automatically, but she stood up and waved in his direction.

When his gaze locked on hers and his face relaxed into a smile, she realized Kelly was right. Sam had been looking for her in the crowd.

The realization warmed her far faster than the wool mittens and blanket did, and her heart did a summersault when he returned her wave. No warm and fuzzy, she reminded herself.

The Eagles kicker put them on the board first with a field goal, and the offense maintained the lead by getting the ball in the end zone twice. The defense played a fierce game as well, holding the other team to two field goals.

Once the clock started ticking down toward halftime, Jen kept an eye on the end of the bleachers. When Sam had called her the night before to tell her how his dinner with Sheila had gone, he mentioned that he'd invited her to the game, but that she'd miss the beginning due to work. He'd sounded really solid on the phone, which Jen thought was amazing. In the five weeks or so that Sam had been back in Stewart Mills, he'd done a lot of work on putting his past behind him and reconnecting with his mother. It looked to be paying off, and she was happy for both of them.

And sometimes, when she let her guard down, she thought

about how much healing Sam had done since he'd been back, and wondered if he'd stay.

That would be a serious problem as far as their fun fling went, she thought. It was one thing to hold her emotions in check when she was doing it for a limited time. But if she just kept on seeing him every day, it was going to get a lot harder to lie to herself. And to him.

When she finally spotted Sheila, looking up at the stands with obvious trepidation on her face, Jen stood and waved to her. Sheila waved back and then Jen gestured to the seat next to her. Nobody wanted to walk into a crowd and sit alone.

"Sam said you might come," she said once his mom had said hello to Gretchen and Kelly and settled next to Jen on the wool blanket. "I'm glad you made it."

"Me, too." She sighed as she looked at her son, who was currently in what looked like an intense conversation with PJ. "He looks so different out there, in that shirt and looking all official."

"He's a great coach," Jen told her. "I don't think Coach McDonnell is an easy man to substitute for, but he's done so well. The kids really love and respect him, and so does everybody, really."

"I think it's wonderful that you two are seeing each other," Sheila said.

Jen was thankful the woman's gaze was locked onto Sam because her expression was probably something like *oh, crap*. She had no idea what to say to that, since she wasn't sure if that information had come from Sam during their dinner or from the Stewart Mills grapevine.

If there was one thing Jen was absolutely sure of, it was that Sam wouldn't be comfortable with her talking to his mother about him or their relationship or practically anything of a personal nature.

"He's a great guy," she finally said. She felt as if she was repeating herself with how great Sam was, but at least it was noncommittal.

When Hunter Cass found a hole in the defensive line and broke free for a thirty-yard touchdown run, everybody jumped to their feet, screaming and stomping. It was a good distraction and hopefully the subject of her and Sam seeing each other was closed.

Who would have guessed a fun fling could be so complicated?

Sam snapped the clean flat sheet so it fell over the bed, crooked and folded over on itself. He swore under his breath and tried again. Making a bed wasn't one of his more finely honed skills, but he wanted clean sheets because Jen was stopping by anytime.

Somehow, after the game, he'd snuck a few minutes away from the team to say hello to his mom. She'd seemed shy in front of the others, but she smiled and told him she was proud of him. And after she left, Jen had been there to tell him it was a great game.

And he'd told her if she wasn't doing anything later, maybe they could get together. Since she was going to be hanging around town, she offered to come to him this time. It was only later, when he was picking up stuff around the apartment, that he realized he could probably have used some time alone to process how he felt about the day before seeing her again.

Spotting Jen and his mother together in the stands, their heads close as they talked about who knew what, had felt like running into a brick wall and being knocked on his ass. He couldn't get past the wall and couldn't seem to get over or around it in his mind.

Casual, fun flings shouldn't sit and be chummy with a guy's mother. He wasn't sure if that was a rule but, if it wasn't, it should be.

Logically, he knew that Jen and his mother knew each other. Hell, Jen knew her better than he did. But it had made him uncomfortable in a way he couldn't define. Maybe it had been the illusion of having his family cheering him on, the way Mrs. McDonnell and Kelly had done for Coach when Sam was playing.

He and his mom were trying to be a family. But he and Jen weren't, and he'd reached a point where he wasn't sure if he was shaken because it looked that way and he didn't want it to, or if it was because it had looked that way and he wished it was true.

If he didn't hit the road soon, he was going to be in trouble.

He was already having a hard time imagining a day without Jen in it. Even when they were too busy to get together privately, they saw each other at school a lot. They texted and sometimes even talked on the phone just because it was easier. And because he liked hearing her voice.

When he went back to Texas, he knew he wouldn't call her. It would only prolong the process of letting go of each other and getting on with their lives. Jen wasn't going to find herself a perfect husband if she was at home on the phone with him.

And, God, that made his stomach ache.

He almost jumped when there was a knock on the door, and he took a deep breath before opening it. Fun. Casual. Friends with benefits, as Coach had said. He just needed to keep it more about the benefits.

"Hey," he said when he'd let her in. "Did you enjoy the game today?"

"Of course." She kissed him hello before peeling off her coat and draping it over the back of a chair with his. He didn't have a coat closet. "They're so good this year. I mean, they were good before, but I think almost losing the program made them realize how much they love it and they're bringing that renewed passion to the field."

"They have a pretty decent coach, too," he joked.

"That they do." She looked around his apartment, but then stopped when she saw the line of little pumpkins on his counter. He'd forgotten about them. "What is happening right now?"

"Some movie that half the team wanted to take their girlfriends to is playing about forty minutes from here and they played a good game, so . . . I'm babysitting pumpkins." He wasn't surprised when she gave him a *really?* look. "I have to write down when I pretend feed them and pretend change them and stuff, so I have alarms set on my phone."

"You can't just write down some random times for each pumpkin?"

"That's cheating."

She laughed at him. "You can't be serious."

He had to admit it was a little ridiculous. "I was bored."

The last thing Sam wanted to admit was that he'd been curious about the health class assignment. If it really simulated having to care for a child, would he be up to the challenge? Even though it was stupid, because he was starting to seriously doubt he'd ever be a father, he threw himself into babysitting the little baby pumpkins to the best of his ability.

Until he lost track of which one was which and screwed up the times. Then he realized that taking care of seven miniature, misshapen pumpkins with faces painted on them was nothing like caring for an actual child.

"I'm not bored now," he said, looping his arm around her waist and pulling her close.

She wrinkled her nose like she wasn't in the mood. "Before you get your hopes up, this isn't a sexy week for me, if you know what I mean."

It took him a few seconds to catch on, and then he smiled through the disappointment. "Okay. Should I be afraid?"

She laughed and shook her head. "I don't get really moody, but you might want to hide any potato chips you have in the house."

"I ate the last ones about an hour ago."

She frowned. "Okay, you should maybe be a *little* afraid."

"Do you want to watch a movie or something? There must be something on TV on a Saturday night."

"Sure."

And that's how Sam found himself curled up on the couch, watching an action movie they'd both seen a dozen times, with the woman he was supposed to be keeping at an emotional distance.

He should have offered to take her out, he thought. Once she'd told him about her period, the best move would have been to get out of his apartment and out of sight of the bed, but instead they were having a movie night. With her body tucked against his and a fleece blanket thrown over them, the last thing they had was distance.

He squirmed a little, which only made it worse because the couch wasn't really big enough for both of them, so her body was pressed pretty closely to his. He really liked her body a lot and not being able to put his hands on her was killing him.

"Do you want me to move?" she asked.

Desperately. "Nope. I'm good."

"I can feel how good you are right now, actually."

"Sorry. Ignore it and it'll go away. Eventually."

She laughed, which made her body shake, which wasn't going to help *anything* go away. Then she threw back the blanket and sat up on the edge of the sofa.

"You really don't have to move," he said, but she gave him a smile that made him even harder, which he hadn't thought was possible at that moment.

Then she pushed the blanket back even more so she could tuck a finger under the waistband of his sweatpants. When he realized where she was going with that, his balls started aching in earnest.

"You don't—" The words choked off when she ran her hand over his erection through the fabric and he forgot what he was going to say.

He lifted his hips when she started working his waistband down, lifting it up and over his dick, which twitched at the brush of her hand. He'd skipped the briefs after his shower since he hadn't intended to have any clothes on for long, so after one easy tug, there was nothing between her hand and his flesh.

Sam closed his eyes, moaning when her fingers stroked the length of his dick. She had long, slender fingers that closed around his throbbing erection, and he had to clench his teeth hard to keep from begging her to take him in her mouth.

She teased him, stroking him lightly before tightening her grip. Her tongue flicked over the head and he shuddered. This was *not* going to take long, he thought, even though he'd do his best to savor every minute. Or second.

He groaned, a harsh and guttural sound, when she finally closed her lips around him. As she stroked down his length, her lips followed. The heat of her mouth was almost his undoing, but he clenched his jaw and dug deep for self-control.

When she shoved at her hair, which kept falling in the way, he put his hand under the blond length of it and splayed his fingers to capture it all. Then he closed his fingers, holding it out of her way, and she smiled.

It was the smile that did him in—the way her lips curved around the head of his dick—and his fingers tightened in her hair. She must have sensed he was about to lose it, because she wrapped her fingers around him and moved her fist in time with her mouth. Taking him deeply, she sucked lightly as her mouth retreated and her hand squeezed as it slid over the flesh her mouth had made slick.

He groaned as he came, trying not to pull her hair, but not able to think about anything but the powerful orgasm. She took him deep into her mouth again, swallowing, before kissing his stomach and smiling up at him.

"Better?" she asked, her mouth curved in a naughty grin.

He wasn't able to form words yet, so he nodded. Then he summoned the strength to lift his hips again as she pulled his sweatpants back up. Pulling her into his arms, he kissed her hair and held her close.

But after a few minutes, when he was sure his knees would hold him up, he nudged her. "Let me get up for a second."

She moved so he could stand, and he went to the cabinets where he kept his food. After rummaging around for a minute, he found a snack-sized bag of potato chips and brought them back to the couch.

"I forgot I'd bought some of these to have on hand." He pulled open the top of the bag and handed it to her.

"Thank you," she said, giving him a bright smile.

Once he was situated on the couch again and she was curled up against him, munching on the chips, he draped the blanket over them and kissed the back of her neck.

"Do you want a chip?" she asked, offering one over her shoulder.

"No, thanks. I'm good."

"So am I," she said, snuggling a little bit closer.

He was better than good, actually. Though he'd never been a man big on believing in hopes and dreams, Sam knew this was what he'd always wanted. This life with this woman was something he wanted for himself and he couldn't run away from it anymore.

"There's something I need to tell you," he said before he could change his mind.

Jen stiffened, a million thoughts seeming to fly through her head, with most of them being panicked certainty he was about to tell her he was leaving Stewart Mills.

But that was ridiculous, she thought. Even though he looked a lot stronger, Coach hadn't been cleared by his doctor to return to work and she knew without a doubt Sam wouldn't leave the team before he was.

But there was a tightness in Sam's voice that let her know it was something serious. She pushed herself upright and turned on the couch cushion slightly so she could see his face. "What's up?"

He frowned. "It's easier for me to talk to the top of your head."

"I know, but I like looking at you when I talk to you. So what's going on?"

"Neil Page offered me a job as his assistant coach."

Of all things he could have said, that was the last thing Jen expected. She knew Neil slightly, since they'd attended the seminar on sports scholarships for student athletes once, but she didn't realize Sam knew him. Or that Neil knew Sam.

But as Sam explained about the phone call, she realized Neil had probably watched Sam coaching during the homecoming game and saw his potential.

"Are you going to take it?" she asked, not meaning to interrupt his story, but unable to stop herself from asking what she thought was the most important question.

"I don't know." He seemed to be searching her face, looking for her reaction, and she had no idea what he'd see there. Mostly she was still numb. "I have plenty of time to think about it. They haven't even announced the retirement yet—and they don't want that getting back to the team, so this is between you and me—but he wanted to talk to me now in case Coach McDonnell came back and I left."

"So you didn't tell him no?" And what would it mean for them if he said yes? He wouldn't be in Texas. He wouldn't even be an hour away. But he'd be *almost* an hour away. So close and yet so far at the same time.

Sam shook his head. "A smart man doesn't turn down any job offer without considering all his options first."

Was she one of his options? "I . . . wow. Bet you didn't see that coming."

"Nope." He tilted his head, his jaw flexing for a second. "What do you think?"

"I don't know. Does it pay enough? I know they have a big football budget, but it's not *that* big."

"I'm a pretty simple guy. And I'll find a job besides the coaching. It's not really meant to be a full-time gig. At least the job market's not quite as tight down there."

He sounded like he was actually considering it, and Jen's heart squeezed in her chest. "I know a lot of people would love to have you living that close."

"It's close enough, I guess."

Close enough for what, though? For weekend visits to catch up with his mom and his friends. But it wasn't close enough for them to continue their relationship. "Have you talked to Coach about it?"

"Not yet."

That was telling, she thought. For Sam to not look for Coach's advice on what was a huge life decision meant Sam was deeply conflicted. And she forced herself not to read too much into the fact he'd told her before telling Coach McDonnell.

"You must have been flattered when he called you," she said.

"I was surprised. And yeah, I guess it's flattering." He shrugged. "I'll take my time thinking about it. But do me a favor and don't tell anybody, okay? I need to get a better handle on how I feel about it before everybody and their maiden aunt gives me an opinion on whether I should take the job or go back to Texas."

"I understand." She smiled and nudged him with her elbow. "I guess *I* should be flattered you told me."

He didn't smile back. His gaze locked onto hers with an intensity that made her shiver. "Spending time with you is one of the best parts of my life, Jen. That's a part of it, too."

Warmth flooded through her and she leaned down to kiss him before snuggling back into her spot. "I like spending time with you, too."

He kissed her neck and gave her a squeeze before resting his hand on her hip. But even though her eyes were on the television screen, Jen found herself unable to focus on the movie. There was more than a fun fling going on and they both knew it. It had been said out loud in Sam's own way and it couldn't be taken back.

But he'd made it sound like he was choosing between returning to Texas and taking a job that would mean living almost an hour from Stewart Mills. And she wasn't sure where she fit in that decision.

16

Jen looked up from her computer screen when her phone buzzed, blinking rapidly. The information she needed about a scholarship one of her juniors might qualify for in the future was on a website with light blue text on a dark blue background, and she wasn't sure her eyes would ever focus correctly again.

She picked up the handset. "Yes?"

"Cody Dodge is here. Do you have a few minutes for him?"

"Sure. Send him back."

She bookmarked the site to finish reading later and stuck a sticky note with the student's name and the highlights of the information onto the messy pile of sticky notes she'd collected over the day. She'd tried many times to train herself to take notes on the computer's built-in notepad, but she hated flipping between websites and the app and always reverted to a pen and whatever paper was at hand to write on. To avoid writing on papers she shouldn't be using for scratching notes on, she kept the sticky notes next to the pens. It wasn't an ideal system, but it was the only way she didn't lose track of what she was doing.

When Cody appeared in the doorway, she smiled and waved at the chair across from hers. "Good morning, Cody."

"Morning, Miss Cooper. Thanks for seeing me."

"Anytime. What's up?"

"I'm going to see my dad next weekend."

Jen sat back in her chair, trying really hard not to let her shock show on her face. That was probably the last thing she'd expected him to say. "How do you feel about that?"

He shrugged one shoulder and leaned forward to grab the Rubik's Cube off her desk. Jen had learned a long time ago that teenagers talked best if they could fidget. The puzzle toy gave their hands something to do and also gave them something to look at. "It was my choice. I've talked to him on the phone a couple of times."

"But it's your choice to go see him? Nobody's pressuring you?"

"Nope. I talked to Coach about it. Coach Leavitt, I mean."

The morning after the homecoming dance, when he'd left her bed to check his text messages. "Was Coach Leavitt helpful?"

"Totally. He knows what it's like to have a parent you kind of hate, you know? He explained to me how it's different because his old man was mean and abusive and my dad got addicted to drugs after he broke his leg. But he helped me work through a lot of it."

Even though Cody and Sam seemed to have talked about his dad, Jen suspected there were more similarities when it came to Sam's mom. She'd hurt him almost as badly as his father had, but now she was trying to make amends and rebuild their relationship. Much like Bill Dodge.

Either way, it couldn't have been an easy conversation for Sam to have and yet he'd managed to say the right things to help a very confused teenager sort through some pretty tangled emotions.

She asked him some leading questions, and it didn't take very long to figure out that what Cody needed was suggestions on how to express potential feelings to his dad without hurting his dad's feelings. Jen concentrated on imagining what things might be said and felt at a reunion of a father and son in their situation and then walked him through a little role-playing.

"Is your grandmother going to be with you?" she asked, once he felt more confident he'd be able to come up with things to say even if the visit was awkward.

"We're still talking about it. It might be nice to have her in there to help make things easier," he explained, and she nodded. "But if it doesn't go very well, I don't want her to have to choose sides. What do you think?"

"I think Mimi's a pretty wise woman. And she has done an amazing job of loving both you and your dad since the accident without anybody having to choose sides. If she's in the room with you, she won't only get a report filtered through you or through your father. That'll make it easier to talk about it after the fact."

"Thanks, Miss Cooper. I have a test next block I can't miss, so I have to go. But it always helps to talk to you. And to Coach."

"I'm always here for you to talk to. And Coach, too."

"I know. Well, he won't always be here. But there will still be a coach to talk to, so it's cool."

"I guess you're right."

Cody put the Rubik's Cube back on her desk and stood up. "Even though I'll be happy when Coach McDonnell comes back, it'll be kind of sad because it means Coach Leavitt will leave town again. He told me he could never live here. Too much baggage or something like that."

Jen felt her smile freeze on her lips, which was probably a good thing. Maybe the impact Cody's carelessly tossed-out remark had on her wouldn't show on her face.

"I'll let you know how it goes, Miss Cooper."

She fixed a smile on her face. "Definitely. And you have my number. If you need to talk to me over the weekend, just send me a text."

He smiled and gave her a wave before walking out of the office.

Once he was gone, Jen leaned back in her chair and closed her eyes. It was stupid for her to be so rattled by something she already knew. Staying in Stewart Mills hadn't been one of the choices he'd mentioned when they'd talked about the job offer from Neil. And she had to guess Sam had told Cody he could never live in Stewart Mills again the day they'd talked about Bill Dodge, which had been a while ago since it was the morning after homecoming.

Things had changed since then. Their relationship had changed. He'd told her outright that wanting to be with her was a part of it. But *it* hadn't included staying in town, and Jen wondered if she was going to be faced with a choice between Sam and Stewart Mills—the town she'd returned to because she loved it. Because watching the kids grow and helping them plan and achieve better futures for themselves fulfilled her.

She loved her home and her job. But she loved Sam, too. If she had to choose, which could she give up?

Before practice, Sam stopped at the gas station to grab some drinks. He'd stocked up on food at the market, but they didn't have his favorite iced tea.

Janie Vestal was working the cash register, and she greeted him with a smile when he walked in. She and Chase had dated for most of high school, so they'd spent a lot of time together back in the day. They'd split amicably before college and she had a family now, which made him happy. He'd always liked her because she didn't look at him differently than she had anybody else, like some of the cheerleaders.

After saying hello to her, Sam went to the cooler in the back, but there was an empty slot where the iced tea was usually found. And they were the only store in town that carried that particular brand.

After grabbing a bag of chips because he'd skipped lunch, he went back to the counter and got in line behind a guy paying for gas. After a few seconds, Edna Beecher approached, and Sam imagined he felt a cold breeze blow across his face. After glaring at him, she got in line behind him, clutching a package of crackers.

When it was his turn, he set the chips on the counter. "Hey Janie, you guys are out of that iced tea I like. Any chance I can get you to order more?"

"Oh, I think I have some out back," she said. "We haven't had a chance to restock yet, but I can grab you some."

Before he could tell her to forget it—he'd rather go without the iced tea than stand next to Edna any longer than he had to—she was gone. He wasn't sure if she left the cash register unguarded because it was a small town and she trusted him, or if she knew Edna would call the FBI if he even thought about touching it.

She just stood there next to him, like a judgmental statue, until he couldn't take it anymore. "I didn't kill my old man, you know."

Her scowl grew more pronounced. "What are you talking about?"

"You hinted around once that my father didn't really run off and leave us. That we'd taken care of him ourselves somehow. But we didn't kill him."

She scoffed, waving a bony hand in the air. "That was probably just wishful thinking. He was a horrible man."

"You won't get any argument from me."

"I called the FBI on him, but they said it was a matter for the local police. Never did think much of them."

"You called the FBI on my father?" He wasn't sure why that surprised him since she'd probably called the FBI on everybody in town at some point.

"I did. More than once, too. Told them what was going on in your house and told them they needed to come get him or at least get you out of there, but I guess they didn't believe me."

Feeling as though he'd been kicked in the gut, Sam tried to process the conversation, but he wasn't sure he could. Of all the people, it was the Wicked Witch of Stewart Mills who had tried to protect him. "Sometimes the police would come, but my mom lied. She got me to lie, too. She told me we'd starve and be homeless if they put him in jail. We protected him and the domestic violence laws were a lot different then, so there wasn't much the police could do if she didn't press charges."

"I've been watching for him, though, all these years. If he steps one foot in this town ever again, I'll be calling the FBI again and this time I'll make them listen."

Gratitude welled up in his throat, threatening to choke off his words. "Thank you, Miss Beecher. I appreciate that."

"Just looking out for you, and I guess for your mother, too, even if I'm not sure she deserves it. Drinking or not drinking, you're her child. But I look out for everybody in Stewart Mills."

"You sure do." If by looking out for, she meant trying to get 80 percent of the population locked up by the FBI over the last who knew how many decades. But he guessed her heart was in the right place. They'd always thought she was mean-spirited, but it seemed like she was just really enthusiastic.

Janie returned, carrying six cans of the iced tea. "We might be able to order extra for you, you know. Like by the case, so you don't have to deal with the cans."

"I don't want you guys to go to any trouble."

"It wouldn't be any trouble at all."

"I, uh . . . I don't know how much longer I'll be in Stewart Mills." He was going to have to make a decision soon. Being in limbo made everything harder.

"Oh." She sighed and then picked up the scanner to ring up his purchases. "I know you came here just temporarily while Coach was laid up, but you're like part of the community again. It'll seem weird not having you around anymore."

Sam's chest tightened, but he managed a smile and a nod. *You're like part of the community again.*

He could be. The job market wasn't great, but he'd spent

most of his life doing odd jobs before settling into oil-field electrical work. He'd get by. And he'd be able to keep seeing Jen and find out where their relationship was heading.

But he loved coaching the Eagles. Neil Page asking him to be his assistant coach had really driven home how satisfying he found it, and it was one hell of an opportunity.

After he'd gotten his change, he said good-bye to Janie and Edna and after pulling open a bag of chips, he drove to the high school. When he pulled into the parking lot, he dumped the last of the potato chip crumbs into his mouth and then crumpled the bag. He had an open can of iced tea to bring in with him, but he'd leave the other five in the truck, since it wasn't cold enough for them to freeze and explode yet.

He laughed at himself, amused by the fact years in Texas hadn't made him forget how to live in New England. Maybe he'd always known he'd end up back here because nowhere he'd passed through had ever felt like home to him. New Hampshire hadn't always felt that way to him, but it was starting to now. All he had to do was accept Neil's offer and it would be official.

Sam paused in the lobby of the gym, in front of the trophy case. He had a chance to be a part of building a football program that would bring home trophies. Not as a fill-in for Coach McDonnell, but as a real assistant coach with a whistle he'd earned on his own.

He was going to take the job, he admitted to himself. And he and Jen would figure it out . . . somehow.

"Coach!"

Sam took a deep breath, trying to shake off his thoughts of Jen, and turned to watch Cody emerge from one of the connecting hallways. "Hey, Cody. You're early for practice."

"I was on my way to the bathroom and I saw your truck pull in and I wanted to talk to you for a minute."

"Which means you're not where you're supposed to be."

"Dude." Cody showed him a hall pass that clearly said he was supposed to be in the bathroom. "Anyway, I just talked to Miss Cooper and told her I'm going to see my dad."

"You're going to go see him, huh?"

"Yeah. I'm nervous and excited at the same time, I guess. But Miss Cooper wants me to go back and talk to her after I see him so she can make sure I'm okay."

Sam smiled. "She cares about you kids a lot."

"Yeah. She's wicked cool."

"I agree. And I want to hear how your visit goes, too."

He nodded. "Oh and just a heads-up, but Miss Cooper might be mad because I kind of told her about how you said you'd never live in Stewart Mills again."

Sam felt himself go still. "And she was mad?"

"Well, not really mad. But you can kind of tell when you say something that a girl—uh, woman—doesn't like, you know?"

"Yeah, I definitely know."

"I need to get back to class before the bell rings. See you at practice, dude."

Sam nodded before going through the gym to his office and shutting the door. Normally he didn't because closing the tiny office up just made it feel more claustrophobic, but he needed a minute.

One of the kids saying that Sam couldn't live in Stewart Mills shouldn't have affected Jen. She had known that from the beginning, but she also had to know things had changed between them. Maybe he hadn't been clear enough when he told her spending time with her was the best part of his life, but he didn't think that was the case.

Taking a deep breath, Sam made up his mind. When the time was right and they were alone, he was going to tell Jen he was taking the assistant coaching job. And then he was going to tell her he wanted her to go with him.

A fter school, Jen let herself into Coach's house after a cursory knock on the door, just as she'd been doing for most of her life. The knock was mostly a formality, because she didn't need to do it. This house was practically her second home growing up. This house and the Walker farm.

She already knew, from Kelly's text message, that Coach and Mrs. McDonnell weren't home, so she started up the stairs to Kelly's old room. She'd brought a bunch of boxes down from the attic at her mom's request because she wanted to start getting rid of some of the things they'd collected over decades in the house. Since nobody would be using that bedroom in the foreseeable future, it was the designated sorting station.

"Hey," Kelly said when she saw Jen in the doorway. "You are not going to believe some of the stuff my mother's been keeping since . . . hell, before I was born."

"Before you ask, I don't want any of it. Especially if it involves yarn in any way."

She laughed and gestured at the far corner of the room, where a pile of yarn shaped into things sat. "There's a macramé phase and a crocheting phase. And an 'I don't even know what that's called' phase."

"You need a Dumpster."

"You know my mom. She wants to have a yard sale."

Jen rolled her eyes. "Everybody who would want that stuff already has boxes of it in their own attics."

"Trust me, I know. Maybe what I need to do is have a Dumpster delivered to the Walker farm. Then I can tell Mom I'm donating it all because who has time for a yard sale?"

"There's no way she won't hear about that."

Kelly frowned. "There has to be someplace I can hide a Dumpster where my mother won't hear about it five minutes later."

"Vermont."

"Funny." Kelly sighed and sat on the edge of the bed. "This isn't what I wanted to be doing on my time off, but at least it's something to do while Chase is gone."

"I hate to say it, but if your actual plan is to sort this for a yard sale and not just throw it all away, you called the wrong person for help."

"Mostly I was just looking for company. I was talking to myself. So tell me, how are things with you and Sam?"

"Something's changed." Jen set a pile of what looked like twenty oven mitts on the floor so she could sit on the bed, too.

"Something like what?"

Jen shrugged, her mouth twisting in a wry smile. "I don't know. If I knew exactly what had changed, I probably wouldn't have said *something*."

"Funny, smart-ass. But if something changed enough for you to notice, what were the changes you noticed? And you're going to give me a headache playing word games. Just answer the question."

"He said spending time with me was the best part of his life."

Kelly's mouth dropped open. "He said that? Sam Leavitt actually said that?"

Jen laughed. "Yes, he did. It was very sweet."

"And?"

"And I said I liked spending time with him, too."

"That sounds . . . awkward, to be honest."

It sounded that way to her now, though it hadn't at the time. "It wasn't, trust me. Like I said, it was really sweet."

"You're in love with him, aren't you?"

Jen pressed her lips together, as if not admitting it out loud meant it wasn't true. "Okay, fine. Yes. I don't know how it happened, but yes."

"It happened because you like each other and you have a good time and you talk and you have great sex. That's kind of what happens when spending time with each other is the best part of your life."

"Why didn't I learn from your mistake?"

Kelly scowled. "I wouldn't exactly call it a mistake. But the fact I was having temporary fun with Chase while he was back in Stewart Mills and now we're getting married should have been your first clue that's a plan that can go sideways on you."

"I didn't think it would with us. Who would ever believe I'd be attracted to Sam Leavitt, never mind fall in love with him?"

"Just anybody who sees you together."

Jen wanted to argue the point, but she was pretty sure she'd lose. Hell, Kelsey Jordan had guessed they were a couple before they'd even become a couple.

"Okay, so what's the problem?" Kelly asked. "If you're in love with him and, from the sounds of things, the feeling's mutual, you should look happier."

"It's complicated." She couldn't tell Kelly about the coaching job offer. Even though she was one of Jen's best friends and the keeping-secrets rule shouldn't apply, she was also Coach McDonnell's daughter and that made loyalties and promises a lot more murky.

"Do you think he's still going to leave?" Kelly asked.

"Maybe," she was able to answer honestly. It just wasn't Texas he was considering leaving to.

"Maybe you should tell him you want him to stay."

"I don't know. I don't want him to feel pressured to stay here if he really wants to leave." She sighed. "He's dealt with a lot emotionally while he's been here, so I'd just like for him to come around to it on his own."

"Maybe he needs to know he has something—or somebody—worth staying for."

If Jen mustered up the courage to tell Sam that her feelings went beyond enjoying spending time with him and told him she was in love with him, would that influence his decision? He'd said outright he couldn't handle having the opinions of others pushing and pulling in his mind.

But it wasn't just an opinion. She loved him. "I don't know, Kelly. I don't want to push at him, and unless he starts throwing what he owns in the back of his truck, there's no reason to rush."

"So," Kelly said, "now might not be the best time to tell you this, but it really *is* good news."

Jen knew immediately what she was talking about. "Coach can go back to work."

Kelly grinned. "Yeah. His doctor cleared him. Obviously he's not supposed to get too worked up, but he tires a little more easily now. Hopefully that'll keep him in check."

"Maybe now that Dan's wife had her baby and everything's going well, he can do a better job of helping him out, too."

"I hope so. I don't ever want to go through this again."

"Did he tell Sam?"

"Yeah. He and Mom stopped by the school right before practice to tell him and I guess they'll probably tell the team. Dad's ready to jump right in, of course." Kelly sighed. "It's a little scary for me and Mom, but it's good to see Dad so happy again. I think without football, he'd just sit in his chair and fade away, so he might as well be on the sidelines."

"I bet your mom will have spies everywhere."

Kelly laughed. "You know it. But I can't say that I blame her. Doing CPR on him and . . ."

The words died away as Kelly's voice cracked, and Jen squeezed her hand. "He's fine now. Everything turned out okay and, like you said, the football makes him happy. There's not much sense in taking it away from him."

"Even though I worry about it, I can't wait to see him out on the field again."

Jen reached across the bed and hugged her best friend. "I'm so happy for you guys. I really am."

It wasn't a lie. She loved Coach and Mrs. McDonnell like family, and she was genuinely relieved and ecstatic that he'd not only survived his heart attack, but was recovered enough to return to his beloved football program.

And Sam was going to have to move on with his life.

17

Sam faced the team, his heart pounding in his chest. They were having a team meeting in the gymnasium, due to the cold, and Coach was at his side. They'd be taking them out to the practice field together today.

It should have been a happy moment, but he hadn't anticipated it being so hard to hand this bunch of teenage boys he'd barely known only five weeks ago back to Coach McDonnell.

He wouldn't be leaving right away, of course. And there would be a new group of boys to get to know. But he was definitely going to keep in touch with these guys. Especially Cody. And Shawn. Hell, all of them.

"I'm proud of you guys. You all really pulled together when Coach was out and that's what being a team is about." He held up the whistle and smiled. "But now I'm giving Coach his whistle back."

The boys cheered, their joy echoing off the gym walls.

Shawn Riley raised his hand. "Does this mean you're leaving?"

"Yup. I was subbing for Coach."

"So you won't be here for the rest of the season?"

He knew what the quarterback was really asking. If they bucked the odds and made it to the championship game, would he be there to see it?

With the entire team watching, waiting for his answer, Sam admitted to himself that even if he hadn't accepted the job offer, he would have stuck around for the rest of the season. There was no way he could have told them no. And now it was time to break the news, since he didn't see a way to dance around it.

"I actually will be around," he said, not surprised when Coach's head whipped around. "That team we beat for homecoming? I, uh . . . might be on the other side of the field next year. I'm swearing you all to secrecy because they haven't announced it yet, but their coach is retiring and the assistant coach is moving up. He asked me to take his place. But I'll be around for the rest of your season."

There was a long silence before PJ finally broke it. "It'll be good for you to experience losing championships for a change."

They all laughed and there was a little more trash-talking before Sam reiterated he was trusting them to keep quiet and sent them out to do warm-up laps.

Left alone with Coach, Sam sighed and shoved his hands in his pockets. "What do you think?"

The older man gave him a long look before nodding his head. "You'll do a good job with that program. You're a natural, son, and I'm proud of you."

Suddenly choked up, Sam nodded and turned to watch the

boys. It had been a long, lonely road, but worth the journey. He'd made the man next to him proud, and he was getting used to the feeling of having a place he belonged. His life was changing for the better, and he had almost everything he needed.

When practice was over, Sam spent the short drive back to his apartment in a low-level inner turmoil he couldn't seem to settle. He'd done it. He'd said out loud he was going to accept Neil's offer and it had felt right at that moment. Now, though, he felt jumpy and out of sorts.

As soon as he walked up the stairs to his apartment, he knew what it was. Jen was sitting on the top step, her hands pulled up into the sleeves of her winter coat. As soon as his gaze landed on her, his heart seemed to skip a beat. Here was his turmoil, life-sized and blond-haired.

"What are you doing sitting here?" he asked. "It's cold."

She shrugged. "I've only been here a minute. I texted you to see if you were around and I was going to wait a few minutes before heading home."

"I forgot to plug my phone in and it died about two hours ago." When she stood and let him pass, he unlocked the door. "Get in here and warm up."

Once they were inside, he plugged in his phone and took her coat to drape over the back of a chair. She looked tired, he thought. Almost as tired as he felt.

"I heard the good news," she said, sitting on the couch and pulling her knees up to wrap her arms around them.

It wasn't because she was cold. He knew just enough about body language to know she was trying to shield herself from him, or from whatever hurt he was about to inflict on her. But he was working his way around to the right words in his mind and he had no intention of hurting her.

"I figured you would."

"Kelly told me. I'm surprised you didn't."

"Coach and Mrs. McDonnell showing up was a total surprise. We talked and then the boys started showing up. By the time I had a chance, I knew it had probably spread through the grapevine and I was going to call you when I got home and could plug my phone in."

"Are you okay? I mean, I know you're happy that Coach is back in fighting condition, but I also know you've gotten attached to the team and you enjoyed coaching them."

"I really have. But I won't be too far away to keep in touch and I'll have a new crop of kids to coach."

"So you're taking the job, then?"

He watched her face as he nodded. She was expressive enough so he knew the lack of reaction there took a supreme act of will on her part. And it was now or never, he thought.

"I want you to go with me," he said.

Her eyes widened and her lips parted as she took in what he said. And then his stomach knotted when her mouth tightened and it wasn't happiness he saw in her eyes.

"You want me to move with you?"

He nodded and went all in. "When I said spending time with you was the best part of my life, what I really meant was that I've fallen in love with you. I didn't plan to. I guess I wasn't really supposed to. But I love you and I want you to come with me."

Jen wasn't sure what was happening or why it was happening so fast. She only knew that everything was tumbling down around her and it was going to hurt.

"I didn't plan on falling in love with you, either, but I did," she said. She watched the lines of his face soften and almost couldn't say what needed to be said. "But you're asking me to leave Stewart Mills."

His jaw tightened again. "It's a town."

"It's *my* town. I left once. And even though my family moved away, I chose to come back here for a reason. I love Stewart Mills and the kids need me."

"I need you."

Jen dug her fingernails into her palms, doing everything she could to keep from falling into a heap of tears. "Why can't you stay here?"

She expected him to pull himself back emotionally. The walls would go back up and he'd close her out. But he walked to her and pulled her into his arms. For a few minutes they just stood in silence, holding each other with his cheek pressed to the top of her head.

"I need to take this job, Jen. I love coaching and I'm good at it. They want me."

I want you. The words never left her lips, though. Sam had come to grips with his past while in Stewart Mills, and this was the brass ring for him. He wasn't that Leavitt kid anymore. He was being invited to be a part of a community that would trust him with their kids. That would support him and maybe in time come to love and respect him like Stewart Mills did Coach McDonnell. She understood why he couldn't say no, even if she wished she didn't.

"Maybe I can commute," he said.

She laughed, a short and humorless sound. "It's obviously been a long time since you've experienced winter up here."

"It's forty-five minutes."

"In good weather. In shitty weather, it can take up to two hours. And by the time practice is over and the temperatures have dropped . . . it wouldn't work, Sam. No matter how much we want it to, that's not the answer."

"So what is the answer?" he asked, but the sorrow in his eyes told her he already knew there wasn't one.

"You need to take the job and I can't leave mine."

The muscles in his jaw flexed and he gave a curt nod. "So I guess we're back where we started, then."

They could never be back there, she thought. She could never go back to a time or place where she hadn't loved Sam Leavitt and lost him before they even had a chance.

"I guess so," she said, unable to do more than whisper.

He released her, stepping back to rest his forehead against hers for a moment. "The last thing I ever wanted to do was hurt you, Jen. I know what this place means to you, so I won't keep asking, but I'm sorry I'm hurting you."

"I know. I wish I could . . ." She let the words die away. Other than rehashing the same points over and over, there was nothing left to say. "We'll be seeing each other around, but it'll be okay. I'm happy for you, though. I really am. And I'm proud of you."

The pain on his face was almost her undoing. "I have to, Jen."

"I know." She kissed his mouth for the last time and pulled away. "And I have to go."

He let her leave without another word, and she managed to make the drive home without shedding a tear. Shock, maybe. But she knew it wouldn't last long. The pain was like an iron corset squeezing her heart, and the tears were going to come.

Once she was safely parked and in her house, Jen took her phone and her favorite fleece blanket into her bedroom and curled up on the bed. Then she pulled up the group chat with Gretchen and Kelly, her thumb freezing over the keyboard.

She stared at the screen for a long time, not sure what she wanted to say. There was so much, but the words didn't come. And she was afraid if they started, she'd be typing into her phone for hours.

Finally, she pulled a Gretchen and communicated her feelings with an emoji. The red heart broken in half said everything, really.

Kelly responded almost immediately. I'm not far away. 5 mins.

The text from Gretchen came about a minute later. Shit. Finishing some chores. Will be there as soon as I can. It was followed by a string of emojis that made her sad.

It was less than five minutes before she heard a car door slam and then her door open and close. "Jen?"

Rather than have a pity party on her bed, Jen got up and dragged herself and her blanket to the couch, getting there at the same time Kelly did. Her friend held out a candy bar, which Jen accepted with a tearful smile.

"That's the emergency chocolate from my cruiser, so it's all I have. Are you okay?"

"Not really."

"Did you tell him?"

"That I love him?" She nodded. "Yeah. He loves me, too."

"Okay, I'm confused. Did you hit the wrong emoji by mistake? Because I know you love him, which means him loving you should be a good thing."

"He's leaving Stewart Mills."

"I . . . What? He told you he loves you, but he's still taking the job?"

"He asked me to go with him and I said no."

"Shit." Kelly plopped onto the couch next to her.

"Yeah." Jen unwrapped the candy bar and broke it in half. She gave Kelly one of the pieces. "Have some chocolate with me."

"At least I can't drink, since I'm on duty," Kelly said. "Getting Gretchen through Alex leaving wasn't one of my finer moments."

Jen was surprised by the laughter that burst out of her mouth. Fifteen minutes ago she would have sworn she'd never laugh again. But they'd all gotten good and drunk when Alex left Gretchen and they didn't think he was coming back. Especially Kelly. "I don't think any of us had any particularly fine moments that night."

"But Sam asked you to go with him?"

Nodding, Jen took a bite of the candy bar and chewed it before answering. "You know I came back here because this is the life I wanted. The kids and their families . . . they're almost like *my* family. I can't leave them."

"Okay, so what are you going to do now?"

Jen wiped a bit of chocolate from the corner of her mouth. "I'm going to do what I was doing before your dad dragged Sam Leavitt into my life again. I'm going to work and keep the kids on track and do a shitload of paperwork and maybe, at some point, I'll meet a guy I want as much as I want Sam."

"Hey, what happened to that guy you were meeting for a second date when I called you from the hospital?"

Jen rolled her eyes. "I called him the next day and he was really pissy because it was rude of mc to cancel on such late notice. And a friend shouldn't be more important than a romantic interest, according to him."

"He was mad you were coming to me when my dad had a heart attack?"

"Yeah, that was the end of any romantic interest. It wasn't going to work out, anyway. I was just trying to get Sam and that night at the dam out of my head."

"Someday you'll meet a guy who'll make you forget Sam ever came back to Stewart Mills."

Jen nodded, grateful she had one last piece of chocolate to shove in her mouth so she wouldn't confess that she knew that guy didn't exist.

"He loves you," Kelly said softly. "Right now things went sideways, but you might still work it out."

"He's choosing a job over me. I should be worth more."

"You *are* worth more. He's a moron." Kelly sighed and leaned back against the couch. "And I don't want to say this because I'm your best friend and I'm totally, one hundred percent on your side and the last thing I would ever want is for you to be an hour away, but you're not choosing him over *your* job, either."

Jen scowled and threw the empty wrapper at her. "It's not just my job. It's my entire life. My home. You guys are all like family to me. And the kids . . . He's choosing strangers."

"You're right. He's an asshole."

Best friends were wonderful things, Jen thought. But then Kelly's cell phone chimed and she read the text with a scowl.

"I hate to do this, but I have a call. You'll be okay until Gretchen gets here?" Jen nodded. "You should text her and tell her I only had chocolate, so she should bring something salty and crunchy. Or alcoholic."

Jen stood, letting the blanket fall away so she could get a hug. "I'll be fine, I promise."

And she was, until the sound of the cruiser's engine faded away. Then she clutched the blanket to her face, sobbing into it, but the release did nothing to ease the ache in her heart.

Jen managed to pull herself together a little before Gretchen showed up, carrying a grocery bag stuffed with every comfort food the market carried, including her favorite vanilla bean gelato. She also brought Cocoa, who gave her a high five and then licked Jen's face as if she could bathe the sadness away.

They curled up on the couch with the remote control, throw blankets, junk food and a big chocolate Lab cutting off the circulation to her legs. Jen didn't mind Cocoa, though. She rubbed the dog's head and got adoring looks in return.

If she didn't have a tendency to work long hours at the school, she would get a dog, she thought. Such simple relationships. Offer love and get pure, unconditional love in return. And it was too late, anyway. She'd already had her heart broken by conditional love.

Kelly had been wrong about one thing. She was never going to forget Sam.

18

Sam pulled his truck into the sprawling parking lot behind one of the wings of the massive regional high school that was going to become the center of his life.

In the week since Jen left his apartment, he hadn't seen her. He knew she'd been at work, but out of respect for her, he hadn't gone looking. And she'd managed to never be in the same hallway at the same time. He felt her absence like a gaping black hole in his life, so he'd decided the best thing to do was start focusing on his new life.

Now he had a meeting with Neil Page and a few potential rental places starred on the real estate app on his phone. There was no reason he couldn't make the drive for the Eagles games as he'd promised the team, while putting some space between him and Jen so they could heal. Or at least not hurt so badly they had to avoid each other.

He walked around the school to the front door and got buzzed in. It was a few minutes before Neil showed up, grinning and with his hand extended. "Coach Leavitt. Good to see you!"

The surge of pride hearing himself called Coach without the title being borrowed from Coach McDonnell fueled him as he got a tour of the school. He'd known it was a big, well-funded institution, but Sam was still surprised when Neil brought them into a waiting area that had three doors leading off of it.

"The sports department," Neil said, before opening the door that had a vinyl football decal clinging to the smoked pane of safety glass. "I'll introduce you to Coach Gaffney."

The man sitting behind the largest desk in the very spacious office looked up when the door opened. The man was even older than Coach, and was wearing a maroon polo shirt and a whistle. "Coach Leavitt, it's good to meet you."

Sam shook his hand, feeling the slight tremor in the other man's otherwise firm grip. "Thanks for the invite."

"You've done a hell of a job with McDonnell's Eagles. They had a rough year and I'm impressed with what you did this season. I was thrilled to hear you're willing to consider our offer."

"It's an honor being asked," he said, and then bit the words off. He hadn't formally accepted the position yet. When he'd reached out to Neil, he'd stopped short of it and instead suggested he get a tour of the school and the community.

And he'd told himself it was because he didn't want to look too eager to accept. There wouldn't be much to negotiate in his contract, if anything, but he didn't want to show all his cards too soon.

But he knew he hadn't said the words because he couldn't bear the finality. As soon as he said them, he'd have to stand by his word and he'd be leaving Jen behind. It was stupid, he knew, since he was going to be looking at places to live while he was here, but he'd been afraid he'd choke on the words.

They talked a little about the football program. Sam knew their record, of course. He'd filled the endless hours without Jen by reading every relevant newspaper clipping and high school football report he could find online. But they talked philosophy and methodology for a while and Sam was pleased they all seemed to have the same priorities when it came to the boys being more important than the wins. Most of the other members of the coaching staff also taught classes, so he didn't get to meet them, but Sam didn't mind. Coach Gaffney and Neil seemed to be on the same page, so he assumed the others were, too.

When they'd talked as long as they could without it being awkward when Sam didn't accept the position, he shook both their hands. "Thanks for the talk. I think I'll go explore the town awhile, and I'll reach out if I have any questions."

"Thanks for making the drive down," Neil said. "We're really looking forward to hearing your decision."

The opening was there, but he still couldn't do it. "I'll let you know by next week."

"Excellent. We hope you'll come on board."

Sam drove around the downtown area until he found a place to park. Then he walked for what felt like hours, checking out the businesses and watching people. It was lonely, walking alone, and thinking about how much he wished Jen were with him, holding his hand and checking out their future, made his heart ache.

It was a significantly larger town than Stewart Mills, but the people seemed friendly enough. He'd probably get to know some of them in time. Find a favorite diner and a favorite market.

Maybe someday it would even feel like home.

A strange skittering sound made Jen look up from her computer just in time to see Cocoa slide through the open door. They'd just waxed the floors, and a chocolate Lab at a full run wasn't graceful when it came to braking to begin with. After barely managing to avoid sliding into the desk leg, Cocoa recovered and walked around to get a high five.

"Hey, Cocoa Bean. What brings you here today?" She ruffled the dog's fur, looking into her big brown eyes and again wishing she had a dog of her own. Maybe her life wouldn't feel so horribly empty now if she had a friend to cuddle with while she watched stupid comedies that didn't make her laugh anymore.

It was another two minutes before Gretchen showed up. "I should have known I'd find her in here."

"Please tell me we're not doing another round of ugly pumpkin babies."

Gretchen snorted. "No. Alex was just running in to talk to the yearbook advisor about some photos real quick but you know how that goes. After fifteen minutes, I decided to come in and use the bathroom, but Cocoa would rather socialize."

"I'm always happy to see her. I wonder if I got one of those little dogs that fit in a purse if I could sneak it into work with me."

"No. I don't care if a dog's the size of a teacup or a small horse. They need fresh air and grass, not cement walls and desk chairs."

"Spoken like a true farm girl." She was right, of course, but Jen still gave a wistful sigh as Cocoa went to explore the garbage can. She wouldn't rummage in it, but there was a banana peel in there that probably smelled intriguing.

"How are you doing?" Gretchen asked.

"I guess you heard he went down and had a meeting. And looked at places to live," Jen said quietly. That had come from Chase by way of Kelly, so she was pretty sure Gretchen knew, too.

"Yeah, I heard."

"I haven't seen him since that night. It's stupid because the longer we go without seeing each other, the more awkward it's going to be when we do."

Gretchen's cell phone chimed and she frowned at the screen. "Of course, now that we abandoned ship, he's done and wondering where we are."

"I'll walk out with you. It'll do me good to get a few minutes of fresh air, even if the air's ridiculously cold."

Gretchen just laughed at her. She spent most of her life outdoors and didn't mind the cold nearly as much as her friends did. "You do realize it's not even winter yet."

"How many years have we had this exact same conversation?"

"Every year."

Cocoa was between them, her puppylike exuberance holding all of Jen's attention, which was why she didn't realize until they were halfway across the parking lot that Alex was leaning against the hood of his Jeep, and he was talking to Sam.

Her breath caught in her chest, and she stopped in her tracks. She'd missed him with every fiber of her being, and she drank in the sight of him now. He looked tired, she thought. Whatever he was discussing with Alex looked serious, and she realized how much she missed his laughter. The sound of his voice. His touch. She missed everything about him and she knew when he turned his head and saw her that it was going to hurt like hell.

But she'd gone too far to turn around and run. If she'd been paying attention, she could have said good-bye to Gretchen at the door and nobody would have been the wiser. Now she was committed.

Cocoa barked once, obviously asking Jen why she'd stopped walking for no reason, and both guys looked their way.

She saw the widening of Sam's eyes when he spotted her, and he even started to smile before a flash of sorrow and maybe even regret wiped it away. Jen knew exactly what he'd felt. That initial *Oh, I missed you so much and I'm so happy to see you* followed by the inevitable *but you're not mine anymore*.

Trying to brace herself the best she could, Jen started walking again—much to Cocoa's relief—and plastered what felt like the worst fake smile ever on her face. "Hi, guys."

"Hey, Jen," Alex said. "I guess Cocoa found you, huh?"

"She does have a way of charming her way around the rules," Jen said, holding her hand out for Cocoa to slap with her paw. "I think the principal would put in a doggy door just for her if we had the budget to hire a carpenter."

It was painful to be so close to Sam and not touch him. They weren't even talking, though the awkwardness was masked by Alex and Gretchen telling a story about Cocoa trying to stop Alex from driving away from the bank drive-up window by plopping her butt on the steering wheel because they didn't put a dog biscuit in the drawer with his deposit slip.

"I should go," Sam said when there was a lull in the conversation, and just three little words were enough of his voice to cut through Jen.

"Yeah, us, too," Gretchen said. "I want to get a head start on the chores because Gram's having some friends over, so Alex and I are having a date night."

The way Alex looked at Gretchen made Jen turn away. "Have fun, you two. I'll see you later."

Unfortunately the timing meant walking back into the school with Sam at her side. They didn't make it ten feet from Alex's Jeep before the silence grew so oppressive she had to break it. "How's everything going?"

"Except for missing you so much I can hardly breathe, everything's fine, I guess."

It was so blunt, Jen actually winced. There was no dancing around it or pretending they were doing just fine and dandy. "I miss you, too. But . . . how's your mother?"

He snorted, but must have decided to let the change of subject stand. "She's doing really well. Better than I'd hoped, actually."

"So she's taking you leaving okay?"

"She's glad it's not Texas." He shrugged. "We're going to have dinner once a month, which will be nice."

Which meant at least once a month Sam would be in Stewart Mills. Jen wondered how long she'd have to work at avoiding him before she could casually run into him without feeling as though her heart was breaking all over again.

"It means a lot to the team that you'll be around for games for the rest of the season," she said, desperate for anything to talk about. They were almost to the door and then they could go back to their respective offices and hide some more.

"It means a lot to me, too. And I talked to Cody yesterday. He's doing really well."

She nodded. "I guess it was a really emotional meeting but Mimi told me they all came through it feeling stronger. They're going to try to visit the prison a couple more times before the weather starts turning."

"I'll be keeping in touch with him. With all of them. They're great kids."

"They are."

They paused at the door, waiting for it to buzz. "Jen, there's no reason we can't have dinner or something. I'm not leaving town yet and . . ."

"I can't." Her throat felt tight suddenly and if they'd just release the damn door, she could maybe get to her office before she cried again. She was so sick of tears. "What's the point? It already hurts. I can't get in even deeper and then go through it again."

"You're right. I just miss you."

They heard the click and she yanked open the door. "I miss you, too, Sam. I have to go."

She didn't run, but walked quickly enough that her office door swung shut before the first tear ran down her cheek. For a brief second, she'd considered dinner with him, but he hadn't even gotten the words out before she balked. If they went to dinner, they'd end up in bed again. They'd watch television and read and talk and it would be so much worse this time. This time they'd know they were in love and when it came time for him to move, she wouldn't be able to get through it.

A clean break, she thought. Or as clean as it could be in a town as small as Stewart Mills. It was the only way she could let him go.

"Honey, if you eat any more of that macaroni salad, you're going to have a tummy ache."

Jen knew Gretchen's grandmother was right, but she couldn't help it. "You know nobody else in the world can make macaroni salad like yours, Gram."

She beamed. "That's because I'm the only one who has the recipe. But don't you worry. It's written down in my will so when I'm gone, Gretchen will be able to make it. Or maybe Alex, to be honest. He's a little better in the kitchen than my girl."

"Thanks, Gram," Gretchen said, though Jen noticed she didn't bother denying it.

"Cocoa and I are going to go putter outside for a little bit. I want to organize my garden shed before it gets any colder."

"Thanks again for the macaroni salad," Jen said.

Gram kissed the top of her head as she went by. "When one of my girls calls me up and asks me to make it special, I know to make a big batch, too. There's a dish in the fridge to take home with you."

Jen felt her eyes well up. She couldn't remember ever being gifted with macaroni salad leftovers before. She must have sounded even more pathetic than she thought. After tossing and turning and crying and then tossing and turning some more all night long, she'd curled up on the couch and tried to lose herself in mindless television shows. It hadn't helped, so she'd reached out to her mom.

But her parents had been getting ready to go to an anniversary party for their best friends, and Jen hadn't been able to bring herself to ruin it. Her mother would have stayed on the phone with her for as long as she cried or, worse yet, gotten in her car and driven back to Stewart Mills. So she'd lied and said she had a really bad cold to explain her hoarse voice and obvious congestion and told her to have fun.

Going to Mrs. McDonnell would have been too messy, considering the connection to Sam, so she'd called the Walker farm and thrown herself on Gram's mercy. As usual, the woman didn't disappoint.

Once she and Cocoa had gone outside, Gretchen looked at Jen and shook her head. "Is that what I looked like after Alex left?"

"Of course not. You're you. You probably put on your stoic farmer face and did chores to work through your emotions."

"Stoic farmer face?" Gretchen snorted. "Is that like Kelly's cop face?"

"Yup."

"And what's yours?"

"Compassionate, concerned guidance counselor face, of course." Jen tried to show her, but she was pretty sure her puffy eyes and red nose blew the effect.

Her friend chuckled, but then her amusement faded and she did a pretty good impression of the compassionate, concerned guidance counselor face herself. "What are you going to do, Jen?"

"Probably eat macaroni salad until the carb crash hits and maybe I can finally sleep."

"Is he worth this?"

Jen pressed the heels of her hands to her sore, grainy-feeling eyes to stem the inevitable tears, but they didn't come. Maybe she was literally all cried out. Finally. "He's worth everything."

"Is he?"

She knew where Gretchen was heading, and she shook her head. "You know as well as anybody how much I love what I do."

"I know. And you make a difference, you really do. But I'm worried about you because you're not really bouncing back and I'm afraid you're sacrificing your own happiness for the kids'. You don't owe them that."

"It's not an issue of owing them." Jen set her fork down, having reached her limit of macaroni salad for the moment. "Why did you let me eat so much?"

"I've got a list of things that need doing before snow flies if you want to work some of it off."

Jen laughed. "Therapy for me, free labor for you?"

"You know it."

Pushing back from the table, Jen scraped the rest of her macaroni salad into the garbage and washed her bowl. "What would happen to the kids if I left Stewart Mills?"

"Is that a super-dramatic rhetorical question or do you actually want me to answer it?" When Jen gave her a look, Gretchen shrugged. "They'd hire a new guidance counselor and you'd probably be all up in the hiring process. And then you'd be all up in helping her. You'd be in touch with the kids. And you'd be volunteering to drive up and help her with the college fair and to help her do all the stuff you do now. And you'd be doing it all on top of taking care of your new crop of kids."

"That sounds exhausting. And I'm pretty sure whoever they hired would get sick of me looking over her—or his— shoulder pretty quickly."

"Maybe." Gretchen looked skeptical. "But I think the administration really appreciates everything you do and you'd have some say in the hiring process. They wouldn't hire somebody whose ego is more important than the kids."

"There isn't exactly a line of guidance counselors just waiting to take a job up here in the middle of nowhere."

"Stop."

Jen looked at her friend, her eyebrow arched. "Stop?"

"You're going to go in circles and there are too many people in your head. Make it about you and Sam. Do you want to go with him or not?"

"I do, but I don't see how I can." When Gretchen rolled her eyes, Jen pointed an accusing finger at her. "Don't you dare. You weren't willing to leave this farm for Alex."

"That's different. There were Gram and Cocoa to consider. And this is my home."

"It's not that different. It wasn't just about you and Alex any more than I can make this about just me and Sam. We care about people. We have responsibilities."

"I know. I just . . . I'm afraid for you because I know, if Alex hadn't come back, I still wouldn't feel whole. And I don't want you to give up being happy."

Jen didn't want to give up being happy, either, which spun her right back into the horrible ping-pong game her thoughts had been stuck playing since the night Sam asked her to move away with him.

"You tell your kids they have to fight to make their dreams come true, Jen. If there's an obstacle, they have to find a way around it or over it. You teach them to be determined but also how to compromise. I've personally heard you tell a junior if she sat around waiting for her dream life to just appear in her lap, she was going to grow old without that dream ever coming true. Are you full of shit, Miss Cooper?"

"I'm taking my macaroni salad and going home now," Jen snapped.

"Sure. Go sit on your couch with your leftovers and wait for your dream life to fall in your lap."

"I'm calling Kelly next time."

Sam looked around the apartment that had been his home for the last month and a half, making a mental catalog of his personal belongings. He was pretty sure he'd be able to make it in one trip.

It had been a hell of a day. He'd finally gotten around to officially quitting his job in Texas. And he'd arranged to have the things he'd left behind boxed up and sent to Coach

McDonnell's address. His mom didn't have the space and he didn't have a new address yet. He'd narrowed his choices down to two apartments near the high school but, for the first time in his life, found himself being picky. Neither of them were exactly what he wanted, so he'd found a dozen stupid excuses not to sign a lease.

And he had a voice mail message on his phone from Neil, looking for a commitment. Sam hadn't been busy when the phone rang. He'd seen the name on the caller ID and simply wasn't in the mood to answer it. Now he wasn't in the mood to call him back.

Running into Jen the day before had rocked his world. Turning and seeing her had been a split second of joy followed by what felt like a wrecking ball to his chest. He still hadn't regained his equilibrium and he'd spent more time brooding over her than he had taking care of the things on his to-do list.

After muttering a fairly long string of curses under his breath, he pulled out his cell phone and hit the number for Coach's house. His wife answered on the second ring. "Hello?"

"Hi, it's Sam."

"Sam! How are you doing?"

"Not too bad," he lied. "I'm going a little stir-crazy, though, and was thinking about stopping by for a visit with Coach if he's not doing anything."

"Right now he's just waking up from his customary post-lunch nap. It's a nice day. You two can do some porch-sitting and then you'll stay for dinner."

He hadn't been angling for a supper invitation, especially given the changes to the menu at Chez McDonnell since Coach's heart attack. "I'm not sure about the meal yet, but I'll come get Coach out of your hair for a few minutes."

"I'll let him know you're coming."

He didn't even know what he was going to say, he thought as he walked down the back stairs to his truck. Or what Coach might say. But if there was one man who could help him sort through the chaos in his mind, it was the old man.

Coach met him on the porch with two mugs of coffee that were steaming like crazy in the cold air. "It's not like you to randomly stop by, but it's good to see you."

"I was bored and sick of staring at my apartment walls," he said, even though it was a lie. He'd come for advice and being stir-crazy was just the excuse he'd given himself. "Kind of cold out here."

"Yeah, it is, but you and I always did our best talking out here on the porch. Have a seat."

Coach set the mugs on the table between the two rockers as Sam sat. "I thought coffee was on the forbidden list."

"There's a thing called half-caf that's not decaf, but not fully caffeinated, either. Helen and I compromised and I can have two cups of it before two in the afternoon, and then I have to switch to decaf." He took a sip of his and gave a contented sigh. "You can only go without something out of sheer stubbornness before you realize compromise is a lot better than living the rest of your life without it."

Sam looked out over the street, still quiet at this time of day, especially this late in the fall. "Somehow I get the feeling you're not talking about the coffee anymore."

Coach shrugged. "If something I said resonates with you, I guess you need to ask yourself why."

Sam drank some of the coffee to ward off the chill setting in and then gave an angry shake of his head. "Can we not do this?"

"Hey, I was napping. You're the one who came looking for company."

"I mean, can we not do this thing where you say vague things meant to prod me into having an epiphany? I'm a grown man now. If you want to say something, Coach, just say it plain."

"Okay. You're being an idiot and it's pissing me off."

Sam sat back in the rocker. "Maybe not *that* plain."

"You're a man with a good work ethic. You've got the kind of loyalty that dragged you halfway across the country *twice* to help me out. You're working hard to be a family with Sheila again and that kind of forgiveness doesn't come easy. You took care of my boys and, yes, I know what a help you've been to Cody, especially. People respect you and admire you, Sam."

"Why do I feel like there's a *but* coming."

"Because I haven't gotten to the part where you're an idiot yet. Don't jump the gun."

"Let me save you the trouble, Coach. This job means a lot to me and I'm taking it."

"And there's the part where you're an idiot."

Sam sighed and took another sip of his coffee so he wouldn't say anything rash or disrespectful. He was pretty sure Coach was wrong this time, but he would hear him out. He owed him that much at least.

"I don't know why you're shooting yourself in the foot, son," Coach continued. "It's like you look in the mirror and see the boy you used to be looking out at you. But that's not who we see."

"And that's not who Neil Page saw, either."

"Is that what you're looking for? Validation from

somebody who doesn't know a damn thing about you other than watching you on the sidelines and hearing some stories about how you came back to help me out?"

"I think your meds are addling your brain again." He didn't bother trying to inject any affectionate amusement into his tone. "I've discovered I really like coaching. And I'm good at it. Why is it so hard to believe I'd accept a coaching job just because I want to?"

"Because of what you're leaving behind."

Sam felt a chill and took a sip of the coffee in a futile effort to ward it off. "I asked Jen to go with me, Coach. She said no."

When the slight creaking of the rocker ceased, Sam looked over to see Coach had stopped moving and was frowning at him. And that's when he finally understood what the man was trying to dig down to.

"You thought I was running out on her, didn't you?"

"The gossip in this town ain't what it used to be."

"Probably because it's not really a gossip kind of thing. When you hurt like this, you might tell your best friend, but it doesn't spread around."

Coach started rocking again. "You talking about her? Or you?"

"I told her I was in love with her." He sniffed hard and sucked at the back of his teeth for a second, trying to keep the rise of emotion at bay. "And she loves me, too. But she won't leave Stewart Mills."

"I'm sorry, son. I didn't know it had gone that far."

"It's not just about validation. It's a new life for myself. A new life with a job I want, built on a strong foundation this time. And I wanted her to share it with me, but she won't go. I've hated this town for so long, Coach. And even though I've come to actually like it here, it still seems weird to think about staying here. Calling it home."

"You haven't hated Stewart Mills, son. You've been hating what happened to you here. But you're putting it behind you. I know you are because you're letting Sheila be a mother to you again. The town's just buildings. It's the people that matter."

Sam drank his coffee, rocking the chair slightly, while he considered the people Coach was talking about. The McDonnells. His mother. Alex and Gretchen. Chase and Kelly. The school staff he'd gotten friendly with. The football team. Other students he'd crossed paths with. Hell, even Miss Beecher had turned out to have his back.

And Jen.

"Everybody I care about is in this town," he admitted finally.

"Just as importantly, everybody who cares about *you* is in this town." Coach sighed. "This is your home, and I just hope you realize it before it's too late. And it's not because you were born here. It's because the people you care about are here and you made yourself a place."

"It's hard, after all these years, to wrap my head around being happy here."

"Maybe you're going about it the wrong way. Try wrapping your head around how you'll feel *not* being here."

Lonely. Once again on the outside. And without the only woman who'd ever lit up his day with just a look or a simple touch. "Why won't she go with me, Coach?"

He didn't bother feeling embarrassed by the way his

voice cracked. This man had seen him at his worst and at his best and everything in between.

"It's not that simple, Sam. Let me ask you a question. What would you say if I told you Helen wants me to move down south somewhere? Maybe somewhere warm."

Sam shook his head. "She'd never ask you to do that. This town is part of who you are. Not only the team but . . . oh."

"Yeah. This isn't just the town where Jen lives. It's not just a job. She fights for those kids just like I fought for you. You know how it is here. How bleak the prospects can be. She gives them hope. Gives their parents hope and help and everything she has to give. Have you ever looked through the scrapbooks on the shelf in her office?"

"No." To be honest, he hadn't even known there *were* scrapbooks in her office.

"When the kids go off to college, they send her things. Pictures. Awards. Newspaper clippings. Anything those kids are proud of, they send to their parents and to Jen." Coach paused to take a sip of his coffee. "Now, I'm not trying to say anybody's right or wrong here. That's not my place. I just want you to understand that it's a lot harder for her than simply changing jobs. You're asking her to give up a part of her heart in exchange for yours."

"Shit."

"Ever since you were a teenager, that's been your response to me finally breaking through that thick skull of yours."

"How come your advice always makes things simpler and yet more complicated at the same time?"

"Hell, you coach football for as many years as I have and you'll find yourself talking the same way."

Sam snorted. "It's amazing Kelly's got such a good head on her shoulders."

"Thank God for her mother," Coach said, and then he laughed, his rocker creaking in the cold sunshine.

Jen parked next to Sam's truck and made the long walk up the stairs to his apartment, her stomach in knots.

She looked like hell warmed over, and she knew it. Her hair was pinned up in a sloppy bun. No amount of makeup was going to hide her puffy eyes and the lingering redness of her nose, so she hadn't even tried. She smelled good, thanks to a long soak in the tub with her aromatherapy bath beads that hadn't helped. But that was all she had going for her at the moment.

It didn't matter, she thought as she walked to the door. He'd told her he loved her, so hopefully he'd look past it and be happy to see her. And if she was lucky, he'd be *really* happy when he heard what she had to say because after the worst night she'd had yet and now bolstered by macaroni salad, she'd realized happiness was within her grasp. All she had to do was take it.

When Sam opened the door, her first thought was that he looked almost as rough as she did. His eyes were sad and his mouth looked grim as he ran his hand over his hair.

"Can I come in for a minute?" she asked.

"Of course. Is everything okay?"

She waited until he'd closed the door and turned to face her. "I want to go with you."

His sharp intake of breath made her sorry she hadn't

worked her way up to it, but then he slowly shook his head. "I can't ask you to do that, Jen."

"You're not asking me to. I want to. Unless you've changed your mind, which is fine. I mean it's not fine, but I'll pretend it is and get out of your way."

Sam closed the distance and pulled her into his arms, squeezing her so hard she could barely breathe. But she didn't care as long as her arms were around him. "I will never change my mind about you."

"I don't want to spend the rest of my life without you in it, Sam. That's more important than anything."

"I told them no."

She went still, the room silent except for the thumping of his heartbeat against her ear. "What?"

"I thanked them for their interest, but told them I wasn't interested in leaving Stewart Mills."

She tilted her head back so she could see his face. He didn't look like a man who regretted the decision he was talking about. "When did this happen?"

"About twenty minutes ago. I was trying to get control of my nerves and then I was going to come see you. You beat me to it."

"Sam." She sighed, tears burning her eyes. "You really wanted that job. You should call him back and . . ."

"No." He put his finger under her chin and lowered his mouth to kiss her.

She sighed, melting against him as every part of her being seemed to sigh in contentment. His mouth was soft and gentle, almost tentative as they savored each other again. It was right, she thought. *This* was right.

When he broke off the kiss and she opened her eyes, she hoped her face reflected the same love and happiness that his did.

But they weren't done yet. "No matter how much you kiss me, you're not going to distract me. You wanted that job."

"I did. But, more importantly, I think I wanted to be asked. It felt good to be wanted because they respected my role in the community and not because I look like a guy who's good at physical labor. I got caught up in that and lost sight of what's important and that's you."

"I should have said yes when you asked me to go with you, though."

"No, you shouldn't. And I shouldn't have sprung it on you like that. We should have discussed it instead of me putting you in a position of just saying yes or no like that. I'm sorry."

"I'm still sorry I said no." He smiled, stroking wisps of hair away from her face. "What will you do for work?"

"I'll find something. I always have in the past. And the rumor about new buyers for the mill is rumored to be more than a rumor."

"Or so rumor has it."

He laughed. "It actually is true. I know because Chase has already talked to them and I already know there will be work to be had."

"What about coaching?"

"I'm pretty sure I know a guy who'll let me volunteer at our high school."

Jen's heart beat rapidly in her chest as it really started sinking in that this was happening. "Are you sure you'll be happy here?"

"I'm already happy here. With you. And since I intend

to stick close to you for the rest of my life, I'm pretty sure I'm going to be a very happy man." He paused to take a deep breath. "You know, for so long I looked around this town and all I could see was my past. But now I see you and I see my future."

"We can make that come true," she said, her voice husky with restrained tears.

"I love you, Jen." He pressed his lips together for a few seconds, his obvious struggle with his emotions tugging at her heart. "I love you. I've never said those words to anybody and I don't know how to prove it to you, but I do."

She stepped closer to him, wrapping her arms around his waist and tilting her head back to look at him. "Sam, you don't have to prove anything to me. I love you, too. And you love me and that's all we need."

"I only need you." He pushed a strand of hair behind her ear. "You accused me once of using you as a comfort object. You're not a comfort object for me because you're not an object. But you *are* my comfort. You make my life everything I wanted it to be just by sharing it with me."

Tears slipped down over her cheeks, but she smiled to let him know they were happy tears. "You're really staying?"

"If you'll have me."

"Oh, I'll have you, Sam Leavitt. I called dibs, and I'm keeping you. Forever."

Epilogue

November . . .

Dylan Clark met them at the Stewart Mills town line in his cruiser, pulling in front of the first bus with his lights flashing and siren wailing. The cars behind the buses laid on the horns, and people spilled out of the houses they passed to wave to the football players cheering and yelling out the open bus windows.

Sam looked across the aisle at Coach McDonnell, who was sitting behind the driver and watching the boys by way of the huge mirror over the driver's head.

Stepping out onto the sidelines of the University of New Hampshire's football field with Coach for their division's championship game was a moment that would be forever at the top of Sam's lifetime highlight reel. He'd given Coach back his whistle, but had been given one of his own when he accepted the position of assistant coach. The stipend wasn't much, but it wasn't about the money, anyway. He wanted to give back to the community he'd made peace with and would call home, and to the man who'd been like a father to him.

The boys had played one hell of a football game—both teams had—and when the Eagles pulled out the win in over-time, it was almost as emotional as the day he and Chase and Alex and the others had won the first trophy.

And Jen had been in the stands, right behind the bench where he could see her and get an encouraging smile to keep him going. The others were with her, of course—Kelly and Chase, Gretchen and Alex, his mom and Mrs. McDonnell—but whenever he looked in that direction, his gaze naturally fell on her beautiful, beaming face.

And now they were returning in triumph, announcing to everybody within earshot of the sirens and horns that the Stewart Mills Eagles were champions again. The cruiser led the buses and cars on a parade lap around the town square before they pulled up along the curbs and shut off the engines.

It was the weekend before Thanksgiving and the temperature was hovering around the forty-degree mark, but nobody seemed to care about the cold or their holiday to-do lists. There was a championship to celebrate.

Barbecue grills had been thrown in the back of pickup trucks, and Don and Cassie Jones had already offered boxes of burger patties and the fixings from O'Rourke's freezers in the event of a big win. People brought whatever food they had available with them, from pasta salads to half-eaten bags of chips, and it was one hell of a party.

Sam managed to avoid manning the grills, but keeping

an eye on the teenagers and making sure the cans they were carrying around only had soda in them was a full-time job in itself. At least it was a job he could do with Jen at his side and her hand in his.

He saw his mom from a distance, in a conversation with some women that involved a lot of hand movements and laughing. For the first time, seeing her made him smile without hesitation and he didn't poke at his happiness for her. They were looking forward, and she was a little stronger and a little more confident every time he saw her.

As if she felt his gaze on her, his mother turned. He lifted a hand to wave, and she smiled before excusing herself from her friends. He and Jen changed course to meet her halfway across the grass.

"Congratulations!" She was grinning, but her hands stayed at her sides, and he watched her fingers curl into fists.

Impulse made him let go of Jen's hand and open his arms. His mom didn't hesitate, and stepped into his embrace. He hugged her, giving her a squeeze. Her eyes were a little shimmery when the hug ended, but she was beaming.

"The boys did good," he said.

"Of course they did. They have a great coach."

"Why thank you, Sheila," he heard Coach McDonnell say from behind him, and they all laughed.

"They have a pretty great assistant coach, too," his mom said.

"That they do." Coach's hand fell on his shoulder. "I'm proud of *all* my boys."

Sam nodded, the sudden lump in his throat keeping him from saying anything. He wasn't surprised when he felt Jen's hand slip into his and give it a little squeeze.

"I just wanted to say hello to Sheila for a moment," Coach said. "Helen's making me up a plate because she doesn't trust me not to fill it with coleslaw and potato chips, but she's letting me have a cheeseburger, so I'm not complaining."

Sam watched Coach McDonnell walk away, thankful yet again for the man's strength. If not for his constant mock-complaints about Mrs. McDonnell's stranglehold on his diet, it would have been easy to forget he'd had a heart attack so recently. But his back was straight and his stride was long, and Sam had no doubt the man would be on the sidelines with him for years to come.

"I should get back," she said. "They're thinking about starting a book club that meets every other week and they invited me to come."

"I'll catch you later," Sam said, giving her another smile. It felt good to have a mom, he thought when she smiled back.

Once they were alone, Sam and Jen started walking again, waving to the kids who were scattered all over the square. Some of them would be graduating soon, but he knew they'd keep in touch. And there would be new boys on the team to help mold into football players and damn good young men. He'd go home to Jen every night, and they'd have his mom over for dinner.

"Do you think they're starting a real book club?" he asked Jen, since his mother was on his mind. "Or one of those book clubs that's really an excuse to get together and drink wine?"

Jen shook her head, chuckling. "The woman in the blue sweatshirt Sheila was talking to is also a recovering alcoholic. They won't be drinking wine, and she'll enjoy having friends to talk about books with."

"That's good, then."

"Hey, there are the others," Jen said, pointing to a spot near the covered bridge where there was a small group of folding chairs. Alex and Chase were there with Gretchen and Kelly, and Alex beckoned them over when he saw them.

"Great night," Chase said, taking a seat on one of the metal chairs before wincing. "A little chilly for metal chairs, though."

"I'll stay standing," Alex said, and the rest of them agreed, except for Sam.

"While you guys were sitting in the stands, I was on my feet for that game. I can handle a little cold." He sat and then scratched behind Cocoa's ears when she stood in front of him and then collapsed against his knees. The dog sure knew how to get attention when she wanted it. Once she'd had her fill, she offered her paw for a high five and then went to collapse next to Alex and Gretchen again. If Sam had to guess, he'd say she managed to beg more than her share of people food at the cookout and was too full to do anything but stretch out on the grass and snore.

"That's one hell of a sight, isn't it?" Chase said, nodding his head toward the other end of the square.

From the covered bridge, the giant blue and gold banner hanging at the top of the old brick mill's wall was visible. PROUD SUPPORTER OF EAGLES FOOTBALL.

The new owners of the mill would need some zoning concessions to make the property work for the manufacturing business they were putting in, and they'd decided to make nice with the town by offering to ensure the football team had funding until the school budget recovered and could reflect the employment opportunities and contribution to the tax base they brought to Stewart Mills. Jen had stepped in at the last minute and gotten some promises for the music department, too, so everybody was happy.

Including Sam and Chase, who would be working together to oversee the refitting of the mill. When that work was complete, Sam would stay on in a maintenance supervisory role while Chase would move on to whatever the next building job was, as long as it was close enough for him to be home by dinner. He was done in New Jersey. And a whole lot of unemployed people in Stewart Mills would be drawing steady paychecks again.

"I can't believe how much has changed since spring," Kelly said. She was standing behind Chase's chair, her arms wrapped around him and her chin resting on his shoulder so their cheeks were almost touching. "The town was in a grim place. It looked like the end of football, and the kids were going off the rails."

"And three best friends were all single with no hope of love on the horizon," Gretchen added.

Jen laughed. "We sure fixed the hell out of that."

Alex slid his arm around Gretchen's waist and kissed her neck. "I'm pretty sure if you three women decided you wanted to take over the world, we'd all be in trouble."

"Eagles Fest was enough," Kelly said, and they all laughed.

"I think all three of us would agree Eagles Fest was the best thing that ever happened to us," Chase said, his gaze still on the sign. "But I'd be lying if I said I'm sad we won't have to do it again."

"Watching from the stands is as close as I ever want to come to playing football again," Chase agreed. "I never felt as old as I did when we were facing these boys across the line of scrimmage."

"Hell, we're not old," Sam said, snagging Jen's hand and pulling her onto his lap. He kissed her before she leaned against him, resting her head on his shoulder. "We're just getting to the good part."

If you enjoyed Sam and Jen's story, keep reading
for an excerpt of Chase and Kelly's story in

Under the Lights

*The first book in the Boys of Fall series
by Shannon Stacey*

Available in paperback from Jove Books

With his business partner off to who-knew-where with the money he'd drained from their accounts, and his girlfriend currently stripping their apartment of any sign she'd ever lived there, the last thing Chase Sanders wanted to do was answer the damn phone.

It was only nine in the morning and he'd already fielded a call from their lumber supplier, wanting to know why their check had bounced. That was followed up by a call from his girlfriend's new boyfriend, wanting to hash out who owned the television before the guy carried it out to his truck.

Former girlfriend, he corrected himself as the phone kept ringing. Maybe he'd hit the shitty-day jackpot and it was his doctor calling to tell him he might have contracted some horrible disease. Probably from his girlfriend—*ex*-girlfriend— and her new boyfriend.

At the fifth ring he glanced at the caller ID, and the area code snapped him out of his funk—603. And the prefix numbers were from his hometown. Why the hell was anybody calling him from Stewart Mills, New Hampshire?

He tempted fate and picked up the phone. "S and P Builders."

"Chase Sanders, please," said a woman whose voice he didn't recognize, not that he would expect to after fourteen years away. Her tone was warm, and maybe a little sexy, but he braced himself for bad news because that was just how his luck was running at the moment.

"This is Chase."

"My name is Kelly McDonnell." The last name landed a sucker punch to his gut. "You probably don't remember me, but—"

"Don't." Chase was struck by a terrible certainty she was going to tell him Coach—her father—had passed away, and he didn't want to hear it. He had to make her stop talking.

"I'm sorry. Don't what?" She sounded confused, not that he could blame her.

He could deal with Rina reacting to the increase in penny-pinching by finding herself a new guy who wasn't losing his business. He could deal with Seth Poole reacting to the decline in the construction industry by pinching the few pennies they had left and running. But he absolutely couldn't deal with hearing Coach McDonnell was dead. Not today.

"Hello?" she said. "Are you still there?"

What an ass he was. This call couldn't be easy for the man's daughter. "I'm sorry. Go ahead."

"But you said 'don't.'"

"I was talking to my dog." Not that he had a dog. Rina

didn't like dog hair and had refused to budge, even when he'd told her some of those froufrou ankle-biter breeds didn't shed.

"I'm Coach McDonnell's daughter and I'm calling to talk to you about a very special fund-raising festival we have planned for the summer."

Fund-raising festival. "So Coach isn't dead?"

"What?"

"Sorry. Didn't mean to say that out loud."

"Why would you think that?" Her voice was still sexy, but it wasn't warm anymore.

"You're calling me, out of the blue, after fourteen years. I thought you were going to ask me to be a pallbearer or something."

"You've been gone fourteen years, but you think I'd ask you to carry my father's casket? If he was dead, of course. Which he's not."

"You wouldn't ask me to be a pallbearer, but you'll ask me for money?" Not that he had any to give.

"No." He heard her exasperated breath over the phone line. "Can we start over?"

"Sure." Wasn't like the conversation could go any worse.

Chase tried to remember what Coach's daughter looked like. She'd been a sophomore during his senior year, so he probably wouldn't have paid much attention to her if she hadn't always been around because of her dad. Thick, straight blond hair. Not much in the way of a rack, but she'd had killer legs. That was about all he remembered. Oh, and that she hadn't liked him much, for some reason.

"Things are bad in Stewart Mills," Kelly said. He wasn't surprised. Things were bad all over and New Jersey certainly wasn't a picnic at the moment. "The school budget's been whittled down to bare bones and they cut the football team."

He waited a few seconds, but she didn't tell him why she called to tell him that. "And you want me to . . . what, exactly?"

Over the line, he heard her take a deep breath. "I want you to come home."

"I'm not sure what you mean by that, but I *am* home."

"We need to raise enough money to fund the team until the economy swings back around, and we're starting with a two-week-long fund-raising festival. We're hoping to get as many players from the first Stewart Mills Eagles championship team as we can back to Stewart Mills to take part in the events."

"When? For how long?" Not that it mattered.

"Next month. We'd love the whole two weeks and we're hoping for at least the closing weekend, but we'll work around any commitment we can get."

"I wish you all the best, but—"

"Let me tell you some of the events we have planned," Kelly interrupted. "Besides the standard bake sales and traffic tollbooths, we're planning a street fair and—most exciting of all—an exhibition game featuring the alumni players versus the current team. We'll wrap things up with a parade on the Fourth of July before the fireworks."

Getting the crap beat out of him by a bunch of teenagers on the football field wasn't very high on Chase's to-do list. "I have a lot going on. Work and . . . stuff."

"My dad had a lot of work and *stuff* going on, too, but he was there for you. How many hours did he spend with you over the years, making sure you didn't flunk off the team? Bet that college degree came in handy when you were starting your own business."

He leaned back in his chair and groaned. "That's a dirty play."

"There's a lot riding on this. I'll do whatever I have to."

It might be a slight exaggeration to say he owed everything to Coach McDonnell, but not much. Even if Chase's life was currently going to crap, he'd had a lot of opportunities over the years he wouldn't have had without a stubborn old man who refused to give up on him.

"I'll see what I can do." There. That was vague and noncommittal.

"I hope to hear from you soon. Without the Eagles to coach, I don't know what'll keep my dad going."

Even as he recognized her lack of subtlety in laying on the emotional blackmail, his heart twisted and he heard himself say, "I'll be there. I'll make it work."

"Great. I'll be in touch soon with more details and to nail down the dates." She was smart enough to end the call before he could talk himself out of it.

Once he'd hung up, Chase laced his fingers behind his head and stared up at the ceiling. He hadn't thought about Stewart Mills in ages, but now that he had, he couldn't help but crave a little one-on-one time with Coach McDonnell. He loved his parents, but they'd been either unwilling or unable to keep their thumbs on him academically or be a shoulder when he needed one.

He sure as hell could use a shoulder to lean on right now, as well as some pseudo-paternal advice. Besides, if he couldn't straighten out the mess his partner had made in the next month, a couple of weeks wasn't going to hurt. For Coach, he'd make the time.

If there was one thing Kelly McDonnell had learned in her years as the daughter of the Stewart Mills Eagles high school football coach, it was that hesitation got you sacked. If you wanted to win, you had to pick your play and execute it with no second guesses.

And as much as she'd also learned to hate sports analogies during those twenty-eight years, this one she had to take to heart. She was fighting for her dad and for her town, and she couldn't lose, so she had to execute the only play she had left in her book.

It was crazy, though. *She* was crazy. Hail Mary passes didn't even begin to describe the desperate phone calls she'd made. But they were going to work, and that made all the trouble worth it.

She already had several commitments. Alex Murphy, defensive tackle, had been hard to track down but agreed to come back after she reminded him of the many times her father had bailed him out of jail after fights and taught him to channel his aggression into football. The quarterback, Sam Leavitt, was coming all the way from Texas. The son of an abusive drunk, he was probably the kid Coach had cursed the most, loved the most and done the most for. And Chase Sanders, running back, had bowed to her not-so-subtle pressure as well and was driving up from New Jersey.

So, the good news—Chase Sanders was coming back to town. The bad news—Chase Sanders was coming back to town.

"Officer McDonnell?" Kelly looked up when the school

secretary said her name, shoving Sanders to the back of her mind, where he belonged. "Miss Cooper's available now."

Kelly nodded her thanks and made her way through the maze of short hallways—one of the joys of a hundred-plus-year-old brick school—until she came to the guidance counselor's office. She didn't have to worry about getting lost. Besides the fact that she'd walked the same halls as a teenager herself, as a police officer she'd spent a lot of time in Jen Cooper's office. The budget didn't allow for a full-time school resource officer, but Kelly filled the role as best she could anyway.

She'd barely closed the door behind her when Jen pointed at her and said, "You *have* to save football."

Kelly laughed at her best friend's irritation and sat in one of the visitor chairs. "You know I'm trying."

"The boys are already getting into trouble. Since March, when the budget for next school year was decided, they've been sliding, and now, with this school year almost over and finals right around the corner, they're losing their minds." Jen leaned back in her chair, rocking it as she always did when agitated. "Without the threat of August football try-outs to keep them in line, I don't know how some of them will stay on track this summer."

"I'm going to put them to work. If they want to play this fall, they'll have to work for it, even if it's doing car washes every Saturday all summer."

"Hunter Cass hasn't done any homework for over a week. I had him in today and he told me since he didn't need to maintain at least a C average to keep his sports eligibility, he didn't see the point."

Kelly shook her head, feeling a pang of sadness. Hunter

had struggled to keep a D average through middle school, and only the promise of playing football got him to work hard enough to stay above the cutoff. With the help of the peer tutoring program Jen had started, the running back was carrying a B-minus average before they announced the program cuts.

Like Chase Sanders, she realized. Football had inspired him to do better academically, too, and he'd made something of himself. The difference was that Chase had struggled with learning techniques, and Hunter just didn't give a crap.

"When we get a few more details nailed down, we'll be able to start putting the kids to work. Once they can see there's something they can do to save their team, they'll get back on track."

Jen leaned forward so she could prop her elbows on the desk. "What if they put in the time and the work and it's not enough?"

That would be so much worse for the boys, so Kelly was going to make sure that didn't happen. "It'll be enough."

"Where are the alumni going to stay?"

Kelly appreciated the switch to talking about things they *could* control. "To save money, we're boarding them with families in town. It's a little awkward, but since our only motel has plywood on the windows, it would cost a lot to find someplace else for them, and then we'd have to provide transportation, too. My mom decided to ask around, and she's in charge of matching them up."

"Who gets to stay with Coach?"

Kelly rolled her eyes. "Chase Sanders."

She appreciated the battle Jen fought to hide it, but her

friend couldn't stop the grin. "Was that your mom's idea . . . or yours?"

"Mom's." Boarding the guy she'd had a crush on in school at her parents' home, where she spent a lot of her time, would never have been her idea. "And I never should have told you I liked him, even though that was a *long* time ago."

Jen picked up her pen and started doodling on a notepad. "He's not married, is he?"

"I don't think so. The only guy who mentioned having to talk to his wife was John Briscoe. Remember him? Tall, skinny, played wide receiver."

"Vaguely." Jen sighed and set the pen down, which was good since she was really burning through the ink, judging by the number of doodles already on the pad. "I'm losing them, Kelly."

"The most important thing is that they see us fighting for them."

Jen nodded, but Kelly wasn't surprised at the lack of conviction on her friend's face. They both had front-row seats to the toll the economic downswing was having on the town's kids. With their parents fighting unemployment, bankruptcy, foreclosure, depression and each other, the children were falling through the cracks. Alcohol-related calls were on the rise, as were domestic calls, and lately the Stewart Mills PD had seen a sharp increase in the number of complaints against teens. Drinking, smoking, trespassing, vandalizing, shoplifting. The kids were doing more of it, there was less tolerance for their behavior and their homes were pressure cookers. Somebody had to fight for them.

Kelly had to make their fund-raiser a success, no matter

what, not only for her dad but for the entire town, too. She'd work her butt off and schmooze and beg if she had to. She'd also do her best to ignore the fact that Chase Sanders would be sleeping in the room where she'd spent her teenage years daydreaming about him. She had no idea which task would be more difficult.

C hase managed to bash his knuckles twice on his way down the stairs with the last of Rina's boxes, which did nothing to improve his mood.

She'd moved the bulk of her stuff out already, but as he'd packed his own belongings over the last few weeks, he kept finding things of hers. He'd tossed those items in separate boxes and then, when he was sure he'd gotten everything, he texted her to come and get them. She'd come up with a lame excuse and sent Donny, her new boyfriend, instead.

Nothing soured a day like having to play nice with the guy who'd been banging his girlfriend.

"That's the last one?" Donny asked after Chase tossed the box into the back of the guy's truck.

"Yeah." He was about to walk away, when Donny stuck his hand out. Chase stared at it for a few seconds, debating on punching the guy in the face, but he'd been raised better than that and shook his hand.

"No hard feelings," Donny said.

Chase squeezed, tightening his grip until the man Rina had chosen over him winced. Then he turned and went inside, slamming the door a little harder than was necessary. That was enough playing nice.

With the exception of the duffel bags by the door and a

few odds and ends on the kitchen counter, almost everything he owned was in boxes in a storage locker, waiting to be moved to a new, much smaller apartment the weekend after he returned from Stewart Mills.

By downsizing his life, groveling and bargaining, he'd managed to clear up most of his business woes. And, most importantly, he'd sold the engagement ring he'd bought Rina back when times were good and he was feeling flush. Every time he'd thought he was ready to pop the question, though, something had held him back, and the ring had stayed hidden in the bottom of a beer stein from college, under miscellaneous guy debris she had no interest in sifting through.

He wasn't sure why he'd never asked her to be his wife, yet considering she was living with Donny and the ring was paying not only for his trip to Stewart Mills but also the first and last month's rent on a new place once he found one, it was a damn good thing he hadn't.

After one final look around, Chase tossed his stuff into his truck and hit the road. It was a nine-hour drive, so if he pushed straight through, he'd get into Stewart Mills early evening. If he was going to be any later than that, he'd spend the night in a motel and arrive in the morning.

He had one quick stop to make before he left town. When he'd told his parents he was going back to Stewart Mills and why, his old man had called him an idiot, and his mom had told him to swing by and pick up a pie. It was intended as a hostess gift for Mrs. McDonnell, but Chase was afraid if Coach's wife had ever had his mom's pie and remembered the experience, she might not let him in the door with it.

His parents' home was in a small neighborhood made up mostly of retirees, though his mother still worked. She claimed she enjoyed doing insurance claim work for a large auto body shop, but Chase suspected she couldn't handle her husband 24/7. Nobody could. Today she was home, though, her shiny compact car squeezed into the driveway alongside the massive Cadillac that Bob Sanders had bought back during Clinton's first term in the Oval Office.

His mom was on the sofa when he walked in, watching some kind of cooking show. "Hi, honey. Your father's out back."

It was the standard greeting, but he stopped and kissed her cheek on his way through the house. "Hi, Ma."

His old man was on the tiny dock that matched all the other tiny docks up and down the canal that ran through the neighborhood. He had a bulk package of cheap chicken drumsticks and was shoving a couple of pieces of raw poultry into each of his wire traps. Ma would be making fresh crabmeat-salad sandwiches for lunch.

Chase hated seafood. Especially crab.

"You heading north today?" Bob asked when Chase reached the dock.

"In a few minutes. Ma made a pie for Mrs. McDonnell."

"Lucky her."

Chase grinned and shoved his hands in his pockets, but the smile faded as the silence stretched toward awkward. They'd never had a lot to say to each other, but their relationship was particularly strained at the moment.

Bob Sanders made no bones about being disappointed—and maybe a little embarrassed—by the failure of Chase's business, no matter how much of it was due to the economy and Seth's financial shenanigans rather than mismanagement on Chase's part. Chase's impending return to Stewart

Mills had also dredged up his buried resentment that his father had written him off as stupid, and it had taken Coach McDonnell to show him he wasn't.

Bob lowered the last trap into the water, shoved the empty chicken packaging back into the plastic shopping bag and turned to face Chase. "Get everything straightened out?"

"More or less. Got most people willing to wait for pay until the lawyers catch up with Seth. Scraped together enough to stay out of bankruptcy court, and managed to find contractors to handle the jobs I can't afford to do now. Things are tight, but I'll probably get to keep my shirt."

"And you think it's a good idea to go to New Hampshire right now?"

Yeah, he did, because Coach needed him. "Probably not, but I'm going anyway. This mess will still be here when I get back."

Chase followed his dad back to the house and, since the conversation seemed to have run its course, he got the pie and got the hell out of there. He thought about ditching the hostess gift in a rest area trash can, but if his mother tried to call him at the McDonnells' and the pie—or lack of one—came up in conversation, he'd never hear the end of it.

He turned the music up too loud, drove a little too fast and drank way too much coffee, but he pulled into Stewart Mills a little past six. A perfectly respectable time to show up on Coach's doorstep.

As he drove through Stewart Mills, though, he noticed the town had changed a lot, and not necessarily for the better. A lot of For Sale signs. A few bank auction signs. They'd obviously done some restoration work on the historic covered bridge, but it didn't distract from the dark, silent shell of the paper mill looming behind it that used to be the life-blood of the town.

There was also a new stop sign, he realized *as* he went through the intersection. Without stopping.

And the Stewart Mills Police Department had a fairly new four-wheel-drive SUV, too.

There hadn't been a stop sign at that intersection fourteen years ago, Chase thought as he pulled off to the side of the road, making sure there was plenty of room for both his truck and the SUV with the flashing blue lights.

It was one hell of a welcome home.

FROM *NEW YORK TIMES* BESTSELLING AUTHOR

SHANNON STACEY

Defending Hearts

Globe-trotting photographer Alex Murphy returns to
Stewart Mills for a football fund-raiser, but stays to
document the football team and the town's changes.
Since his project includes photos of the Walker farm,
he rents a room there.

Needing money to save the family farm, Gretchen
Walker doesn't have time to deal with the sexy photographer in her house. After all, Alex is a man with
no sense of home, and to her, home is everything. But
when she finds herself falling for him, she'll be forced
to decide where her dreams really lie...

shannonstacey.com
penguin.com